I07611132

MURDER AT 30,000 FEET

BOOKS BY

SUSAN WALTER

Good as Dead

Over Her Dead Body

Lie by the Pool

Running Cold

Letters from Strangers

Murder at 30,000 Feet

SUSAN WALTER

MURDER AT 30,000 FEET

BLACKSTONE PUBLISHING

Published in 2026 by Blackstone Publishing
Cover and book design by Larissa Ezell

Printed in the United States of America

First edition: 2026
ISBN 979-8-228-35733-4
Fiction / Thrillers / Suspense

Version 1

Blackstone Publishing
31 Mistletoe Rd.
Ashland, OR 97520

www.BlackstonePublishing.com

"Never wait for trouble."
—Chuck Yaeger,
Pilot, Trailblazer, Troublemaker

PROLOGUE

Eye of the storm

"Good evening, this is your captain speaking," the pilot of Pioneer Air Flight 868 announced, rousing passengers from their slumbers. His voice was like liquid moonlight, lustrous and deep. They might have let it lull them back to sleep, if not for what he said next.

"I'm afraid I have some bad news."

Eyes opened. The accountant in 22A held her breath as she imagined herself on a game show. *Name three people you never want to give you bad news. One: doctor. Two: airline pilot . . .*

"Several clusters of storm cells have converged unexpectedly," the captain said, before she got to three. "The squall line stretches a hundred miles in both directions. I can't get around it, we're going to have to go through."

DING.

The "fasten seatbelt" light went on. Nervous fliers looked down at their laps. Among the passengers were a high school baseball team on their way to a tournament, family members, friends, and frenemies attending a destination wedding, and a tattooed rock star heading home after a gig.

"I just turned on the fasten seatbelt sign. Out of an abundance of caution, I'm going to ask you to put away all electronics and push those carry-ons under your seats."

There was a flurry of movement. A high schooler watching *Top Gun* on an iPad pretended not to hear. His neighbor elbowed him in the ribs. "Dude. He said to put all electronics away."

There was a brief stare down, but the iPad found its way into the seat back without a scuffle.

"I'm going to do my best to fly between the cells, but we may experience some moderate turbulence. Shouldn't last more than a minute or two."

The bridesmaid in 28D wasn't concerned. She'd recently ridden *Twisted Colossus*, the harrowing steel rollercoaster at Magic Mountain. That was at least five minutes. And she'd survived.

"Flight attendants, please take your seats."

Two of the three flight attendants, the female crew lead and her male newbie, slid into rear-facing jumpseats at the front of the plane, while the third found an empty seat in the main cabin.

A batting coach in an exit row tightened his seatbelt as he looked out the window. *Thump-thump . . . thump-thump . . .* The red beacon on the wing mirrored his beating heart. Clouds rose up like wispy smoke, turning the indigo sky to ash. They were flying into the soup.

The hum of the engine went from alto to baritone. Most of the passengers intuited—correctly—that the change in tenor meant the pilot was slowing down, but only the engineer in 12D knew it was to reduce stress on the airframe. If you try to power through turbulence, he understood, it could rip the plane apart. The safest course is to ride them.

The aircraft quivered as they bounced along the pockmarked air. Tray tables rattled. Seatbelts strained against jiggling thighs and laps. 12D counted his inhales and exhales to quiet his unease. *Sixteen . . . seventeen . . .* And then they were back riding smooth sky. Ten uneventful seconds turned to twenty, then thirty, then sixty.

"Was that it?" the bridesmaid in 28D asked.

"I think that was it," a groomsman across the aisle answered.

"Hell yeah!" whooped someone in the back who'd had three gin and tonics. And everyone who didn't know what it feels like in the eye of a storm laughed.

"Rita," the jumpseated male flight attendant said, pointing at the tattooed rockstar who was on his feet, reaching for something in an overhead bin.

"There's always one." She reached for the intercom to tell the rocker to sit his ass down. As her hand closed around the handset—

FWUMP! The plane bucked like an angry horse, nose plunging toward earth as the tail kicked the sky. The guitarist whipped back into his seat. As he hurried to reclip his seatbelt—

BAM! A guitar case toppled out of that open bin, ricocheted off an armrest, then tumbled end-over-end down the aisle.

The plane leveled off long enough for one collective gasp—

Then dropped like a skydiver in freefall.

Passengers shrieked as the guitar case slammed against the ceiling. The bridesmaid in 28D white-knuckled her armrests like she was back on *Colossus*. Some passengers reached for the hand of the person sitting next to them. Others prayed in hushed whispers with eyes shut tight.

Rita looked down at her balled fists, then flexed her hands and pressed her palms into her thighs. People would look to her to know how serious this was, and she didn't want to give them reason to panic. The only thing worse than turbulence was panic. Well, except for that other, unspeakable thing.

The left wing dipped as the plane banked, carving a C-shaped trough through the clouds. As the airframe shook, the engineer imagined rivets vibrating out of their sockets and the aluminum panels of the plane's exoskeleton peeling away one by one.

Captain Brett Bancroft, a retired navy pilot who'd flown with the Blue Angels, depressed the Push-To-Talk button on his sidestick.

"Miami Central, this is Pioneer 8-6-8. We experienced a loss of altitude due to turbulence, we're recovering on a zero-eight-zero heading and climbing back up to flight level three-zero-zero."

"Roger that 8-6-8," the controller responded over the comms. "Hold heading zero-eight-zero and resume FL three hundred. You should find some clearer air up there."

"From his lips . . ." Bancroft quipped to his first officer, who wasn't nervous, not really.

The captain rolled the sidestick and the craft surged forward and up.

"He's trying to break through the eyewall," Rita told her rookie flight attendant. "Almost there." The shoulder harness bit into her neck, but she made a point not to grimace.

The airframe was rattling like a tambourine. As she considered calling the captain to ask how much longer—

POP!

A sword of electricity struck the plane's midsection, then exploded into a hundred thorny tendrils of light. The cabin lit up like a Christmas tree as white-hot lightning seized it in its grasp. This was a new experience, even for Rita. As she looked at the passengers from her rear-facing jumpseat, her mind flashed to the famous painting by Edvard Munch, only with one hundred and twenty-seven faces screaming instead of one.

"Oh God," her male underling murmured. She grabbed his arm and gave it a squeeze.

"It's OK, Alphonso. Lightning can't hurt us."

And then, as if to prove her wrong, the cabin lights flicked off and they were plunged into darkness.

"Oh God!" Alphonso said again, louder this time.

"What's happening?" a passenger cried out. "Turn on the lights!"

Rita let go of Alphonso's arm and reached above her head. Her fingers found the airphone. She yanked it from the cradle.

"Captain Bancroft?"

No answer.

"Captain, are you there?"

Still no answer. Because, she realized, when the lights went out, they took the comms with them.

"What does he say?" Alphonso asked.

"He's working on it." Rita hated lying to her colleague, but he was already on the verge of panic.

She sat in darkness, gripping that phone for ten, twenty, thirty seconds, as if squeezing it might bring it back to life. In the absence of sight, the sounds took center stage—moaning, whimpering, a choked sob. In the jumpseat next to her, Alphonso recited the Lord's Prayer between ragged breaths.

The aircraft ascended sharply. As the G-force pinned the passengers' tears to their cheeks, they thought of spouses who'd stood by them in hard times; children they should have hugged more; friends, grudges, debts they wished they'd forgiven. And then, like closing a window against the wind, the plane leveled off and the turbulence stopped. Seconds after that, the cabin lights went back on, dimmed and tranquil, as if it had all been a dream.

"Well, that was one for the memoir," Captain Bancroft said over the PA as Rita set the handset back in the cradle. "Yes, that was lightning. It temporarily short circuited our avionics, but all systems are back online. Should be smooth sailing all the way to San Juan."

The cabin erupted into applause. Everyone was cheering.

Well, not everyone.

"I'm gonna puke," the kid with the iPad said, pushing his way into the aisle. He sprinted to the lavatory. Opened the door. But he didn't go in. Because someone was already in there. Slumped on the floor. Face bashed in like someone had taken a baseball bat to it.

Because someone had.

SPECIAL AGENT SAM COOPER: Officer Renaldo, this is Special Agent Sam Cooper of the FBI Violent Crimes Division. DHS briefed us on the situation up there, I'll be your POC going forward.

FEDERAL AIR MARSHAL CARLOS RENALDO: Yes, sir. Good evening, sir.

COOPER: Bring me up to speed.

RENALDO: Looks like we've had a homicide while in flight, sir. In one of the aft lavatories.

COOPER: You have a suspect?

RENALDO: No sir, not yet.

COOPER: I'll have a team of field agents meet the aircraft the moment it lands, but you're on your own while you're in the air.

RENALDO: Yes, sir.

COOPER: I need you to keep those passengers calm and in their seats until my team can take over.

RENALDO: Understood.

COOPER: I trust you've been briefed on our code of conduct.

RENALDO: Sir?

COOPER: Be polite, be professional, and have a plan to neutralize anyone who poses a threat.

RENALDO: Copy that.

COOPER: You and those passengers are in a sardine can thirty thousand feet above the earth with a cold-blooded killer, Renaldo.

RENALDO: Yes, sir, I'm aware.

COOPER: Watch your back.

PART

The Calm Before

001

CHAPTER

001

Federal Air Marshal Carlos Renaldo was a practical man. Some might say fastidious—not that they are the same thing. Two prongs of the same fork, perhaps.

He liked to play a game with himself as he went through his morning routine. He called it "snake in the grass," because snakes are the most efficient hunters in the animal kingdom. And also, people are afraid of them.

He slithered out of bed on the side closest to the bathroom. It was five strides to the john, and a ninety-degree pivot to the sink. The only time he had to backtrack was to get to his dresser, which was across from the bed. His socks and underwear were next to each other in the top drawer, separated by a bamboo slat. He pulled them out at the same time, so he only had to open the drawer once. His joggers were in the bottom drawer, which he opened with his foot. T-shirts were in the drawer directly above. He always wore a plain white one for working out, and the white ones were always on top. Three drawers, four items, *bing, bang, boom.*

The kitchen was at the bottom of the stairs. He kept the glasses in the cupboard next to the sink so he could fill and chug without moving his feet. His sneakers were by the front door, under the wooden bench where he sat to put them on. There was no prize for his efficiency, just the satisfaction that every movement had a purpose.

When not in the sky, he ran six miles at six a.m. every day. When you cross time zones for a living, having a routine is vital to your sanity. If he beat his eight-minute-mile pace, he'd round out the workout with sit-ups and push-ups. He promised himself fifty minutes of exercise every day. If he did less, he was only cheating himself. He had a pull-up bar in his kitchen doorway, which he used when he was waiting for his toast to pop. No wasted minutes. That was his game. That was his way.

He ate his toast with two egg rounds from Costco, then went upstairs to shower. He'd let his jet-black hair grow long in the front to offset the military vibe of his sculpted shoulders and tapered waist. As an air marshal, he was undercover so didn't wear a uniform. The only mandatory accessories were his badge, flex-cuffs, and Glock 9mm, which he holstered on his right hip, then covered with a sweater or loose-fitting polo. He wasn't a blazer guy. Too stiff, and not his style.

His itinerary had been sent to him the night before. It was a typical Friday. A quick, morning flight up the coast to San Francisco, back down to San Diego, then an afternoon flight to San Juan. He'd get a ten-hour rest in Puerto Rico, then do the whole thing in reverse. The weekly Puerto Rico flight was his baby. He'd been doing it for over a year. He'd lived on the island from birth to age eight, his fluency with the language and culture made him a natural choice. Plus, it was a helluva lot better than boring, back-to-back trips to Sacramento or Seattle. But that's not why he'd requested it.

He pulled on a pair of dark-wash jeans, a heather gray polo from Ralph Lauren, and his vintage Members Only windbreaker, then stuffed a change of clothes in his backpack, along with a toothbrush, deodorant, sunglasses, and a razor with a fresh blade. He liked a close shave. And the opportunity to flaunt that the rules of commercial flight didn't apply to him.

As he waited for his Uber, he took out his phone to check on Katie. He found it amusing how many people got caught in a lie because of something they posted on their socials. Not that knowing what someone did last summer was his job. He was a glorified security guard, not a secret agent. All that was relevant was what he observed in real time. Who's fidgeting? Texting? Overdressed? Underdressed? Drinking? Eating? Using the bathroom a lot? Or not at all? If he saw something, his job was to act, not ask questions. The FBI did the investigating. He was just the bouncer.

He had an Instagram account, but there were no pictures of him or anyone he knew on it. His username, RogerDodger98, was based on a pretend love of the LA Dodgers, and all his posts were baseball related. Every Puerto Rican kid knew baseball, it was as beloved on the island as Jennifer Lopez and La Bamba. His knowledge made for a convincing cover story. Most air marshals picked something dull—a real estate developer or business consultant—to explain why they traveled so much. But, if asked—and he often was—he told people he was a scout, traveling the country to find talent for a team he was not allowed to identify. Cool, right?

RogerDodger98 didn't follow Katie, but he searched for her so often her profile came up as soon as he typed the letter "K." She had started using a beauty filter which made her look like an anime cartoon character, but her smile was still perfectly crooked and showed off her one dimple. There were new posts about her cat (shedding, always shedding), her morning coffee (the other love of her life), that hike that "almost killed her." He chuckled to himself, charmed to the core. One day he'd slip, and she'd find out he had an Instagram account, and not just to back-up his cover story. But for now, peeking in on her was his secret pleasure.

He checked his watch—a 1963 Rolex Submariner left to him by his hard-living, Irish father, whose other gifts included sea green eyes and a jaw as square as a shoebox. It was 7:42 a.m. Assuming no flight delays, he would be seeing her in just over five hours. And then it would be another six hours at thirty thousand feet before he got her to himself. He was supposed to sleep during his ten-hour turnaround in Puerto Rico, but that was the only time he saw Katie all week, and he wasn't going to waste it sleeping.

A white Explorer rounded the corner. He checked his Uber app to confirm the plate number, then his flight tracker to confirm his departure time. Every other day he was laser-focused on his job.

But today his mind was elsewhere.

CHAPTER

002

Francesca Kessler decided not to water the garden. What did she care if the potted geraniums died? She wasn't coming back here.

The trip came at the perfect time, but that's not why she'd volunteered to chaperone. Nobody wanted her to come, but they couldn't say no to her after what she'd been through. The Crestwood High School Baseball Booster Club was paying for everything, including the cab that was due to arrive any minute. Every time she thought about backing out, she reminded herself that no one ever got what they wanted by staying in their comfort zone.

Puerto Rico is part of the United States, she didn't need a passport, but it was still zipped in the inside pocket of her purse, along with a tin of breath mints and Matthew's baseball cards from the one season he played for Crestwood High. Well, half a season. The cards were Penelope's idea. The kids thought they were stupid—they hated having to pose with their bats on their shoulders and gloves in the air. But the parents ate them up, and at twenty dollars apiece, they made a tidy profit for the Boosters. Francesca had bought six of them. If she did the math, she'd realize she was the one paying for her cab ride to the airport. But no matter. The cards were worth way more to her than that.

She looked down at her watch. She was an anxious traveler. She wasn't afraid the plane would crash, that would almost be a relief. No, she was anxious about the other stuff. Would there be traffic on the way to the airport? Would the security line take forever? Had she forgotten something? The worst part was right after the plane landed, when everyone took out their phones to call people who wanted to know they got there safe. That part made her feel like dying.

She set down her purse to use the bathroom one last time. She'd designed the downstairs powder room herself. Rick thought the crystal chandelier was over-the-top, but she loved how it cast tiny rainbows on the walls when the sun hit it just so. Out of all the decorative touches she'd made over the sixteen years they'd lived there, she was going to miss that chandelier the most.

She checked her reflection in the mirror as she washed her hands. Her heart-shaped face was framed by a layered bob that bounced off her shoulders in loose waves. She'd been blessed with thick, chestnut brown hair that, after forty-two years on her head, had not given way to even one strand of gray. Her weary, brown eyes were framed by lashes that barely needed mascara. Her father-in-law had called her "a looker," which was embarrassing to someone who considered her looks the least interesting thing about her. But her father-in-law didn't talk to her anymore, and she imagined he had a new moniker for her now.

It was a perfect spring day, full of lemony sunshine and cool breezes, so she decided to wait outside. Her black Samsonite looked like everybody else's, so she'd tied a lavender ribbon around the handle so no one would grab it by mistake. As she rolled it down the front walk, she eyed the geraniums, sighed, and stopped. It wasn't their fault she'd lost the house. She reached behind the ficus to turn on the water, then unspooled the hose and moistened the pots.

The cab arrived while she was returning the hose to its resting place. She waved and hurried over to meet the driver before he honked. She wanted to be remembered as a courteous neighbor, even though she was quite certain she'd be remembered for something else.

"I'll get your bag," the cabbie said, taking the suitcase from her. He was nearly twice her age, but she let him. As he wrapped his hand around the handle, she noticed he was missing a finger. Not the whole finger, just the top half. Like so many things, it made her think of Matthew. He'd wanted to make her a birdhouse for Mother's Day, but when the hammer missed the nail, the project was abandoned for the emergency room. As they rolled him into surgery, she remembered thinking how losing the use of that finger for weeks, months, possibly forever, was the worst thing that could happen to a kid. She had no perspective back then.

She glanced up at the house. She and Rick had moved into the two-story Spanish Colonial when she was five months pregnant. She knew she was having a boy and wanted a big backyard for him to play in. The house itself was nothing special, but she could fix that. And she did, over time, replacing the scuffed tile with gleaming hardwood, installing new kitchen cabinets and bathroom fixtures, sprucing up the front walk with terracotta pots. The best memories of her life were made in that house. And also the worst.

She clutched her purse to her chest as she slid into the backseat. She peeked in the front pocket to make sure she had her phone, even though she'd already checked when she left the house, and again when the driver was loading her suitcase into the trunk.

"Airport?" the cabbie asked as he got behind the wheel.

"Yes."

"When's your flight?"

"One o'clock."

"Oh, you got plenty of time."

She wanted to tell him that assuming everything will be fine is how people get hurt, but that was a lesson you had to learn the hard way.

He popped the car in gear and pulled away from the curb. She willed herself not to look back. It was just a house. The stuff that had made it a home had been taken from her long ago. Letting go was part of life. Something we do along the way and at the very end.

The car bumped over the pothole that refused to stay fixed, past a basketball hoop that nobody used anymore, the house that went all out on Halloween—

"Stop!" Francesca called out, surprising even herself. The cab lurched forward as the driver hit the brakes. "I'm sorry. Can you go back? Just for a minute."

The driver met her eyes in the rearview, then wordlessly turned the car around.

"Just pull into the driveway. Please," she said, making a mental note to tip him extra.

Francesca gripped her purse as she punched in the code and slipped under the opening garage door. She took the stairs two at a time. Matthew's room was at the end of the hall. His door was closed, as it had been since she'd boxed up his stuff two weeks ago.

She pushed the door open and stepped over the threshold. Her son hadn't set foot in this room for almost three years, it was crazy to think there would be any traces of him. But she'd earned the right to act a little crazy.

She sat on the bare mattress and peered out the window into the backyard. In all the years they'd lived here, she'd never done this. Is that why she came back? To know what the world looked like to him before that terrible night? Parents make countless decisions, each one pushing the trajectory of their child's life a millionth of a degree in one direction. Cornflakes or eggs? Public school or private? Baseball or track? Rick made his opinions known, but she was the decider. How many decisions would she have to take back for her son to still wake up to this view? A hundred? A handful? One?

The cab driver honked the horn. It was time to go. As she walked out of Matthew's room for the last time, she didn't cry. But she didn't let go either.

CHAPTER

003

"Francesca!" a woman's voice called out over the airport din. "Over here!"

Francesca looked over her shoulder to see Penelope Abernathy waving her manicured hand above her head like the beauty pageant winner she once was.

"You aren't going to the gate already, are you?" Penelope asked as Francesca approached. Her heavily made-up eyes were shaded by an enormous, black-and-white striped sun hat that reminded Francesca of cartoon prison clothes. Francesca thought about telling the reigning Crestwood Baseball Booster Club president she couldn't get sunburned inside the terminal, but surely she knew that.

"Our flight is delayed, did you see?" Penelope asked, showing her a notification on her phone.

"I brought a book. I was just going to read at the gate."

"Come with me."

Penelope slid the straps of her Louis Vuitton tote over her shoulder and marched toward the first-class lounge. The scent of gardenias and money wafted over Francesca as she followed in her wake.

"She's with me," Penelope said to the uniformed gatekeeper. Francesca wasn't sure, but it looked like Penelope pushed a twenty into his hand.

Francesca had never been in Pioneer Air's first-class lounge, or any other first-class lounge, and she was disappointed to discover how unimpressive it was. Chocolate brown club chairs were arranged in little foursomes like seats on a train, and the textured ivory carpet was as bland as cottage cheese. The only thing that made this place special was the cost of admission. Kind of like that Louis Vuitton bag.

"There's drinks and snacks at the bar," Penelope said, reading Francesca's mind. Francesca wasn't hungry, but after that twenty-dollar bribe, she thought it rude not to partake, so she helped herself to an oats-and-honey granola bar and a Coke.

"You're one of those people who can eat whatever you want and not gain weight, aren't you?" Penelope said, eyeing Francesca's diminutive waist. Francesca smiled weakly. She didn't want to invite comparison.

"I ran this morning," Francesca said, to be kind. Poor Penelope had so many unrealized aspirations. Being crowned Miss Kentucky was supposed to be her jumping-off point, not her peak. Her sons were her chance to achieve the glory that had evaded her. All three played baseball at Crestwood High. The first two, Nolan and Ryan—named for the pitcher, obviously—were talented, but abandoned the sport like a broken toy as soon as they graduated. Her last hope, a six-foot tall senior named Ace, wasn't living up to his given name and was currently being retooled as an outfielder.

"They have beer and wine," Penelope said, grabbing a mini of Chardonnay from the beverage cooler. "Free of charge." *Is it really free, though?* Francesca thought but didn't say out loud.

"Thanks, but I don't think I'm allowed to drink while I'm working." Unlike Penelope, who was tagging along to make sure Ace made the team's Instagram, Francesca had responsibilities as a teacher-chaperone.

"Coach is drinking." Penelope pointed to a ruddy-cheeked Irishman nursing a Heineken at a window table. "I got him in too. Poor guy doesn't know what to do with himself." Francesca observed that he was reading scouting reports, as if he knew exactly what to do with himself.

"I'll stick with soda, thanks," Francesca said, cracking open the can. A bartender appeared out of nowhere and handed her a glass. "Oh, thank you."

"Once you fly first class, you can never go back to coach," Penelope said as she whipped off her hat and shook out her freshly blown-out hair. There was a word for people like Penelope, but Francesca couldn't think of it right then. "If you have enough miles, the upgrade costs you almost nothing."

Tone deaf. That was the term she was looking for. Two words, not one.

"Coach looks lonely," Penelope announced. "Let's go rattle his cage."

Francesca followed Penelope to Coach Callahan's table. A trim, flaxen-haired forty-something, Brendan "Cal" Callahan got drafted by the Red Sox out of Stanford but only pitched one season at Fenway Park. Still, as the coach who helped Chicago Cubs MVP Trey Turnberry go pro right out of high school, he was a bit of a local celebrity. Players hardly ever got drafted without playing at least a year or two of college ball. Turnberry's signing set the baseball world on fire. Kids came from all over San Diego County for Coach Cal's program, some even farther.

"You ready for another beer?" Penelope asked, plopping down across from him.

"Nah, I'm good." As the president of the Boosters, Penelope held the purse strings of the program, so he added, "Gotta keep my wits about me," to stay on her good side.

Coach pulled out a chair for Francesca. "Thank you for volunteering to join us."

"Happy to help," she said as she sat.

"Is Ace leading off?" Penelope asked, squinting at the lineup card.

"Still working it out." He folded the card in half and tucked it in his binder. He had to start the Booster Club president's son, just like he'd done with her other two, whether or not the boy had earned it.

"Where are the boys?" Francesca asked, suddenly wondering if, as their teacher-chaperone, she should be with them.

"The other coaches are corralling them at the gate," Cal said. "Don't worry, we have plenty of eyes."

Francesca smiled through her confusion. If they had plenty of eyes, why was she here?

Ever the mind-reader, Penelope said, "You'll have plenty to do once we get to Puerto Rico." Francesca snuck a glance at Coach. He was not as good a liar as the Booster Club president. Francesca's cheeks flushed red hot at the reminder that nobody needed her, not really.

"Well, it's very pleasant in here," Francesca said, raising her glass in a gesture of appreciation.

"After what you've been through, you deserve it."

Coach Cal's eyes flicked up. Francesca's hand shook as she took a sip of her Coke. She deserved a lot more than a few hours in the first-class lounge.

And this trip was her chance to get it.

Dear Friends and Family,

We are thrilled to announce that we are embarking on a beautiful journey together. With immense joy in our hearts, we invite you to join us as we exchange vows and begin our married life.

In the spirit of adventure, we have chosen the stunning island of Puerto Rico as the backdrop for our wedding. Surrounded by the shimmering Caribbean Sea, under the warm tropical sun, we will be saying our "I do's" in a beachside ceremony.

Your presence will add immeasurable happiness to our special day. Join us as we celebrate love, laughter, and a future filled with endless possibilities.

DATE: 19 April 2026
TIME: Five o'clock in the evening
VENUE: Beachside Oasis Hotel and Resort, San Juan, Puerto Rico

For more details and travel information, please visit our wedding website: **www.BillyandJilly.com**

CHAPTER

004

"Who wants another drink?" William "Billy" Wilcox asked after the airline announced the flight to Puerto Rico was delayed.

"Bring it!" shouted Jilly Azarian, his bride-to-be, as she swigged the rest of her whiskey sour and slammed down the glass. Yes, they were Billy and Jilly—well, her given name was Jillian, but no one would call her that anymore.

Their wedding-goers, twenty-three people in total, had taken over the terminal two airport bar, and were unfazed to learn they would be stuck there for two more hours.

"That's my wife," Billy peacocked.

"She's not your wife yet," his best man corrected him.

"I'll marry her in this bar if I have to," Billy shot back.

Jillian blew him a kiss. He pretended to catch it and press it to his heart. If you didn't like them, you might find their theatrics annoying, or perhaps wonder if one of them was over-compensating.

Ding-ding-ding-ding-ding. Someone found a spoon and clinked it against their glass. Within seconds, the bar was filled with a symphony of stainless steel on stemware. Billy slid his hand around Jilly's waist, and they kissed like one of them was going off to war.

"Get it!" someone whooped, and the whole bar erupted in applause—minus one.

"You OK, Angie?" a groomsman asked the maid of honor, who was holding a Diet Coke in her not-clapping hands.

"Fine. I'm not a good flier."

"Maybe you should switch to tequila."

She forced a smile. She was a perfectly fine flier. "I'll be OK."

So there was no mistaking the back-up singers for the star, Angie and the four other bridesmaids were all wearing matching hot pink T-shirts that said, "Jilly's Bitches." Jilly, whose white tee read "Queen Bitch," wore white jeans to match and a sparkly, faux-diamond tiara that somehow had survived the security checkpoint. Jilly was a good match for Billy, but also a terrible one. As many in the wedding party were starting to realize.

"Fireball!" someone shouted as the song by Pitbull came on and the waitress appeared with hot cinnamon shots for the whole crew. Billy and Jilly stood up to help her pass them out—Jilly, to the groomsmen, and Billy, to the maidens.

"M'lady," the groom said to Angie, setting the shot down in front of her. His breath was thick with booze. There was no middle ground with him. He was either dry or soaked to the bone.

"We had a deal, Billy," she said, quietly enough so no one would hear. Jilly, with her wide face and deep-set eyes, was no match for dark-eyed, long-limbed Angie in the looks department. But she had something Angie didn't: tolerance.

"Let it go, Ange." Billy, meanwhile, was a three-sport athlete with a body to match. Blue-eyed and butterscotch blond with a smile that could melt cheese. Stand him next to Ryan Gosling and you wouldn't know which one was the movie star.

"You tell her, or I will," Angie said.

Their eyes locked. One of the bridesmaids looked over at them, so he smiled. "So glad you could make it, Ange." Angie felt a surge of irritation. He was going to have to deal with her, whether he liked it or not.

"To Billy and Jilly," one of the groomsmen shouted.

"For evah and evah," a bridesmaid chimed in. And everybody drank. Except Angie. And not just because she knew the couple was doomed.

"Why aren't you drinking, are you pregnant or something?" Billy's college roommate asked, glancing at her untouched shot. And she almost told him.

"Nah, she's just got sour grapes," the best man said, and Angie's irritation swelled to outrage.

"I never wanted to marry him."

"So you say."

OK, maybe not "never," just not now that she knew what he was. Angie had compassion for Billy. She knew alcoholism was genetic and often triggered by childhood trauma. Billy's father, who was nursing a beer two tables over, was as mean as an alley cat, and preferred reprimanding his only son with a belt instead of words. His mother tried to leave the marriage five times and succeeded on the sixth by taking her own life. Billy was twelve. He coped by disappearing into sports, setting himself up for abuse by more unbalanced alpha males—a football coach with a foul mouth, a basketball coach with broken dreams. Only his baseball coach had treated him like he mattered, but baseball season only lasts three months—not nearly long enough to undo the damage from the other nine.

Billy and Angie had been high school sweethearts. After graduation, he went to Arizona State on a baseball scholarship. She stayed behind to tend bar and save money. She was smart enough to go to college, just not smart enough to figure out how to pay for it. Despite the distance between them, they remained a couple for the four years Billy was at ASU. He came back to Crestwood with a degree in business administration and a drinking problem. When he refused to get help, she left him. Not because she didn't love him, but because she loved herself.

It was eighteen months later when he started dating her best friend. Jillian had asked for her blessing, and she'd reluctantly given it. She wasn't jealous, that's not what the dread in the pit of her stomach was about. Jilly had a troubled past too. And she knew Billy would show her his trick to escape it.

Billy and Angie were each other's first loves. There would always be feelings there. Angie wasn't attracted to him anymore, but the same could not be said for her ex. He still came into her bar, even though there were other choices with better food and atmosphere. He came after work. He came to watch football on Sunday morning. And he came the night of his bachelor party, by himself, with a mission.

Angie watched as Billy and Jilly hooked their elbows together and threw back their fireballs. She didn't want to be a party-pooper. But Jilly deserved to know what Billy had done. Even if it meant the end of their friendship.

TRAGIC HIT-AND-RUN SHATTERS COMMUNITY

Beloved Teen Baseball Enthusiast
Matthew Kessler Remembered
by Maryanne Kennedy, Staff Writer

Crestwood, CA, May 13, 2023—A close-knit community is in mourning after a hit-and-run incident claimed the life of 15-year-old Matthew Kessler, a freshman at Crestwood High School.

The incident occurred last night at approximately 9:30 p.m. near the vacant lot off Maple Drive. Matthew, a rising baseball star, was rushing to catch up with his teammates when he was struck by a speeding vehicle. The driver fled the scene and is still at large.

Despite the best efforts of medical personnel, Matthew succumbed to his injuries at Mercy Hospital later that night. The entire community is grappling with the loss of a young life that held so much promise and brought joy to those around him.

"Matthew was not just a player, he was the heart of our team," said Coach Brendan "Cal" Callahan. "His energy, determination, and sportsmanship were unparalleled. He had a natural talent for the game, but it was his kindness and encouragement that set him apart."

Local law enforcement is actively investigating the incident, urging anyone with information about the reckless driver to come forward. "We are determined to bring the person responsible for this tragedy to justice," said Sheriff Alan Eckles. "We urge the community to assist us in any way possible to ensure that Matthew's family receives the closure they deserve."

The mayor's office has released a statement saying, "The town of Crestwood stands in solidarity with Matthew's parents, Rick and Francesca Kessler, as we all mourn the loss of a bright young star whose light was tragically extinguished too soon."

Rest in peace, Matthew.

CHAPTER

005

Francesca finished her Coke and stood up to go. "I'm going to head to the gate to check on the boys."

Coach Callahan stood up too. "I'll go with you."

Penelope looked at them like they were crazy. "You realize you're going from *Downton Abbey* to *Lord of the Flies*," she said. Both remained standing. "Suit yourselves."

Coach Cal stepped aside and indicated for Francesca to go ahead. As the baby-faced gatekeeper smiled and opened the door for her, Francesca couldn't help but wonder how many twenties were stuffed in that puffed-out pants pocket.

Light from the midday sun poured through floor-to-ceiling windows, making the marble and concrete floor sparkle like a sea of diamonds. Francesca walked next to Cal in silence, letting the sounds of foot traffic and roller bags swirl with her thoughts. She hadn't been alone with Coach Cal since he'd dropped by her house with the contents of her dead son's locker. That was nearly three years ago. Not that they were alone here, in the middle of terminal two, on a busy travel day. But her discomfort remained. Every conversation they'd ever had was about Matthew. How strong his throwing arm was getting. How they were moving him to shortstop. How he should start coming to the off-season program, work with a conditioning coach, what a natural talent he was. And then what a horrible tragedy this was, how much all his coaches and teammates would miss him, how sorry they were for her loss.

Francesca tried not to wince as the backs of her shoes rubbed her skin raw. She wasn't one of those cool teachers who wore Converse and cargo pants to school. It was hard enough to get the kids to take her seriously in leather pumps and boxy blazers.

"So, what exactly are my responsibilities?" Francesca asked, breaking the stiff silence between them. She snuck a glance at his profile, wondered if his ears were red from the beer or the question.

"Honestly? I think it's just a by-laws thing, to have another teacher here, since some of the kids are minors."

"I see." Francesca wasn't sure how she felt about that. If she wanted to be irrelevant, she could have just stayed home. But then again, if she didn't have an official agenda, she could focus on hers.

"They're good boys," the coach said. "The coaching staff will keep them in line." Francesca wasn't sure if he was trying to make her feel better or worse.

They reached the gate. The boys were all there, dressed in shiny tracksuits, their matching backpacks at their feet. She counted eighteen baseball-capped heads, all tilted down, staring at their phones. She knew several of the seniors from Matthew's brief stint on the team, and most of the others from her classes. Sometimes she played a trick on herself, focusing her eyes on something in the distance so the foreground would blur, and Matthew could come back to her. Forever frozen in time, he'd be the youngest one there, shorter and skinnier than the other players, but with feet as big as pontoons. His coaches used to marvel at those feet. Meant he was going to be tall, they said, not knowing why their prediction was incorrect.

"I was surprised you wanted to come," Coach said. Then, a little more boldly, "Why did you want to come?" She didn't want him to see the sheen in her eyes, so she answered without looking at him.

"Wasn't I meant to be here?"

Cal turned his gaze back to the boys. The time for condolences had long since passed. Besides, he'd said how sorry he was a million times a million different ways. Francesca didn't blame him. Yes, they'd had a game that night. But once he dismissed his players, he wasn't responsible for what they did.

"I'm glad you came," Coach said, because it was the polite thing to say.

"I didn't have any spring break plans. Except for moving. And I'm letting the movers do that."

"A move for the better, I hope?"

"We can't afford the house anymore," Francesca replied, even though she was no longer a "we." If they were still a "we," they'd be able to afford it just fine.

"I'm sorry, I didn't mean to pry."

"You didn't pry. I offered. I'm moving in with my sister until I find a new place. She's still getting organized, so the timing was perfect. Plus, I'd have driven those movers crazy, hovering over them like a helicopter."

All of this was true. Yet it was still a lie. Movers were coming. And she preferred not to watch them dismantle her life one box at a time. But the movers weren't the reason she was flying all the way across the country. It was what was due to arrive, not what was being taken away, that she was trying to escape.

"I'm still technically married," she said to explain the ring on her finger. "Papers will be waiting for me when I get back."

The admission caught in her throat. She let herself wonder, just for the briefest of seconds, that if she stayed in Puerto Rico, maybe she'd never have to sign them.

"That's hard," Coach offered.

"Life is hard," Francesca reminded him, because she knew he'd been through it too.

"'If you're going through hell, keep going.' Winston Churchill," Coach said.

She responded with a quote of her own: "'No more tears now; I will think about revenge.' Mary, Queen of Scots."

And the coach known for rousing pep talks fell uncharacteristically silent.

SPECIAL AGENT SAM COOPER: So they did it with a baseball bat?

FEDERAL AIR MARSHAL CARLOS RENALDO: I'm not a forensics expert, sir, but that would be my guess, given that there's one on the lavatory floor covered with blood.

COOPER: Leave it where it is, we want that crime scene undisturbed.

RENALDO: Copy that.

COOPER: Who else has seen the body?

RENALDO: Just the teen boy who discovered it. And the three flight attendants.

COOPER: Tell me about the boy.

RENALDO: He's in high school. Said he's traveling with the baseball team.

COOPER: So he's one of the ball players?

RENALDO: Yes, sir.

COOPER: Keep him away from the other boys. We don't want him working them into a frenzy.

RENALDO: Yes, sir.

COOPER: We're running background checks on all the passengers and crew. I'll let you know if we need you to babysit anyone for the remainder of the flight.

RENALDO: Copy that.

COOPER: Nobody leaves that plane until we make an arrest. That's from the Deputy Director. I don't care how much they cry.

RENALDO: Yes, sir.

CHAPTER

006

"Billy, you need to slow down," Walter Wilcox said, putting a hand on his son's shoulder. "You're making an ass of yourself."

"Did I mention how glad I am that you're coming to the wedding?" Billy said, absorbing the blow like a seasoned prize fighter. "No? Huh. Maybe there's a reason for that." Billy drained the rest of his beer, then signaled to the waitress to bring him another. Most of the twenty-two member wedding party had stopped drinking after their fireball shot, but if they couldn't keep up with him, that was their problem.

"You don't want to be remembered as a drunk on your wedding weekend." Walter's hand tightened around Billy's shoulder. Billy swatted it off.

"It's my party. I'll do whatever the hell I want."

"Your party?" his father mocked. "I didn't realize you were paying for everything."

"It's a party in my honor. Me and Jilly." Billy knew people thought he was marrying for the money, because yeah, Jilly's family was loaded. But fuck them and their ignorant assumptions.

"Yeah, well, the bride's mother is over there trying to talk her out of it." Walter indicated with his head. "Keep it up and she might just succeed."

Billy looked over at Jilly. She was deep in conversation with her mother. Neither were smiling. For a second, Billy almost believed him.

"You don't know what they're talking about."

"Everyone knows what they're talking about." Walter pulled out a stool and sat down across from his son. "Everyone who's not wasted."

Billy met his father's iron gaze. Years of hard living had carved sagging crescents under his eyes, but the rage behind them still burned bright. It didn't scare Billy like it used to. He had the alcohol to thank for that.

"You can't ever be happy for me, can you?" Billy had spent his entire life trying to please his father. From those early days on the playground when he did laps on the monkey bars until his palms were pink and blistered to cheating on his math final so he could graduate with honors. Once upon a time, Billy would have sold his soul to get an "atta boy" from his dad. But not anymore.

"I just don't want to see you ruin a good thing," Walter said. If it hadn't come from his father, Billy might have taken the warning to heart.

"Like you did, you mean?"

Billy didn't decide his mom's suicide was his father's fault until he got to college. Meeting new people meant telling the story, and every good story needs a villain. But what Billy didn't, or *couldn't*, acknowledge was that their family's story was still being written. It didn't start, or end, with Walter. Violence, like blue eyes and bunions, ran in his family. Billy was both the product and a continuation of it.

Walter opened his mouth to return his son's barb but was interrupted by a voice that brought him back to better days.

"Hi Walter," Angie said, taking father and son by surprise.

"Angela! I forgot you were going to be here."

"Maid of honor," she said, pointing to her shirt.

"Right. Of course."

"I was hoping to steal Billy for a few minutes, if I may?"

She looked at Billy. On a scale of one to ten, his desire to continue their conversation from earlier that afternoon was a one. His desire to continue talking to his dad was even less.

"Yeah, sure," Billy said as he stood.

"See you on board," Angie said to Walter, then headed for the exit. Billy followed her without looking back.

"Aren't you going to tell your bride?" Angie asked, stopping at the threshold.

"Tell her what?"

"That you're stepping away." He did not, in fact, want to tell Jilly he was sneaking off to talk to his ex-girlfriend, because that would invite the dreaded, "What about?"

"She'll figure it out."

Angie was already texting.

"What are you doing?"

"Telling her I'm borrowing you."

"Why the hell would you do that?"

"Because she's my friend, and I don't fuck around on my friends."

She hit "send." Across the bar, Jilly looked down at her phone, then up at them. Angie gave her the thumbs-up, and Jilly, while clearly a little confused, smiled and gave it back.

"Great. Now what's she gonna think?"

"Hopefully that we're planning a surprise for her." That this was indeed what they were doing did not have to be said.

They walked in silence for a full minute, past a souvenir shop, a Wetzel's Pretzels, a line of people waiting for coffee at Starbucks.

"I think you should tell her before we get on the plane," Angie finally said as they neared their gate. Billy stopped abruptly and she nearly bumped into him.

"Jesus, Billy!"

"Why do you want to hurt her?" he hissed. "I thought she was your *friend*." He leaned into the word friend, like she was the backstabber.

"Don't make this about me."

They were standing in the middle of the busy thoroughfare. Travelers whisked by them on both sides. A woman who had to go around them gave Angie the side-eye.

"Let's talk over there," Angie said, tilting her head toward the empty gate next to theirs. Billy begrudgingly followed. She stopped at a row of chairs by the window. She didn't sit, so he didn't either.

"This is supposed to be the happiest week of her life," Billy said, folding his arms across his chest.

"Yeah, well maybe you should have thought of that before you showed up at my bar." She raised an eyebrow at him, daring him to disagree.

"All guys do stupid shit at their bachelor parties," he said, parroting back something bartender Angie had once told him.

"So just say that. Then tell her the stupid thing *you* did."

Anger rose up from the pit of his stomach. "Why are you doing this?" Yes, he'd made a mistake. But she didn't have to make such a big fucking deal about it.

"Because what you did was wrong."

"Jesus, Angie. Why do you have to be so dramatic?" She didn't answer, so he added. "Get over yourself already."

"I could report you."

"For what?"

She raised an eyebrow. He shook his head. She was out of her depth.

"It's your word against mine," he said, because this was America, where people are innocent until proven guilty.

"You would deny it?"

"Well, I don't remember you saying no."

"Are you kidding me?"

"It's not like we've never done it before," he reminded her. "Everybody knows you were crazy about me." He thought he had her. But then she surprised him.

"I have a recording."

"What?"

"You heard me." His mind raced through the possibilities. There wasn't a hidden camera in that office . . . *was there?*

"You have a video?"

"Audio."

He felt his eyebrows contract. "You made an audio recording of us?" And she dropped a bomb.

"No. You did."

ANGIE'S VOICE: Hi, it's Angie. Leave me a message so I can call you back.

COMPUTER VOICE: At the tone, please record your message. When you are finished recording, you may hang up, or press one for more options. BEEP.

BILLY'S VOICE: Ange? Ah shit. You're probably at work. It's . . . I dunno, like . . . almost two. I'm going to swing by.
(Long pause . . . some muffled noises . . . thumping . . . crunching . . . two minutes of silence. Then, the sound of a car door opening and closing . . . swishing sounds . . . footsteps maybe? . . . the sound of a heavy door whooshing open.)

BILLY: Is Angie here?

UNFAMILIAR MALE VOICE: (muffled)

BILLY: Office?

UNFAMILIAR: I'm heading out. Lock the door behind me, would ya?

BILLY: Sure.

UNFAMILIAR: Have a good night.

BILLY: You too.
(Heavy door closes. The thunk of it locking . . . swishing sounds . . . a beat of silence.)

BILLY: Hey.

ANGIE: Oh my God, Billy! You scared me!

BILLY: How was your night?

ANGIE: What are you doing here?

BILLY: I came to see you.

ANGIE: Wasn't tonight your bachelor party?

BILLY: Meh. It was lame.

ANGIE: You're not allowed to be in here.

BILLY: Who's gonna know?

ANGIE: I mean it, Billy.
(The click of the office door closing . . . footsteps.)

ANGIE: What are you doing?

BILLY: You look beautiful.

ANGIE: You're drunk.

BILLY: What, I can't tell you you're beautiful anymore?

ANGIE: You're getting married in seven days.

BILLY: So I have seven more days.

ANGIE: I'm tired. I'm going home.

BILLY: What happened to us, Ange?

ANGIE: You're in my way.

BILLY: We used to be so good together.

ANGIE: Move, Billy.

BILLY: She's not like you.
(Muffled sounds . . . creaking . . .)

ANGIE: Billy, stop it.
(More creaking sounds)

ANGIE: Let go of me.

BILLY: You know you want it.

ANGIE: Get the fuck off me, Billy.
(Scraping and thumping sounds.)

ANGIE: Get off!

BILLY: Shhhhh . . .
(More thumping sounds . . . muffled breathing.)

BILLY: You smell so good.

ANGIE: Stop! Billy you . . . (inaudible) . . . not OK. Stop. STOP!

BILLY: I want to breathe in every inch of you.
(Muffled crying.)

BILLY: Shhhh. It's OK. It's just me. We love each other.
(Furniture rattling . . . more muffled crying.)

BILLY: That's it . . . that's it . . . Oh God.
(Silence.)

CHAPTER

007

"The little hot dogs are delish," someone behind Federal Air Marshal Carlos Renaldo said as he surveyed the food in the first-class lounge. "But the egg rolls taste like cat turd, consider yourself warned."

He turned to meet the gaze of the professionally-coiffed blond sitting on a nearby barstool. She wasn't his type, but he still checked her out, as was his habit and also his job. She was tall—five foot ten before those three-inch heels, big-boned with an oval face. Her accent had a southern twang: high society, not trailer trash. The boobs were real but the eyelashes were fake, just like her too-perfect teeth.

"I'm not really an egg roll man," Renaldo said, tucking an unruly strand of hair behind his ear. He tried to avoid talking to other passengers, but that didn't mean he couldn't be polite. It had been an uneventful morning—a quick there and back to San Francisco, then a leisurely stroll to the lounge to wait for his flight to San Juan. He didn't like being idle, but anticipation made his weekly reunions with Katie all the more exciting, so he took it in stride.

"Why they would serve deep fried flatulence to people crowding into a hermetically-sealed flying soda can is beyond me," the woman said as she tossed her hair. "Smells bad enough in there already."

Making a fart joke to a stranger was ballsy, and he found himself drawn to her like you might be to a car wreck.

"I'm not a fan of fried food under any circumstances," Renaldo informed her as he helped himself to four of those little hot dogs and something that looked like quiche.

"Then I guess you're not from the South."

Puerto Rico was the farthest south you could get without a passport, but he knew she meant the figurative south, not the actual.

"No, ma'am."

The woman moved her purse off the barstool so he could sit beside her. He hesitated. It was against his rules to get chummy with strangers, but snubbing women like this outspoken southern belle never ended well, and he was there to diffuse conflict, not incite it.

"Thanks," he said as he set his backpack down and slid onto the stool. His sidearm was on the hip closest to her, so he glanced down to make sure his windbreaker was covering it.

"I'm Penelope," she said, extending a manicured hand.

"Carlos."

"You a frequent flier?"

"Well, I'm not here for the food." He hoped his quip didn't sound flirtatious. She had an obscenely large diamond on her left ring finger, which didn't make her harmless—quite the opposite. In his experience, the bigger the diamond, the more desperate the wearer was for attention.

"Are you traveling for work, then?" she asked, taking a dainty sip of her wine. He couldn't tell her traveling *was* his work, so he just nodded. "Where are you headed?"

"San Juan." Because of his Irish features—light eyes and square jaw—people rarely guessed he was from the island.

"Oh!" she said, unable to raise eyebrows that were Botoxed in place. "I'm headed there too!" He tried not to grimace. He shouldn't have let himself be lured into conversation. But before he could excuse himself, she asked the dreaded question. "What type of work do you do?"

"I'm a scout," he said, as he'd rehearsed a thousand times.

"What kind of scout?"

"Baseball."

"College or pro?"

He popped a hot dog into his mouth. He sometimes got that question. "Pro."

Normally telling a woman he lived and breathed baseball shut her right up. In the rare instance she had questions, they were painfully basic—*"How many games do you go to? What do you look for in a player? Find any good ones this season?"*—and he could bluff his way through.

"Where are your top prospects coming from?"

The word "prospects" made him reach for his water.

"Usual places." He had no idea which programs were hot and didn't dare guess in front of this woman, who for all he knew worked for ESPN.

"I heard the SEC was a disappointment this year," she said with a sideways glance like he was meant to confirm or deny.

"You a scout too?" he asked, a little afraid he might not like her answer.

"Worse. I'm a baseball mom."

She smiled like he was meant to laugh, but he didn't take the cue.

"And I played," she added. "Softball, that is. A league batting champion, no less."

"Impressive."

She bowed her head at the compliment.

"Tell me about your son," he said, knowing his best escape was to make the conversation about her.

"I have three. Nolan is my oldest, he was a walk-on at Cal, but they didn't need a middle infielder, so he didn't play." She rolled her eyes like that annoyed her.

"Ryan, my middle one, could have gone to SC on a full ride but became an actor instead." She spoke the word "actor" like it was on par with robbing banks. "His claim to fame is a Doritos commercial." That eyeroll again.

"Ace is my youngest. He's a fastballer playing left field." She grimaced like this was a fate worse than that Doritos commercial.

"Who does your Ace play for?" Carlos normally avoided asking too many questions, but he wanted to keep her talking so he could finish his snack.

"Trey Turnberry's former team," she said with a conspiratorial smile. Trey Turnberry was the hottest player in baseball. Any scout who was actually a scout would know what team that was.

"Tough act to follow," he offered because he had no idea.

"I'll tell you what's tough," Penelope said. "Having every athlete under the sun bum-rushing our program." She punctuated her complaint by biting down on a piece of cheese.

He nodded like he felt her pain. "It's never good for the sport when all the good players flock to the same college." The statement was vague enough, it shouldn't have aroused suspicion. But for some reason, when he spoke the word "college," she stopped chewing, just for a tiny hint of a second.

"Well the real winner was the NCAA, don't you think?" she asked. Her nostrils flared like a rose blooming. On any other day, he might have recognized it as her tell. But he was in a good mood today—spirits were up, guard was down.

"Absolutely."

CHAPTER

008

It could have been a careless mistake. Or an unrelated generalization. But Penelope was suspicious by nature, as people who stretch the truth often are.

"Well, the real winner was the NCAA," she said, because it would be out of character for her to let it go.

The "scout" nodded in agreement. "Absolutely."

And that's when she began to wonder if "Carlos"—if that was his real name—might not be what he said he was. Because Trey Turnberry never played a single NCAA game, given that he was drafted right out of high school. Any scout worth his frequent flier miles would know that.

So what was going on here? She didn't think he was flirting. Yes, he had swagger, but he was also twenty years her junior. Fine, *thirty* years. Then again, he had looked her up and down like guys do when they want you to know the store is open. And he'd seemed strangely charmed by her fart joke, which was impertinent, even for her. Was that it, then? Was he flirting? Or was he just being a man who pretended he knew something he didn't because that's what men do?

"What team did you say you scout for?" she asked.

"I didn't." He pantomimed zipping his lip. *Yup. Flirting.*

"Been doing it a long time?"

"Feels like forever." *Forever? Plll. . .ease!* She suppressed the urge to snort. He looked barely out of college himself.

"Well, the Cubs got themselves a winner, that much is for certain."

"Fact," the scout agreed. At least he knew Turnberry played for the Cubs. *Typical man in a man's world. A woman with his sub-par knowledge would be fired on the spot.*

She was salivating to brag about her connection to this once-in-a-generation player. Her oldest son, Nolan, was close friends with Trey Turnberry. They were in the same graduating class at Crestwood and played middle infield together. She knew his parents. She'd even talked to them about their son's decision to go pro at the tender age of nineteen. Disappointingly, she couldn't tell him all that now, not after she'd played along with his gaffe about Trey playing in the NCAA. It was a shame she had to walk away. She quite enjoyed looking at him. But she didn't talk to dopes, not even ones with hard bodies and great hair.

"I need to go charge my laptop, excuse me."

She whisked her tote off the bar, then strode toward the table where she'd sat with Francesca and Coach. Even though her laptop was fully charged, she still plugged it in, because unlike the bullshitter at the bar, she knew how *not* to get caught in a lie.

As she logged onto the free Wi-Fi to check her email, she tried not to let the man's behavior upset her. Men always assume women don't know anything about sports. She was herself an athlete—a Division 1 All-Star, no less. Yes, it was softball, but that's only because girls weren't allowed to play baseball, even if they could throw, hit, and slide as well as any man. Which she could.

She logged onto her bballboosterprez email to wrap up any unfinished business before her five-day trip. It was time to order the senior gifts. They were doing gold-plated rope chain necklaces this year, with pendants engraved with each player's name and number. Yes, they were pricey, but the Booster Club was flush, thanks to her. Besides, this was her last year as president, she wanted to go out in style. Ace and his fellow seniors deserved something special after what they'd been through.

Losing a teammate is traumatic. The program nearly fell apart after Matthew Kessler died. It was no easy feat keeping it together—harder than most people knew.

She opened the order form to review the name of the eight seniors who would be getting a necklace. It should have been nine. She'd contemplated ordering one with Matthew Kessler's name on it to give to his mother—he'd be a senior this year, if not for the accident—but that felt macabre. Almost as macabre as Francesca taking the place of her dead son on this trip. For the life of her, Penelope couldn't understand why Francesca Kessler had volunteered to come.

Unless she wanted to ruin it for everyone else.

FEDERAL AIR MARSHAL CARLOS RENALDO: What's your name, son?

KAI RIVERS: Kai Rivers.

RENALDO: And you're on the baseball team?

KAI: Yeah. I play centerfield, mostly.

RENALDO: Tell me what you saw when you opened that lavatory door.

KAI: I saw . . . a body. On the floor, not moving. There was blood everywhere.

RENALDO: What did you think happened?

KAI: At first I thought it was because of the turbulence. Like maybe they got stuck in there. And, y'know . . . got tossed around.

RENALDO: But you don't think that anymore?

KAI: Not after I saw the bat.

RENALDO: Whose bat is it?
(No answer.)

RENALDO: The FBI is going to question everyone on this plane the moment we touch down.

No one gets off until they have a suspect. You want to sit here forever?

KAI: No.

RENALDO: Then I suggest you tell me what you know.

GATE ATTENDANT: Attention all passengers on Flight 868 with continuing service to San Juan. Due to the delayed departure of the previous leg of this flight, FAA safety regulations require us to make an unscheduled crew change.

The reserve crew has been called up, and we will be boarding just as soon as they are in place. We apologize for this inconvenience and appreciate your patience and understanding.

We kindly ask that you remain in the boarding area for further updates. Once again, we apologize for the delay and thank you for your cooperation.

CHAPTER

009

Cathy Yap was on her Peloton, riding into the fat burning target zone, when her phone rang. She grabbed it off the bookcase without missing a single RPM.

"This is Cathy."

Since divorcing her husband two years ago, Cathy, or "Yappy," as her friends called her because she liked to talk and to call her anything else would be a missed opportunity, had traded her Xanax for spinning, her graying bob for a purple pixie cut, and realized her lifelong dream of traveling the world by becoming a flight attendant for Pioneer Air.

"Yap, it's Suzie," the scheduler said. "Check your CCS, you're on 868 to Puerto Rico."

"Wait, seriously?"

"Yes, seriously."

"Yessss!" she said as she pedaled and pumped her fist. Cathy had bid for the Puerto Rico trip many times, but it was popular, and she was a newbie, so had never gotten it. "What day?"

"Today."

She slid the phone from her ear to look at the time. Flight 868 was scheduled to leave at one o'clock. It was one fifteen.

"Oh, shit!"

"Yeah, I know."

"I'm on my way."

She jumped off the bike and took the fastest shower in the history of showers. Pioneer had three standard uniforms. Cathy hadn't shaved her legs for six days, so she went with the pants, which suited her stick-straight shape better anyway. She dried her short hair upside-down so it would have lift—at five foot one she needed all the help she could get. She didn't have time for elaborate makeup—a sweep of mascara and lip gloss would have to do. Her standard-issue black carry-on was already packed, but she snuck a bathing suit and a tube of sunscreen in the front pocket because she had never swum in the Atlantic and wasn't about to miss her chance.

Cathy didn't have to tell anyone she was making an unplanned trip now that her fifteen-year marriage was over. It had been a good marriage between two people who loved their jobs and each other. Those days, Cathy was breaking sales records as a realtor, scooping up clients like fallen leaves. She knew the history of every nook and cranny of Crestwood, which neighborhoods were on the rise, and where that guy from that show lived and why he moved here. And, thanks to her gift of gab, all her clients did too.

If not for the incident, Cathy would still be married to Brendan, in a job that kept her close to home and to him. He was a creative lover, handy around the house, and a decent cook. But what he did—or, rather, *didn't* do—made it impossible to sleep in the same bed with him anymore. Or look at him over morning coffee. Or kiss him at the end of the day. People thought she was crazy to walk away from a lucrative career. She figured if she was going to blow up her life, she might as well do it properly. At forty-four, she was the oldest recruit in the Pioneer Air Flight Attendant Training Program. And the most enthusiastic one. She was making a fraction of her previous salary, but the adventure was priceless, and she'd never looked back.

Parking was expensive at San Diego International, so she Ubered to the airport, arriving a little after two, and went straight to the gate.

"You're the first one here," the gate agent said.

"How come the call was so last minute?"

"Flight from LA is arriving too late, the crew will expire before they land in Puerto Rico."

Cathy nodded. As someone who once worked seven days a week, the concept of a union telling you that you had to rest was strange to her. But rules were rules, and she respected them, especially when they resulted in an unexpected opportunity.

"Who's the purser?" Cathy asked, hoping it was someone who might enjoy her "yappy" side. Being able to talk nonstop was one of the things she enjoyed most about being a realtor, and her special skill was not always appreciated at thirty thousand feet.

"Rita Salazar," the gate attendant replied. "Flight's not full, so it's just you, her, and Fonzie."

Fonzie was a newbie like her, and she knew him well, as they often wound up on the flights nobody wanted—Denver (turbulent), Phoenix (hot), Calgary (boring). Cathy couldn't remember if she'd worked with Rita. She was racking her brain to conjure her face when someone tapped her on the shoulder.

"Hey, Cath."

She knew the voice, of course. If you tallied all the voices she'd heard in her lifetime, his would be the one she'd heard the most.

She turned to face him. "What are you doing here, Brendan?"

"I'm on your flight." He was wearing his usual—baseball cap and emerald, school-issued pullover with the team logo stitched where a breast pocket should be. "Taking the team to a tournament."

She looked out into the waiting area. In her excitement over landing this assignment, she hadn't noticed the eighteen boys wearing the exact same hat.

"It was bound to happen eventually," she said flatly. San Diego International wasn't massive like LAX or JFK. The odds of seeing somebody she knew were high, given that she was there twenty days a month and knew a lot of people.

"Well, I won't keep you from your duties," Coach Brendan Callahan said. "Just wanted to say hello." Then he smiled and went back to his team. As she watched him sit down next to a dark-haired woman in a linen blazer and stiff-looking slingbacks, she thought her eyes were playing tricks on her. A guilty conscience could conjure ghosts. Was that what was happening here?

She blinked and stared. She knew teachers were asked to chaperone, and that they took turns, but surely Crestwood had a staff member her ex-husband hadn't betrayed.

"The plane is in its final approach, the new departure time is 3:05," the gate attendant said. Cathy was too busy staring at Francesca Kessler to respond. Going on a field trip without the son who was supposed to be on it had to be the worst kind of torture. Was she a masochist?

Or something else?

FEDERAL AIR MARSHAL CARLOS RENALDO: Did you bring a baseball bat on board?

ACE ABERNATHY: Am I in trouble?

RENALDO: Why, did you do something?

ACE: What? No!

RENALDO: Baseball bats are prohibited by the TSA. How'd you get it past security?

ACE: My mom brought it.

RENALDO: Your mom?

ACE: She thinks it's lucky.

RENALDO: So your mom's the one who snuck the bat onto the plane?

ACE: She got it to the gate, then she made me take it.

RENALDO: Why would your mom need a bat on the airplane?

ACE: She didn't want the airline to lose it. Trey Turnberry signed it. She says it's a collector's item.

RENALDO: How old are you, Ace?

ACE: Eighteen.

RENALDO: So not a minor anymore.

ACE: I didn't do anything.

RENALDO: Why do you think I'm questioning you? (Beat.)

RENALDO: No one's getting off this plane until I get my questions answered.

ACE: Does this have something to do with Mrs. Kessler?

RENALDO: Mrs. Kessler?

ACE: The biology teacher. No one knows why she's here. I mean, doesn't she have something better to do on her spring break?

RENALDO: Did you do something to her?

ACE: Me? No! I was fifteen.

RENALDO: Fifteen when what? What happened to Mrs. Kessler?

ACE: Her kid was killed in a car accident.

Matthew. It was all over the news. They never found out who did it.

RENALDO: You think someone on this plane had something to do with that?

ACE: I don't know. You're the cop.

CHAPTER

010

Federal Air Marshal Carlos Renaldo could feel the big-haired baseball mom staring at him from across the first-class lounge. He chided himself for chatting her up. Nothing good ever came of talking to strangers. Nothing bad had either. One might say he was overdue.

He was tired of sitting, so he popped the last little hot dog in his mouth, slung his backpack over his shoulder, then made for the exit. He nodded in her direction as he passed her table, then looked away before she could return the gesture. He wasn't here to make friends, but he didn't want to be a prick. Don't be nice. Don't be rude. It was a fine line to walk, and he wished he'd walked it better.

He arrived at the gate just as the plane was pulling up. Through the window overlooking the tarmac, he could see the baggage trolley piled high with suitcases. As it lurched forward and an electric blue Tumi teetered off the top, he tried not to roll his eyes. You think when that sharply dressed gate agent sets your suitcase on the belt that the baggage handling process is orderly. And for the first five minutes, it is. But as soon as that bag leaves the terminal, it's monkeys slinging mud. Baggage handlers don't care about your custom-tailored Armani or that one-of-a-kind flea market find. Once your suitcase escapes your watchful eye, it's flung downfield like a football at the two-minute warning. And don't get him started about baggage claim. You're not allowed to leave your bags unattended for a hot second when you check in, but you could take any suitcase on the carousel when you check out and no one would even notice.

The plane came to a stop, and as an unseen operator steered the passenger bridge toward the door, he couldn't help but smile. He wouldn't be able to exchange more than a few words with Katie while in flight, but that was half the fun. Pretending they were strangers while texting what they would do to each other when they got to the hotel made for tantalizing foreplay. It was risky business. If his bosses found out, he'd be fired on the spot. Then again, he wouldn't be an undercover terrorist hunter if he was afraid to take risks.

He hung back as the other passengers jockeyed for position. Normally their impatience annoyed him. It was an airplane, not a buffet dinner, there was enough stale air for everyone. But today he shared their eagerness.

He reminded himself that he was here to do a job and started checking out the other passengers. This flight always had an interesting mix. He observed Patagonia-clad backpackers, laptop-toting business travelers, leathery-skinned seniors enjoying too much sun in retirement. Budget cuts had made air marshals a rarity on domestic flights, but Puerto Rico's neighbors (Venezuela, Columbia, Panama) were known to have lackadaisical security, so DHS liked to have eyes on flights going in and out of San Juan. Besides being on the lookout for suspicious behavior, he scanned the crowd for repeat customers who might have an agenda other than visiting their moms.

As he surveyed the waiting area, his gaze paused on a tattooed Latino man holding a guitar case. It was cliché to suspect there might be a weapon in there, but also, in the right hands, a guitar could be used as a weapon. As could many of the items people legally brought onto planes—a trophy won at a golf tournament, a ThermoFlask of hot coffee, tweezers, nail clippers, cigar cutters, even a run-of-the-mill ballpoint pen. His job was not to look for weapons. It was to look for people who might want to use one.

He surveyed the gaggle of teenage boys. He'd traveled with sports teams before—gymnasts with hair pulled into tight ponytails, long-legged volleyball players, tournament bowlers with twelve-pound balls that could split your skull in two. But this was his first baseball team.

The first thing he noticed about the players was their age. They were babies. OK, not babies, but still smooth-faced and innocent. Correction: innocent-looking—he knew better than to assume. He thought back to the woman from the lounge, wondered which one was her son, then wondered why he cared. He dismissed it as curiosity, momentarily forgetting it was his instincts that made him good at his job.

His gaze traveled across the players to a couple in heated conversation by the window at the neighboring gate. She was in a hot pink T-shirt with writing he couldn't read. He was in an untucked, white linen button-down and faded blue jeans. She held her arms tightly across her chest, he was gesticulating like a batter arguing with an umpire over a bad strike three call. Suddenly, the man's hand curled into a fist, and for a second Carlos thought he might strike her. But she didn't flinch. Either she knew he wouldn't hit her, or she knew he wouldn't hit her *here*. He made a mental note to keep an eye on him.

"Ladies and gentlemen, we have a number of passengers getting off the plane here in San Diego," the gate agent announced. "Please stand back so they can deplane. Thank you."

Carlos shifted his gaze back to the herd. Predictably, nobody moved. At times like this, he wished he wasn't undercover so he could order everyone to back the fuck up.

The deplaning passengers were not his problem, so it must have been those killer instincts that compelled him to look at the stream of people emerging from the jetway. At first, he was confused. Katie wasn't supposed to get off until they got to San Juan. Yet there she was, in her form-fitting ruby red dress, striped scarf caressing the hollow of her neck. He looked up at the revised departure time. Did a quick calculation in his head. And wasn't confused anymore.

"Aww shit," he muttered under his breath.

He'd missed the announcement, didn't know there'd been a crew change.

"Shit!"

He skirted around the growing crowd to follow her. She and the two other LA-based flight attendants were walking in lockstep toward the crew lounge, heels click-clacking against the marble floor. He whipped his phone out of his pocket and opened his Signal app. No messages. When did she know she'd been bumped? And why hadn't she texted?

She was walking fast, but he was walking faster, closing the gap between them. He couldn't call out. He couldn't let her get away either.

The trio of flight attendants stopped at a closed door with no sign: the crew lounge. He knew the drill. She'd been bumped from the Puerto Rico flight, but she was still on the clock and couldn't leave the airport. They called it being on reserve. Like a doctor on call.

One of her fellow flight attendants, a busty redhead with coffin-shaped nails, punched a code in the keypad and turned the knob. The threesome filed inside.

As the door wafted closed, Carlos extended his leg and caught it with his foot. He used his heel to pull it open, then reached out and grabbed Katie by the wrist. She gasped and spun around. He opened his mouth to say her name, but she cut him off.

"Can I help you?"

She was doing him a favor, acting like she didn't know him. If their relationship got out, she'd get a slap on the wrist, he'd get a whole lot worse. This was an airport, there were cameras everywhere. But also, he loved her. He had never said the words out loud, but he knew it with his whole heart. He loved her laugh, the wiggle in her walk, the way she always botched the punchline when she told a joke.

"I need to have a word with you," he said.

"You can't come in here."

"So come out."

"You OK, Katie?" the redheaded flight attendant asked, looking over her shoulder at the two of them.

He let go of her wrist. Katie retracted her arm and looked down at his foot, still holding the door ajar.

"Carlos, I have to go," she said in a hushed whisper.

"How come you didn't tell me you got bumped?" He knew the answer, he could see it in her eyes.

"We need to cool it for a little while." But it still hurt to hear her say it.

"What's a little while?"

"I don't know."

"Did something happen?" Behind her, the redheaded flight attendant was staring.

"I'm just not into it anymore, Carlos."

"Into what?" he asked, hoping—*praying*—that he misunderstood. "Me? You're not into me?" And her non-answer confirmed his worst fear.

"You're going to miss your flight."

And then she turned her back on him and walked away.

He removed his foot from the crack and the door wafted closed. He stood there in stunned silence for several seconds, his heart in splinters in his chest. They weren't boyfriend and girlfriend, so you couldn't call what just happened a breakup. But whatever they'd had together, she just ended it.

He wanted to scream. He wanted to punch something—hard. Still, he had a job to do. So he put his agony in his pocket and headed for his gate.

SPECIAL AGENT SAM COOPER: Cooper.

FEDERAL AIR MARSHAL CARLOS RENALDO: Agent Cooper, it's Officer Renaldo.

COOPER: Go ahead, Renaldo.

RENALDO: Sorry for the incoming call, but I was able to find out who that bat belongs to.

COOPER: Go on.

RENALDO: His name is Ace Abernathy. He's a senior at Crestwood High, plays on the baseball team.

COOPER: You talked to him?

RENALDO: Yes, sir. I asked him how he got it on board. He said his mom snuck it through security.

COOPER: Why would she do that?

RENALDO: Apparently she thinks it's lucky.

COOPER: Lucky?

RENALDO: You know how baseball players are.

COOPER: OK, we'll do a deep dive into the family.

Thank you for that intel. I'll let you know if it proves helpful.

RENALDO: Yes, sir. Oh, and one more thing. I asked him if he knew why I wanted to talk to him, and he asked if my questions about the bat on board had something to do with the death of Matthew Kessler.

COOPER: Who's Matthew Kessler?

RENALDO: His teammate. Or rather, former teammate. He was killed in an unsolved hit-and run.

COOPER: How is this relevant?

RENALDO: I'm not sure it is, sir, other than the fact that the dead kid's mother, Francesca Kessler, is on this flight. Seat 11C.

COOPER: I'll look into it. How's the mood up there? You keeping the passengers out of my crime scene?

RENALDO: Everything's under control.

COOPER: I'll see what I can dig up on the Kessler death. Might be a dead end, but until that plane lands, I don't have many leads to explore here on the ground. I'll let you know if anything comes of it.

RENALDO: Thank you, sir.

CHAPTER

011

"I did *not* need that second fireball," Jilly said, as she bounded up to Billy and pressed her face into his chest. "I hope it doesn't come back to bite me."

Angie took a step back to give the couple space. They were standing by the window at the neighboring gate, waiting for the last of the San Diego–bound passengers to deplane so they could board. Unlike the bride and groom, she hadn't had a drop to drink. Clear head, clear heart. Now was not the time to lose her resolve.

Billy tamped down Jilly's hair to keep it from tickling his nose. It was a movement most people wouldn't even register—small and insignificant, as fleeting as a wink. But isn't that what a trigger is? A tiny echo of trauma, visible only to the victim?

Angie's breath caught in her throat as her thoughts ricocheted back to that night. *"You smell so good,"* he'd said, pressing his face into her hair. *"I want to breathe in every inch of you."* And then his hand was up her skirt, tearing at her panties, yanking them aside to make way for his savagery. If not for the recording, she might have believed him when he'd insisted she wanted him too. He could be very convincing.

"I'm so happy," Jilly cooed, and Angie had to look away. In her bartending job, she had observed many couples over many years. She understood that in any given relationship, there was always one who loved the other more—one who would tolerate bad behavior, give up a hobby, a friend, an ex, to make their beloved happy.

At first, Angie was surprised Jillian had asked her to be in the wedding. Did Jilly think if she made Angie her maid of honor, people would think it was *her* choice, not Billy's, to include Angie in their lives? Because Billy had no intention of giving her up. He'd made that abundantly clear.

The word "rape" felt hyperbolic, but there was no denying that's what it was. "You raped me, Billy," Angie had said, not just there at the gate, but every day since it happened. She said the word to scare him. And to embolden herself. Billy's white man's privilege may have gotten him a free ride to a D1 college, but it wasn't going to get him out of this.

"My dad took care of the bar tab," Jilly said to Billy. "Everyone should be arriving any second."

Angie felt her heartbeat quicken. "I'm going to use the bathroom," she said, backing away from the couple. "See you on board."

She glared at Billy. The command was in her eyes. *Tell her.*

"I love you so much, Angie," Jilly said, letting go of Billy and throwing her arms around her best friend. "Thank you so much for being here." Billy raised an eyebrow at Angie, like *she* was the one ruining everything.

"I love you too, Jills." And she did. That's why she was holding her ground. She was being generous, giving him the chance to confess. She could have called Jilly the very next day. But Billy begged her not to. "Please, let me tell her myself," he'd said. "So I can reassure her it will never happen again." She wanted them to have a fighting chance, so she'd agreed. In the end, the disease convinced him he didn't have to own up to his bad behavior, that Angie would back down. There was a time when she might have. When they were together, he was the star and she was the stargazer, just like Jilly. But they'd been broken up for three years, she wasn't under his spell anymore.

He'd gambled about something else too. When they were together, Angie was on the pill. He'd practically insisted—he couldn't be troubled to take precautions himself. Angie was fine with it at the time. She was raised Catholic, and there were limits to how much she would bend her beliefs. A pregnancy would have been catastrophic. But not as catastrophic as it would be now.

"I'll see you guys on board," Angie repeated, disentangling herself from Jilly. But this time it was the bride, not the groom, who thwarted Angie's plan.

"I should go too," Jillian said, pushing her carry-on toward Billy. "Watch my bag, would ya, babe?"

A slow smile spread across Billy's face. "Of course," he said. "Hurry back," he added for Angie's benefit, not trying to hide his glee.

As a couple, Billy and Jilly almost made sense. He was the prom king, a three-sport MVP with leading-man good looks. *"Billy Wilcox looked at me!"* girls wrote in their diaries. Even his teachers were enamored with him, nudging up his grades to give him an even greater chance to succeed. But the thing about stars is that they eventually burn out. Billy's special brand of currency didn't translate into the post-college world. Off the field, he was a dumb jock whose best days were behind him. Probably his most impressive quality was that he knew that.

Jilly was an ordinary girl made extraordinary by her parents' money. She was likable enough, but the problem with being the girl who gave out Prada phone cases at her catered birthday parties was she'd never know if her popularity was earned or bought. Her grades were good but not great, yet she still landed a spot at Dartmouth, her dad's alma mater. The Ivy League was a wake-up call. She wasn't pretty enough to land a rich man, or rich enough to bring home a pretty one. Humbled, she fell into the arms of a man who'd experienced a similar fall from grace, and their attraction bloomed from how they reminded each other of better days.

"Attention all passengers on Flight 868 with service to Puerto Rico," the gate attendant announced over the din. "We are now inviting our Pioneer Elite and first-class passengers to board, as well as any passengers needing special assistance. General boarding will begin in just a few minutes."

"We'd better hurry," Jilly said, hooking her arm through Angie's.

"Want me to watch your bag too, Ange?" Billy asked. He was practically gloating. He had run out the clock, just as he had done as QB1 in high school, to the frustration of an opposing team that needed to score.

"No thanks," Angie said.

"You sure? I'll be right here."

"I can handle my own stuff."

If Jilly noticed the shots being fired above her head, she didn't let on. "Let's go," she said as she tugged on Angie's arm. "We'll be boarding any minute!"

"Finally! I get you to myself," Angie said, a little too brightly. "We can have some girl talk."

"Don't," Billy mouthed behind Jilly's back.

But the days when Billy told her what to do were over.

SPECIAL AGENT SAM COOPER: Good evening, this is Special Agent Sam Cooper of the FBI. I'm currently driving down to Crestwood, I was hoping to catch Sheriff Eckles.

MRS. BEATRICE "BEA" BOOKBINDER: Oh! Good evening to you too, Agent Cooper! I'm afraid Sheriff Eckles is gone for the day, but let me see if I can get him on the phone for you.
(Brief hold . . . country music plays over the line.)

SHERIFF ALAN ECKLES: This is Eckles.

COOPER: Hello, Sheriff. This is Special Agent Sam Cooper—

ECKLES: Of the FBI, I know, my secretary told me.

COOPER: Sorry to disturb you, but I'm trying to get some background information on the hit-and-run that took the life of fifteen-year-old Matthew Kessler back in 2023.

ECKLES: Terrible night. Just terrible. Worst thing that's happened here since the fire of '54.

COOPER: I see from the police report that you never charged anyone.

ECKLES: Mr. and Mrs. Kessler are the nicest people. I feel so bad for them. But no, we never did find the driver. Wish I could give them closure, but we're just an eight-man force. We did what we could.

COOPER: So . . . no leads?

ECKLES: We had a lot of people through here that night, 'cause of the parade and all.

COOPER: Parade?

ECKLES: For Trey Turnberry. He plays for the Cubs—

COOPER: I know who Trey Turnberry is.

ECKLES: He's kind of a hometown hero. He was born and raised in Crestwood, played for Crestwood High. Until the Cubbies took him.

COOPER: Say more about the parade.

ECKLES: Oh, it was a whole day affair. The Crestwood High School marching band led a procession down Oak Drive—that's our main thoroughfare. There were food trucks and all sorts of revelry late into the night.

COOPER: What about the Crestwood High baseball team?

ECKLES: What about 'em?

COOPER: Were they part of the celebration?

ECKLES: Of course! They had a home game that evening. Trey Turnberry threw out the first pitch. Nearly blew the catcher's mitt off, poor kid.
(He chuckles.)

COOPER: So you saw Matthew Kessler the day he died.

ECKLES: Everyone did. The whole town was at the game. Turnberry was an All-Star that year, the National League starting shortstop. You'd think it woulda gone to his head, but nope, still the nicest guy. Humble down to his bones.

COOPER: Can you think of anyone who might have wanted to harm the Kesslers?

ECKLES: Harm them? Good heavens, no! Mrs. Kessler was a pillar of our community. She and her husband both. It had to have been someone from out of town. We watch out for our own here in Crestwood.

COOPER: Sounds like no one was watching that night.
(Beat.)

ECKLES: Is there anything else I can help you with, Agent Cooper?

COOPER: I'll be in touch.

CHAPTER

012

"Ugh. Why did I drink those fireballs?" Jilly moaned as she and Angie clip-clopped toward the ladies' room. "My insides feel like hot lava."

The late-afternoon sun was caressing the terminal, casting long shadows across the butter-smooth marble floor. There was excitement in the air, the crackle of adventure, the hum of romance. But not everyone was feeling buoyant.

"Whose idea was it to do shots?" Angie asked, to make a point.

"I would have been fine if I'd stopped after one," Jilly said, to undermine it.

The restroom didn't have a door, just an archway in front of a tiled wall that forced you to choose left or right. As they stepped over the threshold, the stench of airport bathroom slapped them like a cold wind. Jilly stopped and pressed her palm into the wall.

"I'm going to be sick," she said, burying her nose and mouth in her elbow. Angie pushed in front of her.

"She's not feeling well," Angie told the person at the front of the line, grabbing the door of an opening stall. "Thank you. Sorry."

She took Jilly by the arm and ushered her inside. "Want me to—?"

"No."

Jilly pulled the door from Angie's grasp and locked it. Somewhere in the hollows, a toilet flushed, and then another, and then the stall door next to Jilly's opened and it was Angie's turn.

As Angie stepped inside, she peeked under the partition to see the bride's feet pointing toward, not away from, the toilet. She felt a flash of guilt. She should have insisted on going in, held Jilly's hair back like she had done for her at prom after too many wine coolers. But then she reminded herself that she still had her friend's back for the thing that mattered. *'Til death* is a long time, and a person deserves to know to whom they're making that commitment.

She did her business, then exited her stall. "You OK in there, Jillian?" she asked through the crack.

"Yeah, be right out."

Angie walked over to the sink. As she dipped her hands under the too-hot water, she wondered what Jillian would do when she found out her fiancé had violated her best friend and his promise in one drunken plunder. Punch him in the face? Punch *her* in the face? Call off the wedding right here at the airport? Is that what she wanted? To hurt the only two people outside her family who ever truly loved her? Yes, Billy's love was twisted by the hands of addiction, but that didn't make it any less real. And Jillian had loved her like a sister since that first day of kindergarten when Angie's mom forgot to send a blanket and Jilly invited her to share hers. Their sisterhood was thorny but loving. Competitive but not destructive. Imperfect but enduring. At least so far.

Jillian emerged from her stall and joined Angie at the sink. Miraculously, her tiara was still squarely atop her head as if she really were a princess. But not a wholly benevolent one. Yes, she'd shared the spoils of her privileged upbringing with others, but only when it served her. Like the time she threw Angie a party on her sixteenth birthday. Angie's parents had offered to host a picnic in the park, but Jillian wouldn't have it. "It's your sweet sixteen! We're doing it in style!" It was only after Angie and Billy broke up five years later that Jilly confessed her real reason for hosting—to steal Billy away from her. "I did it for you," she'd said. "But also for me." And Angie just laughed, because people can't be stolen and rivalry between friends as close as they were was as inevitable as winter giving way to spring.

"Better now?" Angie asked, as Jilly took a sip of water from the bottle in her tote then spat into the sink.

"Much."

Jilly's eyes met Angie's in the mirror. Angie tried to smile like nothing was wrong, but her old friend knew her too well.

"Why are you here?"

The question caught her off guard. Wasn't it obvious? "It's your wedding weekend."

Those fireballs must have shaken something loose, because Jillian suddenly had a bone to pick. "Are you still attracted to him? Is that why you came? To throw a wrench in our plans?"

If Jillian hadn't tried to betray *her* all those years ago, Angie might have found the question odd. But she understood a thing or two about projecting.

"Where is this coming from, Jills?"

"Are you?"

Angie was not into Billy. If she were, she'd be the one wearing that tiara. But what to say? *"I'm happy for you"* was not true. *"I would never do anything to hurt you"* would only be true for a few more minutes. Even a simple *"no"* was misleading because that wrench was in there, and to pull it from the spokes was as dangerous as letting it remain.

"If you don't trust me, why did you ask me to be your maid of honor?" Angie asked, because the only thing she could think of was to turn this back on her.

"Whatever's going on between you two, it stops now," Jilly commanded. "No more sneaking away, no more hushed conversations. I see you."

Angie's heart pounded in her ears. They might not be alone again all weekend. She needed to tell her *now.* In that stinky airport bathroom.

"I love you, Jillian," she said, holding her best friend's eyes in the mirror. "We've always been there for each other. I don't want that to change."

"I don't either." Jillian looked down as she flipped on the water to wash her hands.

"I know your mom's worried about Billy's drinking," Angie started, hoping to ease in through the back door.

"Worried is her resting state," Jillian shot back. "If it's not one thing, it's another."

"I'm worried too, Jills. It was a problem when Billy and I were together, and I don't think it's getting better."

"Yeah, well, for better or for worse," Jilly said. And Angie suddenly wondered, *does she think her money can fix this too?*

"He comes into the bar, y'know." Her heartbeat accelerated. *Here we go . . .*

Jilly pumped the soap dispenser. "And?"

"Not always just to drink." The table was set. She just had to serve the meal.

"I know he likes to party," Jillian said as she lathered her hands. "But he knows my limits. If he ever cheated on me, I would kill him. Without hesitation. And her too." She held Angie's eyes in the mirror.

And Angie lost her nerve.

CHAPTER

013

"Can you watch my bag for a minute?" Francesca asked Cal, pointing to the tote by her feet as she popped out of her chair. "I need to make a quick call."

"Of course. Take your time."

They both knew he didn't really mean she should "take her time," the flight had just started boarding. But she wouldn't be more than a minute, even if Rick picked up.

"Thanks."

She walked to the gate next to hers. It was empty, save for an elderly woman lost in a book. She sat down in a chair by the window and took out her phone. His number was still in her favorites—one of two. She dialed it with one tap, like calling him was the easiest thing in the world.

She pressed the phone to her ear as it rang once, twice, three times. On the fourth ring it went to voicemail.

"You've reached Rick Kessler. Sorry to miss you, but if you leave a message, I'll return your call as soon as—"

Click. That was enough. She just wanted to hear his voice. Like she had every day for twenty years. His voice had reshaped how she saw the world, what she cared about, who she was, and she had no idea what she was going to do without it.

They'd met as undergrads at UC Santa Barbara, during freshman orientation, when they were in line to pick up their ID cards. She was studying biochemistry in hopes of going to med school. He was a theater major determined to become a Hollywood star. He showed up for their first date twenty minutes early. She was still blow drying her hair and answered the door with a hairbrush in her hand. But instead of apologizing, he told her he'd waited his whole life for her and couldn't wait a minute more. He said it with a face as serious as a hurricane. Maybe it was the acting training, but she believed him, and left the apartment with a half-wet head and a wholly-besotted heart.

They were inseparable after that. Her roommates called them salt and pepper for how they always came as a pair. And perhaps for how opposite they were. He was outgoing. She was reserved. He was artistic. She was all science. He asked why. She asked how. He looked for meaning. She looked for patterns. Their common language was curiosity, and they learned more from each other than in all their classes put together.

They got married the summer after graduation when they were both twenty-two. She started med school at UCLA that fall. He took a part-time job in sales that left his afternoons free for auditions. They were busy and happy. And then they were pregnant.

Rick's company offered him a full-time job in San Diego, so they moved. Rick's parents were thrilled to see their son quit the LA acting scene, so they helped with the down payment for the house to keep him away from it. Francesca's transition from med student to mom was seamless. She had already become accustomed to sleepless nights, and she would still be a caregiver, just not to strangers.

The job teaching high school was Rick's idea. Matthew was in preschool, and there were only so many recipes to master and rooms to remodel. Crestwood was in desperate need of science teachers, and her dual degree in chemistry and biology made her a perfect fit. She was able to get her teaching credential online in less than a year and score a full-time position six months after that. She was nervous at first, but she came to love being part of a community that needed her as much as she needed it. Rick's work was up and down, but he happily used the down periods to bond with Matthew. Their projects were legendary—a birdfeeder made from a sombrero, a treehouse shaped like a pirate ship, a quilt fashioned from old baseball jerseys. He was such a good father. When people asked them why they didn't have more kids, they just shrugged. They were happy. Things were perfect—too perfect, apparently.

Unlike childbirth, which hurts for a finite period of time, the pain of child death never goes away. She once described it as swallowing a grenade. The explosion nearly blows your head off, but that's just your introduction. Every day, as reliable as a sunrise, the agony returns. Shrapnel rakes your lungs when you try to breathe, ravages your throat when you try to speak. Somehow, your heart keeps pumping, pushing your pain through your blood like shattered glass. Some days it's bearable. Some days it's not.

There's no manual for how to keep going. If she'd had the courage, she might have chosen not to. She soldiered on for Rick, because somewhere, under all the wreckage, her love for him still burned. And as much as she hurt, she couldn't bear the thought of hurting him.

But now he wanted to be done with it all—his son, his grief, *her*. She remembered the day he deleted Matthew's number from his phone. She was sitting right there next to him. Was he trying to make a point? Giving her an ultimatum? *Move on or else?*

That's when the fighting started. She accused him of trying to erase their past. He begged her to loosen her grip. Like a Chinese finger trap, the harder he pulled, the tighter she held on. She watched in horror as he took down the treehouse, stopped going to counseling, begged her to try for another baby. Another baby? How dare he! It had only been eighteen months since Matthew's death. *He* was her baby. If Rick wanted another one, it would have to be with someone else.

She regretted it as soon as she said it. If he'd been looking for an out, she'd just given it to him. Three months after their fight to end all fights, he got a split-level condo in the center of town to "start fresh." It was what he needed to do to feel "whole" again, he'd said. As if he hadn't once said that about her.

She looked over at her gate. The last of the first-class passengers were trickling on board. She tucked her phone in her purse. As she stood up to go—

BUZZZZ.

She snatched the phone out of its pocket.

"Hi." She knew she sounded eager, and that it was pathetic. But he was the actor, not her.

"I saw that you called."

"Yes, sorry." Was she apologizing for hanging up without leaving a message? Or for all the other things?

"You OK?" he asked.

"Yes." She had a new baseline for OK. "I just wanted to let you know . . ."

But before she could tell him, the gate attendant's voice blared over the airport speakers, stealing her thunder.

"Are you at the airport?"

"Yes. That's why I called. To tell you I was going out of town. In case . . ." In case what? The child was dead, the house was sold, there were no more ties to bind them. "In case you needed to reach me for anything."

"Where are you going?"

"Puerto Rico." She almost added "with the team," but stopped herself just in time.

"That's right, it's spring break."

"I'm just going for a few days," she said, then clarified. "Five." Because she wasn't in the habit of being vague with him.

"Thanks for letting me know."

She peered over at her gate. The line to board was inching forward. She felt bad keeping Coach Cal waiting. But she had to ask.

"I know you were planning to send the papers." Her throat seized up. She would not let him hear her cry.

"I can wait," he said. And just as her old friend denial perked up, he added, "until you're back."

And now the tears came. She'd learned how to cry silently, pressing her lips together to trap the anguish in her throat. She understood why Rick didn't want to spend the prime of his life looking into eyes that had grown dull with grief. But she couldn't let it go just as he couldn't bear to be around it.

"Francesca? Are you there?"

She squeezed her eyelids together and a tear rolled down her cheek. "Send them to my sister's. I'm not going back to the house."

And now it was he who was silent for a beat.

"You moved out," he finally said.

"Movers are coming while I'm gone."

She imagined him in his shiny new condo, wondered if he breathed easier without the stench of loss all around him.

"I have to go. My flight is boarding."

Maybe he was doing her a favor, forcing her to box up what was left of Matthew and sell the house. What was it Hamlet said? Sometimes you have to be cruel to be kind? Rick had always been the kind one, thanking everyone for their condolences, telling them "it's all right," when they choked on how sorry they were. It infuriated her. Probably because she couldn't do it.

"Fly safe, Francesca."

She hung up the phone, looked over at the gate. The baseball boys were in line to board. There were only a handful of players left who'd been on the team with Matthew. Pretty soon they wouldn't remember his name. Which is why she needed to corner them *now*. It was her last chance, really. Yes, it would make them uncomfortable. But that was kind of the point.

SPECIAL AGENT SAM COOPER: Hi, I'm looking for Maryanne Kennedy, Staff writer for the Crestwood Chronicle?

MARYANNE KENNEDY: This is MK, former staff writer, but go ahead.

COOPER: Hello, Ms. Kennedy. This is Special Agent Sam Cooper of the FBI. Sorry to call so late. I'm on my way to Crestwood, and I have a few questions for you, if you don't mind?

MARYANNE: No worries. I'm a night owl.

COOPER: I was hoping to speak to you about a piece you wrote back in May 2023.

MARYANNE: About the Kessler hit-and-run.

COOPER: That's right.

MARYANNE: I was wondering when someone was going to call me about that.

COOPER: Oh?

MARYANNE: The whole thing is sus.

COOPER: What do you mean 'sus'?"

MARYANNE: Suspicious. F'd up.

COOPER: Say more.

MARYANNE: You know I was fired after that.

COOPER: No, I did not know that.

MARYANNE: Yup. Apparently, I asked too many questions.

COOPER: But you were a reporter, no?

MARYANNE: Exactly! I was a reporter, and they canned me for doing my job.

COOPER: What sort of questions were you asking?

MARYANNE: All the questions a reporter is supposed to. What happened? Who saw what? Do they know who did it? Can I talk to the eyewitness?

COOPER: Eyewitness? There's nothing in the police report about an eyewitness.

MARYANNE: I know. They scrubbed his interview. Pretended like no one saw anything.

COOPER: How do you know there was a witness?

MARYANNE: Because I was on scene. Crestwood is a small town. We all heard the sirens. I followed them to the scene of the accident, y'know, to get the story.

COOPER: Go on.

MARYANNE: Anyway, when I was standing there taking pictures, I heard someone tell Sheriff Eckles he saw what happened and wanted to make a statement. Next thing I know, I was fired for trying to talk to him.

COOPER: This eyewitness . . . do you know his name?

MARYANNE: Yeah, of course. Everybody knows his name. He's the Crestwood High baseball coach.

COOPER: You don't mean Brendan Callahan?

MARYANNE: Yup. Coach Cal.

COOPER: Why would the sheriff want to silence an eyewitness?

MARYANNE: I've been wondering that for three years.

CHAPTER

014

"OK boys, let's go," Brooks, the team's batting coach, called out as he stood to wrangle the team onto the plane. "You coming, Cal?"

Brendan Callahan glanced over at Francesca, who was talking on her phone at the adjacent gate. He couldn't board. He was babysitting her carry-on. He'd failed to do right by her son, the least he could do is do right by her bag. No, the accident wasn't his fault. But her prolonged suffering over it was.

Though Matthew Kessler had only been in his program for a few months, it was enough to know the kid was special. He was a tremendous athlete, with great balance and a strong arm. His twenty-four-inch vertical leap rivaled that of the boys on the basketball team, and his hand-bat speed was as fast as any player he'd ever coached—including Trey Turnberry, who'd taken that speed all the way to the major leagues seven years ago, at the tender age of nineteen. Cal knew he wasn't supposed to have favorites, but when you get a kid like Matthew Kessler, you can't help but root for him above the rest. His death was a sword through the heart of their town. He did what he could to tamp the bleeding, but as the saying goes, no good deed goes unpunished.

"Cal?" Coach Brooks repeated.

"Go ahead, I'll bring up the rear."

"Copy that," Coach Brooks said to his boss. Then, to the boys, "On your feet! Get those boarding passes out, let's go!"

Cal watched as eighteen teenage ballplayers lined up behind Coach Brooks—Santiago, Jimmy, Micah, Kai, Javier, Enrique, Christian, Kenny, Danny, Ezra, Shane, Jonah, Kyle, Shawn, Sammy, Ari, Zander, Ace. Every year the names changed, but his love for them remained the same. He'd always thought he'd have kids of his own, but when it didn't happen for him and Cathy, he threw his whole heart into caring for these boys. Some needed a strong hand. Some needed a kind word. Whatever they weren't getting at home, he gave it to them on the field. In return, they gave him the very best of themselves, and the satisfaction that he was doing something important under the guise of a silly game.

His heart broke a little as they filed onto the plane. Every year they seemed to be getting younger, but he knew that was about him. Only one or two of these eighteen boys would continue on with the sport after high school. Luckily, he never thought of his program as a means to an end. The same could not be said for the players—or rather, their parents.

He felt sorry for the boys whose moms and dads were always hovering at practices, shouting at them from behind the fence to *"Watch the ball!"* as if that was the problem. Usually, *they* were the problem. How the heck were these kids supposed to concentrate with their parents squawking at them after every pitch? They laid into him too. The conversations started out friendly enough, with a polite, "Coach can I talk to you for a second?" It was never a second, and they never listened. "He's right where he's supposed to be," he tried to tell them. And when they insisted their son needed more personal attention, he told them some version of "I think he'd perform better with less pressure on him." Everybody wanted their kid to be the next Trey Turnberry. But Trey Turnberry was born a superstar. All Coach could take credit for was not screwing him up.

He tried to have compassion for the overeager parents, especially the dads. He knew many of them were prisoners of their own failed sports careers and couldn't help but take their self-loathing out on their kids.

Why didn't you swing? Slide? Run faster? Jump higher? Try harder? He knew the words hurt. And that some dads didn't stop at words.

Brendan Callahan never aspired to be a baseball coach. When he got drafted by the Red Sox, he thought he'd have a long, lucrative career as a Major League pitcher, retire at age thirty-five, then travel the world on his yacht. But life had other plans. The AL East had some of the best hitters in baseball, and his not-fast-enough fastball and sinker-that-barely-sunk didn't cut it against the bats of Alex Rodriguez and Derek Jeter. God bless the Red Sox, they gave him every opportunity to rise to the challenge, but the harder he pushed, the worse he got. When they didn't renew his contract, he could have done any number of things. He was only twenty-seven, and he had a degree from Stanford. But he couldn't stand the thought of sitting behind a desk all day. So he took the job at Crestwood High.

The program was rinky-dink when they hired him. To his surprise, he liked the job. Working with kids was a rare opportunity to shape not just the player, but also the person. From him they would learn how to be a good teammate, a humble winner, a gracious loser—on the diamond and in life. He knew some of the kids had difficult home lives, and he made sure his locker room was a safe place. He had zero tolerance for bullying, and everyone got to play. He knew he had a reputation among the other coaches as being a "softie." But this was baseball, not the army, and nobody played well when they were afraid.

Coaching high school baseball could be monotonous, but any doubts he had about moving back to Crestwood were erased when he met Cathy in the lobby of Gold's Gym. It was ten p.m. on a Saturday, and they were the only two people in the place. It wouldn't have mattered what time or day of the week it was, or if the place was as crowded as the Rose Bowl Parade, their connection was instantaneous and undeniable.

They made a date for the next day. He took her on a picnic on a scenic vista overlooking the ocean, though she was the only view that interested him. They were engaged within six months and married six months after that. He sometimes questioned their decision not to try harder for kids, but when it didn't come easily, they accepted that it wasn't meant to be. Their lives were full. Between the two of them, they knew almost everyone in Crestwood. She was a member of the Chamber of Commerce, he volunteered for the park service in the off-season. Their family was the whole town. And each other.

He sometimes asked himself, if he died today, was it a life well-lived? His Stanford classmates were saving the planet, curing cancer, sending satellites into space. He used to think teaching those kids baseball was just as important. And then Cathy left him and he wasn't so sure.

They say your life partner is like a mirror, reflecting your choices back at you. When they were married, Cathy's smile told him he was making a difference in these boys' lives, and, by extension, in their community. Then he made a choice that forever erased that smile from her face.

He did not subscribe to the Machiavellian edict that the ends justify the means, not normally. This case was different. There were other factors at play. More personal factors. One boy was dead—there was nothing he could do about that—but another, if the truth got out, would have his life dissected like a frog in biology class. A boy he cared about. A boy who'd tried to blame the welts on his arms and face on yard work or horsing around with his teammates. "How does one kid get hit with so many baseballs?" Francesca Kessler, who had this kid for biology, once asked, and Cal had implored her not to dig any deeper. Then the season was over, and new war wounds appeared, and he had to talk her out of calling child services because as bad as the boy's life was, foster care would be ten times worse. The best he could do was to help the boy punch a ticket out of there by landing a baseball scholarship, so that's what he did.

And, to his astonishment, that boy—now a grown man—was standing a base-path's length away from him here at the airport.

CHAPTER

015

Yes, Billy Wilcox had spotted Coach Cal waiting to board the flight to San Juan. How could he not? He was traveling with the whole damn baseball team. A team Billy used to play for.

He knew he should go say hello, but the shitstorm of his own making was closing in on him. His ex-girlfriend just traipsed off with his fiancée and was threatening to ruin his wedding and possibly his life. He was not in the mood for handshakes and "how-are-you's." Plus, the last time he and Coach saw each other was a day they all wanted to forget.

Prior to that awful night, he loved talking about Crestwood baseball. They had a great team back in the day—made the playoffs all three years he was on Varsity. They were helped by the talents of his teammate, future National League MVP Trey Turnberry, but he'd pulled his weight. Coach Cal used to say they brought out the best in each other. The fact that they both got recruited—Trey by the Cubs and him by ASU—suggested he was right.

Coach Cal was not like the others, in the best way possible. While the football and basketball coaches screamed at them to *"Suck it up!"* Coach Cal said corny-ass shit, like, *"Your glove's an alligator jaw, open it wide,"* and *"Your fingers are fangs, bite down on that ball!"* And his all-time favorite, *"You want to get those single ladies, use your hips! Like Beyoncé!"*—which was followed by the other coaches singing, *"Put your hands up!"* and shaking them above their heads like they were on fire.

Coach was good to him in other ways. Like when he made him stay after practice to field ground balls or add a leg kick to his swing, then took him to Subway or McDonalds to "make it up to him" for missing a dinner he knew no one had made. Or told the principal he'd gotten that shiner from a sharply hit foul ball when they didn't even have practice the day before. He owed a lot to Coach Cal.

The team didn't have money for trips to faraway places like Puerto Rico when he played those seven, eight, nine years ago, but they did go to Vegas once. Coach got a hotel on the strip so they could see what all the fuss was about. They rode the rollercoaster at Circus Circus, played catch across the canals at the Venetian, then chowed down on chocolate cheesecake M&M's at M&M's World. The casinos were all twenty-one and over, but Coach snuck them rolls of quarters and let them each pull the lever of a slot machine once or twice. He wanted them to remember baseball as fun. It's just a game, after all.

Baseball was less fun when he got to Arizona and had a scholarship to service, but Coach Cal had prepared him well, and he played all four years. He was enjoying a rare off-day in his fourth and final season when his former Crestwood teammate Nolan Abernathy texted him that the Cubs were in town, and a bunch of them were going to see them play at Petco Park. "After the game, Trey's coming to Crestwood to throw out the first pitch for the Cougars game," his buddy wrote. "The mayor's making it a freakin' national holiday, with a parade and everything. You should come!"

It was only six hours from Tempe to Crestwood, so he said "Sure, why not?" and made the drive. The Cubs game would be over by the time he got there, but he told the guys he'd meet up with them after. He wanted to hang out with Trey, who he hoped would still be cool even though he was a Big Fucking Deal in the Major Leagues. Also, he could see Angie—they were still hot and heavy then—and it had been a while since he'd gotten properly laid.

He left at nine a.m. and arrived a little after three—just in time for the parade. That's when the drinking started. He didn't know he was an alcoholic, just that when he started drinking, he didn't want to stop. He loved the way his face got buzzy, the weightlessness in his chest, the feeling that he was invincible. He wasn't an angry drunk like his dad. A little bit reckless, maybe. If he hurt someone, it wouldn't be out of rage.

You weren't allowed to bring booze into the ballpark, but they all did, disguising their Tito Mojitos by pouring them into Thermo-Flasks or repurposed Gatorade bottles. The student section was called "The Den," and all the former Crestwood Cougars squeezed in to relive their glory days and steal a toke off whatever the cool kids were smoking.

He was predictably blotto by the time the game ended. Blackouts were a pretty regular occurrence for him, and he had normalized losing long blocks of time. It was Angie who told him what had happened, he had no memory of it. Or his part in it.

He didn't know the boy who died—how could he? The kid was a high school freshman, he was a senior in college out of state. But he did know the kid's mom. He'd had Mrs. Kessler for biology his freshman year. He was pretty sure she was the one who'd told Principal Petersen about all those shiners. She was trying to help him. But you know what they say about *"no good deed . . ."*

"Attention, ladies and gentlemen, Flight 868 with nonstop service to San Juan is now boarding all zones," the gate agent said over the PA. "All passengers may board at this time."

Billy watched as the last of the Crestwood Cougars filed onto the plane. Where were Jilly and Angie? He was about to text them to hurry up when he saw the dead kid's mom walking toward the gate. He was so shocked he nearly dropped his phone. What the hell was she doing here?

He was beginning to think the devil was trolling him. It was the only possible explanation. He couldn't blame his binge drinking for people getting hurt—the boy dying, his ex crying rape—because then he'd have to admit the devil and his drinking were one and the same.

SPECIAL AGENT SAM COOPER: Sheriff Eckles?

SHERIFF ALAN ECKLES: That's me.

COOPER: It's Special Agent Sam Cooper of the FBI again, with a few more questions about the Matthew Kessler hit-and-run, if you don't mind?

ECKLES: I'm here to serve.

COOPER: I wanted to ask you about witnesses.

ECKLES: Yeah, unfortunately there weren't any.

COOPER: No?

ECKLES: It happened after a long day, most everybody was snug in their beds.

COOPER: What about Brendan Callahan?

ECKLES: Coach Cal? What about him?

COOPER: I heard from Maryanne Kennedy of the Crestwood Chronicle that he tried to make a statement.

ECKLES: Ah yes, Maryanne. Troubled soul. You know she was fired right after that, right?

COOPER: So Mr. Callahan didn't come forward with an eyewitness account?

ECKLES: Did you see his name in the police report?

COOPER: I did not.

ECKLES: Well, there's your answer.

COOPER: Why do you think Miss Kennedy would tell me Mr. Callahan saw what happened?

ECKLES: Who knows? For attention maybe? She's a sweet girl, but she was never right in the head.

COOPER: Is there anything else you remember from that night that you think might be helpful for our investigation, Sheriff?

ECKLES: Everything you need is in that report.

COOPER: Right. Well, thank you for your time.

ECKLES: I'm curious, why are the Feds trying to stir up dust in my little town after all these years?

COOPER: We're just looking for the truth.

CHAPTER

016

Flight attendant Cathy Yap was making a fresh pot of coffee for a cranky first-class passenger when she saw Francesca Kessler boarding the plane.

"Francesca! Hi!" she called out, stepping out of the forward galley to greet her former Crestwood neighbor. "It's Cathy." She pointed to herself with two thumbs facing inward. "Cathy Yap."

Francesca looked at her blankly. Cathy noticed the red rims around her eyes but pretended she didn't.

"Y'know, 'Yappy Cathy' . . ." Yap offered, with a self-deprecating smile.

Still nothing.

"Coach Callahan's wife. Well, ex-wife now."

And finally, a gasp of recognition. "Sorry. Of course," Francesca said, then scrunched her eyebrows. "I thought you were a realtor."

"I was. I changed careers after . . . y'know . . ." She didn't want to say the word divorce. She knew Francesca and Rick had recently separated. Even though she didn't live in Crestwood anymore, she still heard the chatter.

"Right. Sorry, I didn't recognize you."

Cathy fluffed her hair. "Purple hair, don't care."

"It looks nice."

She leaned in close. "The airline's not crazy about it," she said with an exaggerated grimace.

"How's that coffee coming?" Rita Salazar said, appearing behind her. Cathy wanted to make a good first impression on her supervisor, and that hair was a lot to overcome.

"Two more minutes," she said to the purser. Then, to Francesca, "I'll catch up with you during the flight."

Cathy ducked back into the first-class galley. As she prepared her service tray, her heart trilled with curiosity. Whose idea was it to invite Francesca Kessler to go on a trip with her dead son's former team? Certainly not Brendan's. She didn't understand how he could even look at her after what he'd done. So did that mean she'd volunteered herself? And why would she do that?

She glanced over her shoulder to see the Crestwood baseball team filing onto the plane. She recognized a couple of the older boys, even though their faces had thinned and their shoulders broadened since the last time she'd seen them. She felt a pang of sadness. She liked going to the games and flaunting her special connection to the team as the coach's wife. She had even convinced her realty company to become a sponsor, personally overseeing the production of the "Sotheby's of Crestwood" banner that hung in left field. She would have happily stayed in Crestwood, hocking houses and cheering for the home team. But Brendan had made that impossible.

Speaking of Brendan, there he was at the end of the procession. He smiled at her as he passed, and she ticked her head in polite acknowledgment. Long days in the sun had aged him . . . or maybe it was that other thing? She hated that she was still physically attracted to him, with his dimpled chin and eyes as blue as the Irish Sea. Still, she couldn't forgive him for what he'd done. It was the one secret she'd kept to herself, only because it wasn't hers to tell.

She turned her attention back to the coffee as the last drops sputtered into the pot. As she filled the mug, a call light in the main cabin lit up.

"I'll take the coffee," Rita said, stepping into the galley. "You go see what 36C wants."

Cathy nodded then scooted past Rita into the aisle. The curtain between first and economy was open, and she could see 36C struggling to get what looked like a guitar into the overhead bin.

"Here, let me help," she said, flipping off his call button.

"I didn't want to move anyone else's things," the man said, raising his hands in the air like she was holding him at gunpoint. "People can be touchy about that."

She checked out his tattoos as he took a step back. He had sleeves up both arms. A fire-breathing dragon on the left, an eagle with talons extended toward his hand on the right. She thanked her Peloton for her strong calves as she went on tippy-toes to move the carry-on to the adjacent bin.

"It'll fit now," she said, stepping aside.

"Thanks, little lady," the guitar player said with the tip of his trucker hat. *Little lady?* Yes, she was small in stature, but if she was older than this dark-eyed stranger, it wasn't by much.

"What kind of guitar is that?" she asked. The aisle was blocked by a woman waiting for her seatmate to get settled, she couldn't get back to the front of the plane even if she wanted to. And she was curious.

"Piano black Les Paul Custom," he said, sliding it into the now empty compartment.

"Vintage or reissue?" She'd had a rockstar client who liked to talk as much as she did and had learned a thing or two about guitars.

"Vintage 1977," he said, looking at her with curious eyes. "Do you play?"

"Just air guitar."

Click. She punctuated her joke by closing the bin. His face erupted in a smile. His teeth looked white as toothpaste against his caramel complexion. She tried to pinpoint his ethnicity. Italian? Mexican?

"You have a gig in San Juan?" she asked, because she had a twenty-four-hour layover and might just go if there was time.

"No, I live there. I'm going home." Ah, he was Puerto Rican. Of course.

"I'm Cathy," she said, offering her hand.

"Marco," he replied, shaking it.

"What's the name of your band? Maybe I'll check it out sometime."

He narrowed his eyes, like he thought she might be playing with him.

"They let us off the plane, you know," she said, and he laughed.

"Sabor Sonic." He rolled the "r" in "sabor," Spanish for "taste," indicating that he spoke the language. "We play the Bourbon Room sometimes, if you're ever in LA?"

"I'm everywhere," she said. "Job requirement." He nodded knowingly. Was she flirting? Maybe a little. Not that he was her type—too tattooed—but it was still fun.

"Hopefully I'll see you at a show." He smiled that toothy smile again. She had no idea of his musical talent, but he had star quality up the wazoo.

She glanced over her shoulder. The aisle had cleared. "I might just surprise you."

She turned and started back toward the front of the plane, past baseball boys with hats turned backward, and what looked like a bridal party, with five bridesmaids in matching pink shirts. Brendan was in the aisle seat of the exit row. She wasn't looking forward to serving her ex-husband, even though she knew he'd be polite. He was never one to stir up drama, even when it was warranted.

She glanced at him as she passed, but he was fiddling with his phone and didn't meet her gaze. Two rows in front of him, sitting by herself, was Francesca Kessler. She had a book in her lap, but was just kind of staring into space, her swollen eyes glassy with sadness. And once again Cathy wondered, *what the hell is she doing here?*

Cathy wasn't a fatalist, but she couldn't help but wonder if the universe was up to something. She'd put in for this flight countless times, and she'd never gotten it. In the fourteen months she'd worked for Pioneer, she'd never been called off reserve for any flight to anywhere. So why today? Why this flight, with these people who had once been family to her? Was there an unseeable force trying to engineer justice long overdue?

As she glanced at Francesca's steely profile, it hit her with such conviction she nearly gasped. She didn't know Francesca's reason for being here, but hers was crystal clear. Francesca deserved answers about what happened to her son that fateful night.

And she was going to give them to her.

CHAPTER

017

Penelope was seated in the third row of first class. There was a time when she could have squeezed her five-foot-ten-inch bod into an economy-class seat, but she had a good forty pounds on that version of herself, and what's the point of having money if you can't use it to make yourself comfortable? Her son Ace wanted to stick with his teammates, so she was sitting by herself with only her torturous thoughts to keep her company.

"Your coffee, Miss?" a flight attendant said, setting a tray on her tabletop. She knew she was being pandered to with the word "Miss." She hadn't been a "Miss" since the outgoing "Miss Kentucky" draped that golden banner across her then-perky double D's. That was over thirty years ago.

"Thank you." She glanced at the woman's nameplate. "Rita."

"I'll have to take it when we taxi, I'm afraid," Rita said, with an exaggerated grimace.

"Not to worry. I'll slug it back like a randy frat boy shooting whiskey."

Rita's smile was forced, but Penelope was used to people pretending with her. When she was young and beautiful, she could charm just about anybody. As her looks grew brash, so did her humor. Her husband had warned her that her barbs could be off-putting. Perhaps that's why she hurled them—so she had something to point to when people turned their backs on her.

As she sipped her coffee, her eyes landed on the couple across the aisle. Their bent elbows were smashed together on the armrest, their fingers threaded together like hands clasped in prayer. The woman was all in white, a dime-store tiara balanced atop flaccid, blond curls. She was no beauty queen, bless her heart. So must be a bride.

The groom was a young Tom Brady with muscular shoulders and a jaw sharp enough to cleave meat. The sight of them, bubbling over with love and promise, made her heart crack down the middle. She was young and in love once. If she'd known she'd never be that happy again, would she still have married him? Hard to say.

She'd had a vision of married life being this beautiful dance—two people twirling in glorious lockstep. Instead of being the dazzling equal partner, she'd morphed into a glorified hired hand. Raising three boys was a slog. Even with twice-a-week housekeeping, the mess was insurmountable. Tricycles, bicycles, skateboards, Legos, bats, gloves, mitts—the toy box was like a clown car, with more pouring out than could ever fit back in. And then there was the food. She bought pasta, cereal, pancake mix, hot dogs, chips, milk, Gatorade not by the case, but by the pallet. Their house looked like Costco after a tornado. There were always floors to clean and uniforms to wash and food to buy, cook, serve, clean up. Her husband worked to pay for it all, but—like all "kept" women—she did everything else. It was a job with no boundaries and no compensation beyond a robotic "Love you" at the end of phone calls and bouquets of flowers on Mother's Day. She took care of those boys out of love. And on the days she was too exhausted to love, out of duty. Those boys would have big, fat, beautiful lives if it killed her. And sometimes it nearly did.

And then, after all that cooking and cleaning and fretting, her children left to make lives without her. She knew a mother's job is to raise the people she can't live without to live without her. Still, it hurt. Ace was the only one left at home, and he'd be gone in a few months. Then what? Her lust for life was as irretrievable as her collagen-rich skin and twenty-five-inch waist. She'd entered marriage as a spritely, young filly. It spit her out as a bloated, liver-spotted crone. Could you blame her for being bitter?

She watched as the bride-to-be rested her head on her groom's shoulder. The tiara grazed his face, and he turned his head in Penelope's direction . . . to catch her staring at him. She knew if she didn't smile, she'd seem like a psychopath, but she was too caught up in her own tragic saga to muster one. Her heart was inflamed with envy. He was at the thrilling beginning, charting a course through seas unknown. She was at the final port, standing on her empty vessel, watching the last of her cargo get whisked away. Yes, after twenty-five years of raising children, she was free. But they wouldn't call it an empty nest if it was supposed to feel triumphant.

She took in the young man's face, the fullness of his lips, the blueness in his eyes. He was an athlete, she was sure of it—he had the kind of confidence you only get by standing at the plate, or in the pocket, or on the free-throw line while the whole stadium waits for you to make or ruin their day. He looked to be about the same age as her oldest son, Nolan. Or maybe exactly the same age?

She stared at him for one, two, three seconds. There was something so familiar about him. Was he on TV? Or maybe she'd just seen him somewhere in the airport earlier. He nodded hello, and she must have nodded back, because he turned his head back around.

And that's when it clicked.

He'd gone to Crestwood High, of course she knew him. He, Nolan, and whiz kid Trey Turnberry had played the infield together—Trey at short, Nolan at second, and Billy—yes, of course it was Billy Wilcox—at third. They were inseparable back then, each pushing the others to play faster, hit harder. Billy and Nolan pushed Trey Turnberry all the way to the Major Leagues. She should have recognized him immediately. Perhaps she'd momentarily blocked it out—understandable, given the sordid turn their story took.

She had to say hello, it would be rude not to. But when she opened her mouth to speak his name, she choked on it. Because if she reminded him how they knew each other, he would be transported back to that awful day. He was getting married. She didn't want to cast a pall over his weekend.

So she closed her mouth and looked away.

CHAPTER

018

Cool ocean air gave way to the stink of stale coffee and jet fuel as Federal Air Marshal Carlos Renaldo stepped off the jetway onto the Airbus. He liked being the last to board, because it gave him a chance to check out his fellow passengers in their seats. He tried not to wait too long—didn't want there to be a big gap between him and the last few stragglers. That might draw attention to him, and the whole point was for him to be invisible.

A flight attendant who wasn't Katie smiled up at him. "Welcome aboard."

He couldn't smile back. Didn't even try.

"Hi, Rita," he said, glancing at her nameplate. He was required to identify himself to a crew member, for obvious reasons.

"I think I'm somewhere near the back?" He took his boarding pass out of his pocket like he needed help finding his seat. His government-issued ID, watermarked with the letters FAM, for Federal Air Marshal, was tucked inside. He flashed it as he opened the folded boarding pass.

"Yes," she said, looking at the ID then back up at him. "30C. That's on the right side, the aisle seat. It's not a full flight, you should have the whole row to yourself."

He refolded the boarding pass around his ID, then tucked them into his pants pocket. "Thanks."

As he stepped into the aisle, he could feel her eyes on the back of his head. He was used to flight attendants checking him out—trying to glimpse the bulge of his gun or the glint of his badge. As if he'd be so careless. He knew travelers were always trying to spot the air marshals. There were how-to articles on the internet. Look for the guy traveling alone, with little or no luggage, who doesn't drink or eat or sleep. Contrary to internet lore, air marshals didn't always sit in the last row—not since all those articles said that was where to look for them. But he liked to sit toward the rear of the aircraft, because he didn't have eyes in the back of his head.

There was an art to checking people out without them knowing. Some of his colleagues wore sunglasses, which he found amateurish, and also kind of obvious. Some tried to blend in by talking on the phone about mundane things, like a child's birthday party or where they'd left the car key, but he didn't want to call more attention to himself by yammering all the way to his seat. His trick was to open a message app and text. That way he could walk slowly without coming off like a voyeur. Sometimes he texted his mom to tell her he loved her. Sometimes he texted his brother about a sports score or upcoming game. On this flight, up until today, he would text Katie—usually to say that the next six hours were going to be torture and warn her that if she was wearing that perfume that smelled like caramel apples, he might just lose his mind.

Pensando en ti, mama, he typed as he started down the aisle. His eyes were cast down, but he could see the passengers in his peripheral vision. He would not let thoughts of Katie distract him. Yes, the relationship was doomed from the start. Still, he couldn't help but wonder why she'd broken it off. Was there someone else? Had he said or done something to scare her away? He'd look through their texts, but not now—now he had work to do.

First class was small—just twelve seats in total. In the first row were two older couples. The couple on his left leaned toward each other in hushed conversation, the one on his right played word games on their phones. In the second row was a snoozing septuagenarian; a fortyish woman in unflattering sweats; a hippy with an unkempt beard; a balding professor-type reading a book. In the third and final row was the angry man from the terminal holding hands with a woman wearing a tiara—a different woman than the one he'd been arguing with at the adjacent gate, which he found . . . interesting. Directly across the aisle from them, in seat 3B, was the woman he'd met in the lounge, sitting by herself, drinking coffee, black. He could feel her eyes on him, but he didn't acknowledge her. He figured once she realized he was in the cheap seats she'd lose interest.

He looked up from his phone and stepped into the main cabin. As he pretended to look for his seat, he tilted his phone up to take a video. This was his second trick. If anyone got up, he would know if they went back to their assigned seat, or to a different one. He kept the phone down by his waist so no one would know he was videoing. Yes, if someone behind him in first class turned around, they might catch him, but why would anyone do that?

Seat 30C was eight rows from the back. There were only about twenty passengers seated behind him, but he suspected that might change as night fell and people went in search of an empty row to steal a nap. Without the promise of Katie's hot breath on his neck, he'd need regular infusions of caffeine to keep him going. Unless something happened and he got to ride adrenaline instead. Not that he hoped for something to happen. Well, at least not something he couldn't handle.

In his six years on the job, he'd only had to reveal himself twice. The first time was on his third day on the job, when a man on a flight to Denver had a heart attack and his wild-eyed wife started pounding on the cockpit door screaming for the pilot to land. Yes, he'd handcuffed the one-hundred-and-twenty-pound woman, and yes, he'd gotten ridiculed for it when word got around. But despite her small stature, her behavior posed a threat, and keeping people safe was his job.

The other time he'd had to spring into action was two months ago, on a flight to JFK, when a woman reported seeing a bomb in the toilet of an aft lavatory. It turned out to be a toy walkie-talkie belonging to a little boy who'd dropped it while taking a whiz then left it there because he didn't want to touch his own pee. He knew he should have been relieved—he didn't know how to diffuse a bomb. Mostly he'd just felt ridiculous.

Other than those two incidents, in six years as an air marshal, he'd done nothing. Nada. Zip. Half a decade is a long time to go without flexing the muscles he'd busted his ass to develop. He'd dared to say this out loud to Katie one time, and she tsk-tsked him. "Be careful what you wish for," she'd admonished. He was too smitten to realize something bad had already happened the moment he fell under the spell of that perfume.

CREW CHIEF RITA SALAZAR: Good afternoon, ladies and gentlemen. On behalf of the entire flight crew, I would like to welcome you aboard Pioneer Flight 868 with nonstop service to San Juan.

We kindly request that all passengers take their seats so we can do our final headcount in preparation for takeoff.

Thank you for your attention, and we look forward to flying with you.

CHAPTER

019

Angie picked at cuticles ravaged by double shifts behind the bar as she choked back rage. Jilly would not leave Billy's side for the next six hours. And even if she did, they were in first class, literally walled off from her seat in coach. The window to confide in her friend had closed. In twenty-four hours, Jilly would be Mrs. Billy Wilcox with no prenup and no escape.

"Your finger's bleeding," the forty-something man in the aisle seat said, looking down at her hand that was resting in her lap. He was a stranger, not with the wedding party. How had he wound up sitting in her row? And what was he doing looking between her legs? As disgusted as she was with Billy, and men in general, she was more disgusted with herself. She had not only failed her friend, she had failed all women, because every rape that went unreported emboldened every man who'd committed one to do it again.

"Thanks," she mustered.

The other bridesmaids, Jillian's sorority sisters from Dartmouth, had bought their tickets at the same time and were clustered together a few rows behind her. Angie's ticket had been paid for by Jilly and bought months before. The gesture felt significant, though she wasn't sure why. Was Jilly afraid she might try to beg off by crying broke? Was she trying to flex? Keep her away from the others? Or was she just being generous since she knew Angie struggled to make ends meet?

Blood had seeped into Angie's nailbed. She didn't have a napkin, so she pressed her fingertip against her tongue to tamp the bleeding. She should have had a manicure before she left—she was the maid of honor for heaven's sake! What a misnomer. There was no honor in what she was doing. As she imagined watching Jilly walking down the aisle to wed her rapist boyfriend, she had a sudden urge to storm off the plane in protest. Jillian thought she was marrying an honest and devoted man. That Angie knew otherwise and was keeping it to herself was not only wrong, it was downright negligent.

So what to do now? The flight was six hours. With the three-hour time change, they wouldn't be landing in San Juan until midnight. Everyone would want to head straight to bed. The morning would be a whirlwind of hair and makeup and giddy anticipation. It was too late. She couldn't stop it. She imagined the part when the officiant asked if there was anyone in attendance who objected to the marriage. If it was cruel to tell her now, it was a hundred times crueler to do it then.

Angie's turmoil turned to panic as she thought about the other potential complication of her silence. It had only been a week since the bachelor party—too soon to know if she was pregnant. If she was, there was no talking her out of having it. Billy would want her to lie, say it was someone else's, anyone but him. It was one thing to stay silent, it was another to make up an imaginary boyfriend to protect a bully. And then there were practical considerations. She was a bartender. She couldn't afford to raise a child by herself. She didn't need his approval, but she would need his help.

She tried to imagine telling Jillian she was pregnant with Billy's baby. "Why didn't you tell me about this sooner?" Jilly would ask, justifiably outraged. Her excuse—I wanted to give Billy the chance to tell you—seemed so flimsy now. She'd told herself she was being kind. The truth was, like so many women who'd been catcalled, harassed, groped, and molested, she was afraid. Speaking out meant confrontation. It meant being accused of inviting the behavior, or worse—lying about it. Coming forward meant facing humiliating questions, like "what were you wearing?"

and "why didn't you tell him to stop?" When you told people you *did* tell him to stop, they'd raise a skeptical eyebrow. It was your word against his. And people would believe him because tsk-tsking a woman was easier than demonizing a man—especially a golden boy like Billy.

"Good afternoon, everyone, and thank you for your patience," the flight attendant said over the PA. "We're just about to close the door and will be pushing away from the gate shortly. Please return your tray tables to their upright positions and make sure your seatbelts are securely fastened."

"Finally!" someone behind her shouted, and a few people clapped. Everyone else on this plane was happy to be going on this trip. She had to tell Jillian what Billy had done—if not tonight, first thing in the morning. Jilly would protest, say it was impossible, he would never do that, which meant subjecting her to that horrifying recording and ending their friendship forever.

She suddenly got scared. What if that recording wasn't enough? If Billy tried to tell Jilly she was saying something different with her body language than she was with her words, who would Jilly believe? Her mind danced with the notion of proof. She thought of a courtroom, lawyers, cops. And then it hit her.

She could tell a cop.

There was no way Jillian would doubt her if she reported the incident to the police. That she'd waited a week was not ideal, but also not unusual—it sometimes took victims of sexual assault months or years to come forward. She would just say it took her a few days to work up the courage. Which, in fact, was true.

She looked down at her phone. She hadn't switched it into airplane mode yet and still had three bars of service. She clicked on the Google app, typed. "How to file a police report online + Crestwood." The form popped up. It was just one page. She could do it right now.

She looked out the window to see flagmen in bright orange vests preparing to push the plane back from the gate. She didn't know how much time she had, it wouldn't be much.

So she started typing as fast as she could.

CHAPTER

020

Cathy Yap closed and latched the heavy door, then started down the aisle for her final cabin check.

"Fasten your seatbelt, please," she said, over and over like a broken record. After sitting their butts in seats, airline passengers are asked to do two things—stow their belongings and fasten their damn seatbelts. It was shocking how many had to be reminded.

"Seatbelt," she said to a woman typing frantically on her phone. The woman didn't look up or comply. "Miss?" She leaned in closer. "Miss?" The man in the aisle seat reached across the empty middle and tapped her on the shoulder. She gasped like she'd been shot.

"You need to fasten your seatbelt, we're about to push away from the gate," Cathy said as kindly as she could.

"Right. Sorry."

The woman clipped her seatbelt, then went back to tapping on her phone. Cathy noticed she was wearing the same hot pink shirt as the ladies a few rows back and couldn't help but wonder if the moniker was meant to be ironic or if they really were "bitches." Since becoming a flight attendant, she'd come across her fair share, but most of them were not self-aware enough to have T-shirts made.

She reached the rear of the aircraft, double-checked that the carts in the galley were secure and the lavatories empty, then stepped back into the main cabin to park her butt in an empty row for takeoff. As she was easing into her seat, she noticed something odd on the tarmac. She leaned toward the window for a closer look. Her pulse quickened. She popped out of her chair and hustled up the aisle, trying not to look alarmed.

"You do a belt check?" Rita Salazar asked as she arrived at the front of the plane.

"Yes."

"Just grab any empty seat, we're about to push back."

"Can I talk to you for a quick sec?" She cocked her head toward the galley, to indicate "in private."

Alphonso, who went by Fonzie, followed them without being invited.

"What's up?" Rita asked. Her tone suggested Fonzie had warned her Cathy was chatty. Which she was. But this was important.

"I don't want to be dramatic," Cathy said, infusing the moment with drama, "but I noticed something odd out on the tarmac."

"When?"

"Just now."

"Go on."

"OK, so I was about to strap in for takeoff—"

"And?" Rita's voice was clipped. *Yup, Fonzie had definitely warned her.*

"And I saw the fuel truck pull up."

"Yes, we always top off before San Juan." Out of the corner of her eye, Cathy saw Fonzie make an "I told you so" face.

"Yes, but it didn't pull up to the fuel port, it pulled up to the cargo hold."

"The cargo hold?" Rita said, like Cathy must be mistaken.

"Yes. The fuel truck driver got out, opened the cargo hold, went back to the cab to grab a suitcase, then tossed it inside."

"He pulled a suitcase from the cab of the fuel truck?" Rita asked, clearly skeptical.

"That's right."

"What kind of suitcase?"

"I don't know, black, small . . . kind of like one of ours."

"Are you sure it was a fuel truck?" Rita asked.

"Well, it wasn't a baggage trolley," she said. *Sheesh, how stupid does this woman think I am?*

"Good afternoon, everyone," a voice interrupted over the PA, "this is your captain speaking. We're just waiting for the grounds crew to push us away from the gate, then we'll be on our way. Thanks for your patience."

"You think I should tell the captain?" Cathy asked.

"You can if you want," Rita said. "But I think if there was something untoward going on, the air marshal would have caught it."

"There's an air marshal on this flight?" Cathy tried not to sound excited, but DHS had grown stingy about placing air marshals on domestic flights and she'd never met one.

"Handsome Puerto Rican guy toward the back. Dark hair. Aisle seat. Right side."

"You mean 36C?" Cathy asked, conjuring the dark-eyed Puerto Rican rockstar. "He doesn't look like a marshal," she added, recalling those tattoos and that megawatt smile.

"They're getting better at disguising themselves," Fonzie butted in. "On a flight to Rome last month, we had a woman marshal dressed up as a nun."

"You got Rome?" Cathy gasped. She'd put in for that trip dozens of times and never gotten it.

"We're about to start taxiing," Rita said curtly.

Cathy didn't want to bother the captain, but also what if this was important?

"I'm going to call the cockpit," she announced, then picked up the handset.

"Hi, Rita," the voice on the other end said. Not the captain, the first officer.

"It's Cathy," she corrected him. "I know you're trying to get us out of here, but I saw something, um . . . unusual out on the tarmac."

"Unusual how?"

She glanced at Rita, who was staring at her like she didn't approve. "Right before we started backing up, the fuel truck driver tossed a suitcase into the baggage compartment."

"OK." *That's it? Just, OK?'*

"Well, I just . . . thought it was a little weird?"

"That someone put a piece of baggage in the baggage compartment?" *Well, when you put it like that . . .*

"Except it wasn't, y'know, a baggage handler."

"How do you know?"

She thought about that. Everyone on the tarmac wore the same navy coveralls. He could have been a baggage handler . . . a baggage handler who was doing his job by getting a forgotten piece of luggage on that plane by hitching a ride on the fuel truck.

"I mean, I guess it could have been," she hedged, her cheeks warming with embarrassment.

"I appreciate you letting us know."

And he hung up.

"What did he say?" Rita asked. Cathy sucked down her pride and told her boss what the twenty-year veteran already knew.

"That it was nothing."

CHAPTER

021

Penelope swigged back the last sip of her coffee, then placed the mug into the outstretched hand of the first-class flight attendant.

"Thanks. I needed that."

"My pleasure."

As the flight attendant moved off, Penelope tucked her tray into the armrest, then turned to look out her tiny window. The tarmac was buzzing with activity—flagmen directing traffic, mechanics slinging tools, caterers delivering food. The employees-only area of the airport was like a secret society, accessible only through unmarked doors and hidden passageways. As worker bees scurried between the planes in coveralls and candy-colored earmuffs, they seemed to her like animals at the zoo, even though she was the one in the cage.

A baggage handler in a bright orange vest drove by on a cart overflowing with suitcases. She was fairly certain hers wasn't on it—her plane was already buttoned up and taxiing. But what if it was? Bags got misplaced all the time—left behind, loaded onto the wrong plane.

"Flight attendants, please prepare the cabin for departure," the captain said in his velvety monotone.

Penelope leaned back in her chair and closed her eyes. If her dresses and sandals got lost in the shuffle, no biggie—she could go shopping in San Juan. The one item that couldn't be replaced was safely stowed in Ace's duffel in the main cabin. People who didn't spend their lives around baseball never understood why the sport is enshrouded with superstition. She saw how they rolled their eyes at the stories of players on hot streaks refusing to change their socks or cut their hair. She'd tried to explain that baseball was a game of failure. If a hitter got on base one out of three times, that was a miracle. A two-thirds failure rate makes for a lot of opportunities to feel hopeless. Players need something to hold onto when things are going well—a bean burrito for breakfast, a rabbit's foot, a bat signed by a Major League MVP.

She turned her thoughts to what she would do for the next six hours—good God that was a long time to sit. She'd brought a book, but she didn't feel like reading. She didn't feel like watching a movie either, even though there were dozens to choose from. What she really wanted was to talk to her co-conspirator who was inexplicably sitting an arms-length away.

Only five people besides her knew the ugly truth about that night. Three of them were neck-deep in it and would never breathe a word. The fourth didn't know the whole story. Billy Wilcox was the fifth. She looked at him, all cozied up to his future wife and wondered . . . did they tell each other everything?

She remembered that day like it was yesterday. Ace was fifteen and in the ninth grade and playing baseball every day. It was three weeks before the end of the school year. The Cubs were in town to play the Padres, so Coach Cal invited Trey Turnberry, the pride and joy of Crestwood, to the game. Turnberry couldn't say no to the coach who'd launched his career, so he showed up in his crusty Crestwood High baseball jersey—God bless him for keeping it—to throw the ceremonial first pitch.

The town went nuts. The mayor had a parade with food trucks and a marching band. Everyone came out. The way people talked about Trey, chests puffed with pride like they had something to do with his greatness, was frankly kind of ridiculous. The only people who deserved credit for his success were Coach Cal, who taught him baseball, and his mother, who did the rest.

Trey wasn't a pitcher, but he still had a rocket launcher for an arm. Instagram feeds across the baseball world exploded with memes of Crestwood High's sixteen-year-old catcher falling backward off a cliff, bursting into flames, disintegrating into dust—that's how hard Trey threw that first pitch. The team scored sixteen runs that night, they were so fired up. The Booster Club made a killing. The raffle for a signed Trey Turnberry Cubs jersey raised almost ten thousand dollars all by itself. It was a perfect day.

Until it all went to shit.

She wasn't an eyewitness, so what she knew—or *thought* she knew—was technically hearsay. She'd never been questioned, which meant she hadn't had to lie. It wasn't a crime to keep her mouth shut. Some might say it was none of her damn business. Honesty may be a virtue, but consequences are what kick you in the ass. A whole lot of people would get hurt if she spoke up. Only two suffered by her silence. And yes, one of them was on this plane.

Keeping a secret is like having a rock in your shoe. Some days you don't feel it at all. Other days it hurts nonstop. A skilled psychologist would probably tell her that her growing self-loathing was caused, at least in part, by that secret slow-rotting inside her. But she had no interest in therapy, or what it might compel her to do.

"Ladies and gentlemen, please turn your attention to your screens for a short safety video," the flight attendant announced. And then Penelope's screen came to life, giving her a reprieve from her torturous thoughts.

She glanced across the aisle to where Billy Wilcox was sitting with his arm around his bride. She felt a pang of sadness as she remembered how he and Nolan were once as inseparable as a pair of shoes. But then a boy was dead, and they never spoke again. And yet they were bound for life. That's what secrets do. She, Billy, and Nolan were flies in a spider web, tethered together by a thread as delicate as it was deadly. To pull on that thread was crazy-dangerous. Was that why she was so tempted?

She knew she shouldn't stare, though he must be used to it. She was good-looking like that once. Did he recognize her? Probably not.

Yes, he'd been to her house back in the day, but teenagers don't pay attention to their friends' parents. Plus, if he knew who she was, surely he would have said hello—his ex-friend Nolan's mother was the last person he'd want to snub.

She wondered what he would say if she refreshed his memory. She'd never gotten so much as a thank you, she was owed that at the very least. That's the sucky thing about secrets. Keeping them makes you invisible. She was no spring chicken, but she wasn't ready to disappear.

FEDERAL AIR MARSHAL CARLOS RENALDO: Tell me about the night Matthew Kessler died.

ACE ABERNATHY: I wasn't there when it happened.

RENALDO: You had a baseball game?

ACE: Yeah. We won, like 16-3, I think? It was a blowout.

RENALDO: What happened after?

ACE: I went home with my parents.

RENALDO: So everyone went home.

ACE: Not everyone.

RENALDO: Say more.

ACE: There's a pizza place down the road. It's like a mile, but you can cut through the field behind the school, that's what we normally did if we didn't have rides.

RENALDO: So a bunch of guys went out for pizza.

ACE: Yeah. I had to take the PSATs the next day, so my mom wouldn't let me go.

RENALDO: Did you see where Matthew went after the game?

ACE: His parents were there, they went to all the games.

RENALDO: But he didn't leave with them.

ACE: Well, I mean, he didn't make it home, so . . .

RENALDO: So he didn't go with his parents.

ACE: I guess not.

RENALDO: How did you hear about the accident?

ACE: From my mom.

RENALDO: She told you about it?

ACE: I overheard her talking to my brother Nolan. He was pretty messed up.

RENALDO: Messed up how?

ACE: I guess it was pretty gruesome.

RENALDO: Your brother was at the scene?
(No answer.)

RENALDO: Why would your brother be at the scene of the accident?

ACE: I don't know. I wasn't there.

RENALDO: Who was he with?

ACE: Some older guys, I don't know who, a bunch of his old teammates came to town for the game. All I know is my parents brought me home after the game, then my mom went back out to pick up Nolan. Next thing I knew she was making him a sandwich.

RENALDO: Because he was upset.

ACE: We were all upset. Matthew was my friend.

RENALDO: What else did your mother say to Nolan?

ACE: Just that everything was going to be all right, she'd take care of it.

RENALDO: What do you think she meant by that?

ACE: I have no idea.

CHAPTER

022

As instructed, Francesca turned her attention to the screen on the seatback in front of her.

"In the event of a loss in cabin pressure," a woman monotoned, "oxygen masks will be released automatically. Be sure to secure your own mask over your nose and mouth before assisting others."

She watched as the mom in the video put on her mask while her unmasked little boy sat beside her. She understood the logic of it—you're no use to your child if you're unconscious—but she wouldn't put her safety before her child's any more than she would turn her face toward a snowball hurtling toward her head—no mother would. She knew this as a biology teacher, as an observer of animals in the wild, but most of all, because she was a mother. Or, rather, *had been* a mother. She would never, under any circumstances, have taken a breath if her son couldn't breathe. And yet, she was on this plane, and he was in the ground.

He'd played well that night—went three for five with a walk and two RBIs. He'd been solid on defense too—threw a runner out at home in a rare 6-2-3 double play that, on any other night, would have made the news. The Crestwood Cougars scored sixteen runs against the Oceanside Sharks as hometown hero Trey Turnberry cheered them on from the dugout. It was the happiest day of her son's life. She could say that definitively now.

She didn't like being the one to tell him he couldn't go out with his teammates after, but he had his PSAT exam at eight the next morning, he needed to sleep. She knew for a fact Penelope was taking Ace home for the exact same reason, and that she was being perfectly reasonable. Rick didn't contradict her, even though she could see the disapproval in his eyes. Let him go for a little while, those baby blues said. But she had paid $150 for that test, and she didn't want it to be wasted.

Matthew's teammates piled into cars headed for Topper's Pizza, the players' post-game hangout. "C'mon Matt," they shouted from open windows as their cars idled in waiting. "Please, mom!" he begged. And she almost gave in. Then she thought of Penelope, who'd raised three boys without being bullied by any of them. "There will be plenty of opportunities to celebrate," she said, thinking it was true.

They started walking through the parking lot. Rick tried to put an arm around their son, but he pushed it away. When they got to the car, Matthew told them he forgot something in the locker room—his water bottle maybe? Whatever it was, it was credible. He threw his backpack in the trunk, then sprinted off. She remembered thinking how tall and lean he looked—not a man, but no longer a boy—and that he needed a haircut. She had a flash that maybe taking that test wasn't that important. If he got a baseball scholarship, no one would care about his test scores. But then again, he could get hurt, or lose interest in the sport, or, or, or . . . She told herself he'd be mad for a couple of hours, and then they'd laugh about it someday. It was just a stupid pizza party.

They waited five, ten, fifteen minutes. Rick went to the field to get him but came back alone. Realizing he'd defied her, they drove to Topper's. Rick waited a beat before going in, as if his hesitation might convince Francesca to just let him be. She didn't want to reward her son for his disobedience, so said nothing.

She stared out the car window as she waited. It was a warm night with only a sliver of moon. The restaurant was packed. Boys in emerald jerseys with eye black on their cheeks and dirt on their pants spilled out onto the outdoor patio. She thought about what Matthew's punishment should be. Mow the lawn? Clean the bathrooms? Lose his phone for a day, the weekend, the whole week? Or was taking the PSATs punishment enough? She knew with teenagers you had to pick your battles. Still, it was too late to unpick this one, and if she let it slide, she would be setting herself up for more defiance. No phone for a day, she decided. It was not much of a punishment, and he'd be at the test for half of it. It was more symbolic than punitive.

"He's not here," Rick said, returning to the car with a bewildered expression on his face. It was that look, not the circumstances, that made her pulse quicken.

She took out her phone. "Where are you?" she texted Matthew.

No response.

She texted again. "We're at Toppers, please come out."

Again, no response.

"This is not like him," Rick muttered, and he was right. Matthew was a good boy, he worked hard, got good grades, didn't lie, rarely ever broke the rules. If not for that damn test they would have let him stay out as long as he wanted.

"What should we do?" she asked. And her husband just shrugged. She opened her phone to look for him on Google Maps, but he'd either turned off the tracking or the phone itself. She didn't know if he'd ever done that before, because she'd never had to use the app to find him.

"Maybe he went home," she said. The one mile drive to their house took twenty minutes because of the game traffic. Matthew could have walked there in half that.

But he wasn't home.

She texted the coach. Then Penelope. Then four other baseball moms. Have you seen Matthew? Nobody had.

Sheriff Eckles arrived at their front door just as they were getting ready to look for him. She'd seen enough bad TV to know the police don't come to your door with happy news. She didn't remember inviting him in, but she recalled snippets of what he said once they were all sitting on her couch. *There'd been an accident . . . vacant lot off Maple*

Drive . . . died on impact . . . first responders . . . emergency room . . . I'll drive you.

She remembered sinking onto the carpet and crying—no, not crying, howling like a madwoman. Rick must have been in shock, because he didn't make a peep. Someone handed her a tissue. One or both men helped her to her feet, then into the squad car, then through the sliding door of the emergency room.

Then they were standing next to a gurney. Rick held her by both shoulders as a gloved hand pulled back the sheet. Her son's face was a ghastly shade of white. His lips were purple like a plum. She threw up in a trashcan. And then they went home.

"We know you have a choice, and we appreciate you choosing Pioneer Air," the woman in the video said. Francesca winced at the notion of choice. She and her stupid choices. Why hadn't she just let him go for pizza with his friends? If she'd let him get in that car, he wouldn't have been crossing that vacant lot in the dark night. He'd be with her, on this plane, going to play the sport he loved.

She knew Coach Cal and the other parents were surprised she'd volunteered to come on this trip. They were careful around her, as if talking about baseball would churn up bad memories. But the memories were ever-present. Being around the team was like standing in a swimming pool in the rain. When you're already drowning, what's a little water falling on your head?

"Flight attendants, prepare for takeoff," the pilot said. She instinctively checked her seatbelt to make sure it was fastened. Did that mean she wanted to live? Yes, but for only one reason.

To get justice for her son.

CAPTAIN BRETT BANCROFT: Good afternoon, everyone, this is your captain speaking. Sorry for the late departure, but thanks to a vigorous jet stream, we'll have a nice tailwind and should be able to make up a little time in the air.

I have us landing in San Juan at approximately 12:02 a.m. local time. Puerto Rico doesn't observe Daylight Savings, so they are just three hours ahead of us here in San Diego. That puts our flying time at five hours and fifty-five minutes, give or take a few.

Our flight plan is going to loosely follow the southern border of the United States. We'll fly over Arizona, the panhandle of New Mexico, then across the great state of Texas.

Once over the Gulf, we'll dip south of Key West, Florida. You can wave to the Bahamas out of the left side of the aircraft and Cuba to your right. Puerto Rico is just beyond the Dominican Republic, bridging the Caribbean Sea to the south and the Atlantic Ocean to the north.

Right now the skies are looking clear, but I'll check back with you if that changes. In the meantime, sit back, relax, and enjoy the flight.

PART

Storm Rolls In

002

CHAPTER

023

"Ladies and gentlemen," Rita announced over the PA, as Cathy mouthed along. "We've reached our cruising altitude of thirty thousand feet and will be beginning our in-flight service." As the newbie, Cathy rarely got to do the announcements but practiced them silently every chance she got.

She unbuckled her seatbelt and headed to the rear galley. The turnover had been so frantic, she hadn't had time to prep the food and beverage carts the way she liked them. Also, she'd been distracted by thoughts of Francesca Kessler and how on earth she was going to tell her that Brendan had not only betrayed the Kessler family, but she herself had known it for nearly three years.

"Hey," Alphonso said as he squeezed in behind her.

"Hey."

"This galley is a mess," he huffed. "Just because those bitches got bumped off the flight doesn't mean they can leave the place looking like they had a frat party!"

This Airbus had an older configuration—the two aft lavatories were caddy-corner to one another, with one off the aisle and the other on the aircraft-left side by the tail. The jumpseat was also on the left side, directly across from the back lavatory. There was a thick, navy curtain they could pull if they wanted to have that rear lavatory to themselves for a few minutes. This flight-attendant friendly configuration had been discarded in the newer planes in favor of another row of seats, but Pioneer had several of these older planes, and Cathy was always pleased when she got one for the tiny respite of privacy it afforded.

As the plane cruised through smooth air, Alphonso and Cathy worked back-to-back in silence. Fonzie inventoried the soda and mixers, while she found the cups, creamers, and napkins and put the coffee on.

"I hope the last crew prepped this ice," Alphonso said as he slid the insert of ice into the top shelf of the cart. "I do not want to fight with it during our service."

"You want the mallet?" Cathy asked.

"Nah, I'll just attack it with minis of Stoli." He made a psycho stabbing motion. Normally this would make Cathy laugh. Today she couldn't even muster a smile. "What's up with you today?"

"Nothing. Just a little distracted." Then, because it would be out of character for her not to spill, "My ex is on this flight."

"Yikes. Sorry," he said, then warned, "try not to take it out on the passengers."

"Maybe just the one?"

"After the service, I'll help you plot his murder if you want?"

And now she chuckled. "Sounds like a plan."

He backed the cart out of the galley. Alphonso always took the front and she the rear. She didn't like walking the whole length of the plane backward. Also, he was wearing loafers while she was in heels.

Her gaze floated over the backs of eighteen baseball-capped heads as they wheeled the cart down the aisle. Flight attendants always start their service in the front of the cabin. There's no logic to it, beyond rewarding passengers who've already been rewarded with better seats. She vowed one day to do the route backward, just to shock people. But today she would shock just the one.

They reached the front of the main cabin. Alphonso parked the cart, and they went to work.

"Something to drink?"

She said those three words so often she heard them in her dreams. She knew passengers regarded her as an overpaid waitress, when in fact she was neither of those things. Flight attendants are "safety officers," and do seven weeks of rigorous training to earn that title. They make less than most waitresses, and despite working under more challenging conditions, aren't allowed to accept tips.

"I got the next two rows," Alphonso said. "Go ahead and pop down to the exit row."

Her chest flooded with dread. The exit row . . . where her ex-husband was seated.

She dragged the cart with her until she was level with the row.

"Something to drink?" Cathy asked Brendan Callahan like he was any other passenger. As he met her gaze, outrage over what he'd done coursed through her veins. Baseball, like her beverage service, was just a cover for their real jobs—keeping players and passengers safe. Maybe her training had changed her. Or maybe time away from Crestwood had given her perspective. What struck her today was not her sudden urgency to speak the truth, but her shame that she hadn't done it sooner.

"I'm OK. I brought my water." He held up his bottle to show her, probably because he knew she didn't trust him. If she did, they'd still be married.

"It's a long flight. How about some cranberry juice?" They always had cranberry juice in the house when they were married. He said it was good for the prostate, even though there was no evidence of that.

"Sure." He had the aisle seat. His batting coach was asleep, his face pressed against the window, with an empty seat between them. This was as close to alone as they would be for the next five and a half hours—if she didn't strike now, she might not get another chance.

She felt his eyes on her as she bent over to look for a can. She was in good shape—her Peloton made sure of that—but she still sucked in her stomach. She wondered what he thought of her purple hair, if he was mortified. Then she reminded herself he had no right to be mortified with anyone but himself.

"Odd choice for a chaperone," she said as she plucked a can of cranberry out of the drawer. She hadn't had time to rehearse what to say, obviously.

"I had nothing to do with it." His tone was defensive. She'd hit a nerve.

"No, I don't imagine." She knew he felt guilty around Francesca, so she turned the knife. "She's been crying."

"How do you know that?"

She raised an eyebrow. There's no crying in baseball, but sometimes he forgot that baseball isn't life.

"Maybe this is cathartic for her," he said.

"You know what would make it cathartic?" Cathy asked as she popped open the can.

His voice got real quiet. "I can't and you know I can't."

She put two ice cubes in a cup and poured. "How about a splash of soda?" she asked because she knew that's how he liked it. And also because what he just said was bullshit and if she didn't change the subject she might throw that cranberry juice in his face.

"Cath . . . it's bigger than just me."

The remark was as maddening as it was predictable. When a parent asked him, *"Why did you . . . bench my kid . . . put Junior in left field . . . let so-and-so pitch into the ninth inning?"* his answer was always *"Because that's what's best for the team."* Some people thought his platitudes *("We rise together or not at all!")* were cowardly and got annoyed. But he saw his players as part of something bigger, and that something bigger had to be protected at all costs.

Over the years, they'd had numerous arguments about his "team first" mentality. "So you'd push someone out of your lifeboat if they were slowing you down?" she'd ask to goad him into admitting his moral code was flawed. Still, he was unflappable. "That lifeboat's no good to anybody if we can't get to shore," he'd respond. "We do it in baseball all the time," he'd explain. "Sacrifice an at bat to score a run, bench your best player to build the confidence of another." Every hypothetical she threw at him, he'd choose what served the greater good. And then it wasn't hypothetical anymore.

Brendan Callahan was born and raised in Crestwood. His parents still owned the house he grew up in, and when he and Cathy were married, they spent every Thanksgiving and Christmas around his childhood dining room table. He was friends with the mayor, the fire chief, and the sheriff and all his deputies. He volunteered for the parks and recreation department during the off-season, spreading mulch and clearing brush. He made his community a better place, just as his community made him a better man—until it didn't.

The day of the accident, her husband woke up a happy man. His team was leading the division, and the player he'd developed from a frisky colt to the black stallion of the National League was coming back to bestow honor on his former team and the town. He'd told her he felt as if the universe was sending him a sign that he'd gotten it right all these years—right job, right choices, right outlook on life.

They drove together to the game that night. She was a volunteer ticket taker and had to be there early too. In the third inning, when Crestwood was already up eight to nothing, she snuck away from her post to join the throngs in the stands. As she looked around at all the smiling faces, she'd never felt prouder. This moment, this team, this outpouring of love and joy, were all because of her husband. He wasn't just the coach of a baseball team, he was the beating heart of their whole town.

As the umpire called strike three for the final out, players, parents, and fans rushed the field, hugging and tackling each other in a tidal wave of excitement. Not wanting to get swallowed up by the crowd, she'd stayed in the bleachers. She knew her husband would find her smiling eyes, and when he did, she blew him a kiss and headed for the exit. He and the players would continue their celebration over pizza and Cokes at Toppers down the street, as they always did after a win. She had no interest in cramming into the restaurant with a bunch of smelly teenage boys. So she got in her car and drove home.

His phone call came after she'd changed into sweats and was scrolling through Netflix. "An accident . . . Oh God . . . limbs aren't meant to bend that way." She'd asked him to slow down, start at the beginning. "I was driving with Coach Brooks, but the traffic . . . so many cars, I got out and walked. I didn't want to miss the celebration. Why didn't I just stay in the car?"

She'd instructed him to hang up and call for help, even though, as he put it, "Only God could help that boy now." He did it anyway, then called her back.

"Tell me what happened, Brendan," she'd commanded gently, in case there was something to be done.

"At first I thought I'd imagined it, it didn't look real," he'd told her. "It was like he got shot out of a canon. He was a rag doll, not a boy . . . He's just a boy. Poor, poor boy."

She let him cry as she put on her coat. "What happened to the car, Brendan?" she'd asked, heading for the door, keys in hand. "Is the driver OK?"

"I don't know."

"What do you mean you don't know?" And his answer nearly stopped her heart.

"They drove away."

He was in shock, she'd reasoned, because he wasn't computing that this wasn't an accident, it was a crime.

Her hand was on the doorknob when she asked the all-important question. "But you saw the car?"

And here's where their memories of that call diverged. Because she was sure he'd said yes. Because after he said it, she told him she was going to grab a pen and paper so she could write down every detail he could remember about that car.

He'd told her he wasn't sure about the color. Not white. That he would have known. His words were intermingled with sobs. *Did he say blue? Or new?* She wrote both words down on her pad. "SUV or sedan," she'd asked, but all she heard was sobbing. "Brendan, focus," she'd urged. "Tell me what you saw." She'd repeated her question—"What kind of car was it?"—and he'd said he was "pretty sure it belonged to—"

The sirens came at the worst possible time, burying his voice under a deafening wail. "Say again? I didn't hear you," she'd said, the tip of her pen on the pad.

"I gotta go, Sheriff's here," he'd told her. And then he hung up.

She went to Google Maps and pinpointed his location. Turns out all she had to do was follow the sirens, the whole police force was there by the time she arrived. Her husband was talking to Sheriff Eckles. She went over to him and wrapped her arms around his middle.

"You told him about the car, right?" she'd asked, because she knew he wasn't thinking straight, and also that the quicker the sheriff gave chase the better chance he had of finding it.

Her husband didn't answer.

"Brendan, you need to tell the sheriff what you saw."

And what he said next ended their marriage.

"I didn't see anything, Cath."

That pivotal exchange played in her mind as she handed her ex-husband his cranberry and soda, as though he was just another passenger.

"Thanks, Cath." He smiled up at her. But she didn't smile back.

"It's time to come forward, Brendan," she said, kicking off the brake on her beverage cart. She knew someone had told her husband to keep his mouth shut. What she didn't know was why.

"Cath, we've been through this—" he started to say but she cut him off.

"That woman deserves to know who killed her son."

"I wish I could help her, but I can't," Brendan said. And, just like when she quit her job and cut her hair, Cathy decided to do what was in her heart, consequences be damned.

"Then I will."

CHAPTER

024

Francesca peered out her window into the darkening sky. The plane was traveling east, away from the setting sun, into an indigo abyss. Coach Cal's comment that they had "plenty of eyes" echoed in her mind. She wanted to be useful. That wasn't why she'd volunteered, but it was a feeling she deeply missed.

It was a classic case of "the grass is always greener." When she was a mom with a full-time job that demanded lesson planning at dawn and grading tests late into the night, she sometimes felt overwhelmed by the additional tasks of being a wife and a mother. Now that Matthew was dead and Rick as good as, she realized having people to care for was the best gift in the world. She wished she could travel back in time, change all those have-tos to get-tos—I *get to* drive Matthew to school, I *get to* make dinner, tidy the house, make my husband and son feel safe and loved. Because good God she missed those things now.

She'd suffered a terrible tragedy, no one could deny her that. But she'd mastered the art of feeling sorry for herself long before the accident. When she was busting her butt to get her grades in and dinner on the table and Matthew to games, *and, and, and* . . . she felt frazzled and put upon. And now that her time and her life were hers, *all hers*, she longed for the chaos. What if the source of her misery wasn't her circumstances? What if it was *her*?

She closed her eyes. *I* get to *go to a beautiful tropical island. I* get to *move in with my sister who loves me. I* get to *discover new hobbies, friends, pastimes, adventures.* She'd lost a son. She'd ruined a marriage. Those were facts. But mourning and moping, those were choices.

If someone were to ask her about her marriage, her knee-jerk reaction was to tell them it was a failure—it was over, after all. But why should the ending define the whole ride? It had been a success for much longer than it had been falling apart. That marriage gave her wonderful memories—opening too many presents on Christmas morning, skiing fresh powder in Heavenly Valley, camping in Yosemite under a sky filled with stars. She got to say "I do" on a beach in bare feet with flowers in her hair, honeymoon in Greece, conceive a child and nurse him on her breast. Just because it was over didn't mean the whole thing was a bust. It couldn't have fallen apart if it wasn't once gloriously whole.

She knew as a person of science that it was more painful to lose something you thought was yours than to never get that thing you long for. People who dream of being rich but remain poor rarely fall into despair, but a millionaire plunged into poverty might never be happy again. That's just how our brains are wired. "Better to have loved and lost than never to have loved at all" might be true for poets and dreamers, but scientifically, it's hogwash.

That didn't mean she was doomed to feel sad forever. With some effort, she could rewire her brain. Call it "counting your blessings" or "mindfulness," the practice of retraining your mind to love your life was neither new nor impossible. As Vincent van Gogh once observed, there's beauty in everything . . . you just have to open your eyes to it.

Rick had tried to teach her how to change her grief into gratitude. He said things like, "when you focus on the good, the good gets better." He bought her a framed picture of Charlie Brown telling Snoopy, "What if today we were just grateful for everything?" But all she felt was anger. And eventually that anger drove him away.

She reached into her purse and pulled out her phone. Maybe leaving town had opened her eyes. Or maybe she was just tired of feeling sad.

Whatever the case, Rick deserved to know he was right. Losing Matthew was only the end of the world if she let it be.

Dear Rick, she typed with her thumbs. She wouldn't be able to send the email until they landed, but she could write it. As I soar toward my next chapter, I can't help but find myself thinking of you. She paused. Did that sound sappy? Hopeful? She was a biochemist, not a writer. She told herself not to worry, she had the whole flight to find the right words. She closed her eyes and let her mind go in search of all the things she had to feel grateful for . . .

"Francesca?"

A woman's voice snapped her back to the present.

"I know we don't know each other very well," Cathy Yap said, squatting down beside her. "But I've thought about you a lot these past few years. Y'know, since you lost your son."

"Thank you," Francesca said, as she'd done so many times when people told her how sorry they were, because she assumed that's what was happening here.

"How are you doing?"

Francesca forced a smile—time to practice her new skill. "I'm grateful for the memories." She would have to work on her delivery, but she got the words out. Fake it 'til you make it, isn't that how the saying goes?

"It was kind of you to volunteer to chaperone," Cathy said, letting *"given what happened"* be implied.

Francesca hesitated before responding. What would she say if Cathy asked why she'd come? She had several responses to choose from. There was the one she gave to Coach Cal—her sister's house wasn't ready, and she had nowhere else to stay. She had the one that would conjure pity—she didn't want to watch the movers dismantle the home she had painstakingly built. She had the one she kept private—she wanted to put off receiving those divorce papers for as long as possible. There was the pathetic one—she was lonely and didn't know what to do with herself. All those possible responses were true. But something else was true. Something she would never say out loud. Because it might frighten

Cathy if she told her these boys were the only connection she had to her dead son and she wanted to shake out every memory of Matthew they still carried, even the bad ones. *Especially* the bad ones. She told herself pursuing justice would not interfere with her budding gratitude practice—quite the opposite. Finding Matthew's killer would simply be something to add to her list of reasons to be grateful.

"It was nice to be asked," Francesca said, even though nobody had asked her.

"We're all so sorry for your loss," Cathy said, and Francesca smiled, imagining this conversation would end like every conversation about Matthew—with a hand squeeze or a hug.

"I imagine it's hard to move on with so many unanswered questions," Cathy continued, stepping out of the script.

Francesca's brow contracted. Where was she going with this?

"It must be so frustrating that they never found who did it." Cathy said this part not as a question, but as an undeniable fact.

"They tried their best," Francesca said, because that's what she'd been told, and to believe anything else would be insane.

"Who?" Cathy asked. "Who do you think tried their best?"

"The police," Francesca said, even though it should have been obvious. "Sheriff Eckles."

"Alan Eckles has been the sheriff of Crestwood for twenty-eight years," Cathy said. "As far as I know, he's never held any other job."

"Well then, I guess he knows what he's doing," Francesca replied, clinging to her quest for gratitude like a buoy in a storm.

"Some might say being an elected official your whole life has the potential to cloud your judgment," Cathy countered. Where was she going with this?

"How so?"

"Your need to stay popular becomes more important than doing the right thing."

"By 'the right thing,' you mean . . . ?"

"Tell the truth."

Francesca's heart did a backflip. "What are you saying, Cathy?"

Cathy lowered her voice. "I'm saying someone on this plane saw what happened and tried to tell the sheriff, but he buried it."

Francesca's pulse quickened. "Who saw something?" she asked. Cathy held her eyes but didn't speak. "Cal?" she guessed. Cathy raised her eyebrows, confirming without confirming. "What did he tell you?"

Cathy leaned in closer. "That he saw the car. As it was speeding away."

Francesca's heart was pounding so loud her ears were vibrating.

"Does he know who was driving?"

"He won't say. Which implies . . ." her voice trailed off. Because if he didn't know who it was, wouldn't he have said that?

"So it was someone from Crestwood!"

"I have to assume."

The synapses in Francesca's brain started rapid firing. If it was someone Coach Cal knew, maybe she knew them too. They lived in the same town, worked at the same school . . .

"Why would he keep that to himself?" She pored through potential suspects as she'd done so many times before—fellow teachers, local business owners, neighbors, students . . .

"All I know is when he called me that night, he'd seen things—*knew* things," Cathy said. "And then the sheriff got to him, and he suddenly forgot."

Francesca felt a prickle of irritation. Alan Eckles had been nothing but kind to her. While others had sent flowers that were dead within a week, the sheriff planted trees that would live on forever. He'd dedicated a park "in loving memory of Matthew," sent restaurant vouchers and movie tickets, came by to check on her long after everyone else had fallen away.

"Who else knows about this?" Francesca asked.

"I don't know for sure, but I think that bossy Booster Club lady."

"Penelope Abernathy?"

"She was there when I got there, milling around . . . a little too close, if you know what I mean?"

Francesca had only known Penelope to care about three things: her appearance, her three boys, and that damned baseball program. Cathy's conspiracy theory was getting wilder by the minute.

"It was wrong of me not to tell you earlier. I'm so sorry, Francesca," Cathy said.

Annoyance rolled across Francesca's skin. The thought that Coach Brendan Callahan, Penelope Abernathy, and Sheriff Eckles had conspired to cover up a crime was positively absurd. Cathy Yap was known to be a chatterbox. She yapped about who got married, divorced, hired, fired, who sold their house, to whom and why. She was always talking. Francesca hadn't known her to make things up, but she wouldn't put it past her.

Maybe it was her lack of specificity ("My husband saw someone but he won't say who"). Or maybe it was that purple pixie cut, that, let's be honest, made her come off as a little unstable. Francesca was too deep in her own personal hell to wonder why Cal had divorced Cathy, but he must have had a reason. Cathy wouldn't be the first person to harbor ill will toward an ex. Or to slander him for hurting her.

"Thank you for telling me," Francesca said, then forced a smile.

Because she didn't believe one word of it.

She knew from Sheriff Eckles that random people sometimes called the tip line claiming to have seen things that made no sense. They do it for attention, he'd said, to feel important. You can't let them drag you down a rabbit hole, he'd warned. She told herself not to let Cathy's insane suggestion upset her. She recalled Charlie Brown's missive to be grateful for everything. Then took a deep breath and ordered her annoyance to go away.

MRS. BEATRICE "BEA" BOOKBINDER: Agent Cooper? This is Bea Bookbinder, Sheriff Eckles's personal secretary. I took the liberty of jotting down your number, I hope you don't mind?

SPECIAL AGENT SAM COOPER: Not at all. Pleasure to hear from you, Mrs. Bookbinder.

BEA: Please, call me Bea.

COOPER: How can I help you, Bea?

BEA: I don't know if this is related to your inquiry, but I handle all the incoming filings, and one came in—well, a few hours ago now, I'm embarrassed to say. I hadn't yet processed it when I answered your call. I'm normally on top of my paperwork, but this came in through our general mailbox and I didn't look at it. Until just this second, I mean.

COOPER: Go on.

BEA: Like I said, it may be unrelated to the matter you and the sheriff were discussing, I don't listen in on his conversations. You have to understand, we have so little crime here in Crestwood! Anyway, I thought it might be what you were calling about, given the timing of it, how it came in right before.

COOPER: I appreciate you bringing it to my attention.

BEA: Shall I send it along, then?

COOPER: Please do.

CRESTWOOD TOWNSHIP POLICE REPORT

(Gray areas are for internal use only)

PERSON MAKING REPORT
(complaints may be filed anonymously)

NAME: Angela Diaz
ADDRESS: 17025 Catamaran Way
PHONE: 619-500-4242
CITY: Crestwood
STATE: California

NATURE OF COMPLAINT: sexual assault
COMPLAINT AGAINST (name/names):
(intentionally left blank)
DATE/TIME: 4.13.26 / 2 a.m.
DATE/TIME REPORTED: 4.19.26 / 3:08 p.m.
INCIDENT LOCATION: *(intentionally left blank)*
DESCRIPTION OF INCIDENT: A man I can identify came to the bar where I work after closing time when I was alone in the office running my totals for the night. He pushed me against the desk and raped me. I have an audio recording of the incident. I'd like to report him for sexual assault.

ELECTRONIC SIGNATURE: Angela Diaz

CHAPTER

025

"Hey, bitches!"

Angie looked up in surprise as Jillian crossed into the main cabin holding five minis of champagne. The rosy pop had returned to her cheeks, as if she'd forgotten all about how her run-in with those fireballs had ended.

"What are you doing back here in the cheap seats?" asked one of the bitches seated behind Angie.

"Getting the party started!" Jillian replied, holding up her minis. Angie felt her pulse quicken. She hadn't expected Jilly to leave Billy's side until the morning of the wedding. This was her chance. All she had to do was muster the courage to take it.

Jillian passed the single serving bottles of bubbly out to her bridesmaids, then backtracked down the aisle to give the last one to her maid of honor.

"Best for last," she said with a wink.

"Thanks, Jills. But I'm not drinking right now." Angie held up her hand in gentle protest, then quickly lowered it so Jillian wouldn't see it shaking.

"Saving yourself for tomorrow?"

"I don't like to drink and fly," she lied.

Jillian raised a skeptical eyebrow. "I don't remember that about you," she said, because they'd gone on several trips together—Cabo for her bachelorette party, Napa for her bridal shower, Jackson Hole for skiing—and Angie had never shied away from an in-flight drink before.

"I don't bounce back like I used to," Angie said, even though the bachelorette party was three weeks ago.

"Fine, I'll drink it then." Jillian turned and faced the other bridesmaids, who were three rows behind Angie and already had their bottles open. "To the best bitches a bride could ever ask for," she said, popping off the cork.

"That's us!" one of the bitches said, and they all laughed.

Angie's heart clouded with sadness as she watched Jillian slug back her champagne—sadness for the future that she was about to ruin but also for the past. People assumed that because Jillian was rich, her life had been easy. But rich-people problems are still problems.

The whole town knew Jillian's father was a playboy. The ladies who lunched clucked about how he would show up at the tennis club without his racket, and the local florist tattled on him for sending flowers to women who weren't his wife. It was even rumored he kept a secret apartment for his revolving door of mistresses. Jillian's mother took her humiliation out on her daughter. If Angie hadn't had a ringside seat for her cruelty, she might have thought the stories exaggerated.

It started with her nose. Jillian's mother thought it was "a travesty" and dragged her to a plastic surgeon to have it fixed when she was twelve. "Just tell your friends you had a deviated septum," her mother had instructed her, as if eighth graders knew what that was. She waited until summer so she could ruin Jillian's vacation instead of her grades. And perhaps give her schoolmates a chance to forget what her nose looked like to make the transformation less glaring.

As the surgeon had warned (and Jillian's mother ignored), narrowing Jilly's nose made her round face look even rounder. So the next summer, inspired by Angelina Jolie's *Maleficent*, her mom sent her back under the knife for chin and cheek implants. Because they were rich, no one called it child abuse. As far as they knew, rich people did shit like that all the time.

When the plastic surgery didn't turn Jillian from an ugly duckling into a swan, her mother simply ignored her—just like her father did, except at close range. That's when Jilly's pill-popping started. In the absence of motherly love, there was Vicodin, Percocet, Xanax, Lexapro—whatever pharmaceutical she could lift from the neighborhood medicine cabinets. When the drugs ran out, she started abusing food—shoving the contents of their double-wide Sub-Zero into her mouth, then bringing them back up in their Kohler self-cleaning commode. Angie's parents didn't buy her Chanel sunglasses or steak dinners at Maestro's, but the hug she got at the end of every day was more than Jillian ever got from her mother.

As Angie watched Jillian polish off her champagne, her resolve swelled. She leaned over toward the guy who had ogled her legs. "I hate to ask," she said to her seatmate, "but my best friend is getting married." She pointed to the Queen Bitch. "Do you think she could sit with me for a minute?"

"No problem," he said, unbuckling his seatbelt. Then to Jillian, "I can move to another row. If you want to sit with your friend?"

Jillian smiled down at him. "Oh! That's so nice of you!"

"Congratulations," he said, stepping into the aisle.

"Thank you!" she beamed. She slid into his seat, then leaned in toward Angie and crinkled her nose. "It's still warm where his butt was." She spied the crescent of dried blood in Angie's nailbed. "What happened to your finger?"

"I picked at my cuticles," Angie said, balling her hand in a fist so Jillian didn't have to look at it. "It looks worse than it is."

"We should have gotten you a manicure." It was passive-aggressive, the use of the word "we," but Angie was about to blow up her life so she let it slide.

"Yeah, sorry."

"It's OK," Jillian said, to make her feel better. Then added, "Nobody's putting a ring on your finger," to make her feel worse. Jillian sometimes copied her mother's *Mean Girl* tactics, and Angie didn't take them personally.

Angie hadn't rehearsed what to say, but what did it matter? There was no easy way. "Listen, Jillian . . . There's something you should know about your future husband."

"He's not the same person he was when you were together," Jillian said. "Anything you think you know about him is old news."

Angie slid her phone out of her purse. "Does six days ago count as old news?" Her cheeks ignited with fear, but her hands were steady.

"What, you mean his bachelor party? He told me all about it."

"Did he tell you this?" She unlocked her phone and turned the screen toward the bride-to-be.

"What is that?" Jillian asked, looking at the screenshot Angie had taken of her police report.

"This should explain it," she said, handing Jillian her AirPods, then pressing "play" on the recording no one wanted to be real.

SPECIAL AGENT SAM COOPER: How's the mood up there? Are you keeping everyone away from my crime scene?

FEDERAL AIR MARSHAL CARLOS RENALDO: Yes, sir. So far the only people outside the crew who know there's been a murder are the kid who found the body and the doctor who examined it. We're keeping them isolated.

COOPER: As long as nobody moves, no one else will get hurt.

RENALDO: Understood, sir.

COOPER: We're looking into the Kessler hit-and-run, seems like there's some funny business there, nice work flagging that.

RENALDO: Thank you, sir.

COOPER: I just arrived in Crestwood. The hit-and-run is not the only lead we're following.

RENALDO: Sir?

COOPER: While I was driving, I got a call from Sheriff Alan Eckles's personal secretary about a police report that had come in earlier today. At first I thought it was unrelated. But then I noticed a stunning coincidence.

RENALDO: A coincidence, sir?

COOPER: It was from someone on your flight.

RENALDO: A passenger?

COOPER: I just sent it to you. Have a look.
(Beat.)

RENALDO: 26A.

COOPER: That's right. Miss Angela Diaz. She filed it at 3:08 p.m.

RENALDO: We left the gate at 3:09.

COOPER: Which means she filed it from the plane.

RENALDO: She said she was sexually assaulted.

COOPER: Last Saturday.

RENALDO: The report doesn't specify who did it.

COOPER: She didn't make it very hard to figure out. She works at a place called the Cliff Diver. We just reviewed the security footage. Because it was less than a week ago, the owner still had it.

RENALDO: That's lucky.

COOPER: Or strategic on her part. There are cameras by both entrances, front and back. He came in through the front.

RENALDO: Bold.

COOPER: The dumb shit parked right by the door. Got a clear shot of his license plate. Took all of five minutes to identify him. Hold on, I'll text you his photo.
(Beat.)

RENALDO: The guy from 3E.

COOPER: That's right. William Wilcox.

RENALDO: Who got on this plane to marry someone else.

COOPER: So it seems. We're doing a deep dive on everyone in the wedding party. I'm pulling police reports from the last five years to see if anything else comes up.

RENALDO: Thank you for keeping me in the loop.

COOPER: Keep the intel flowing. We're going to follow this investigation wherever it takes us.

CHAPTER

026

Penelope was getting restless. Since her flight had taken off, she'd watched a movie, read sixteen chapters of her book, played five games of solitaire, drunk two glasses of wine, and eaten a four-course meal. Busybodies, by definition, don't like to sit still, and she'd been sitting on her duff for over four hours. So—despite her better instincts—when the young lady sitting next to Billy Wilcox got up and left him alone, she seized the opportunity to scratch that itch that had been gnawing at her since before they took off.

"Billy Wilcox, right?" she said, leaning into the aisle toward him. He was wearing headphones and didn't hear her. His outside arm was parked on his armrest. She reached out and touched it with her French-dipped nails.

He looked down at her hand, then up at her face. His bicep strained against his linen shirt as he reached up and took out an AirPod.

"Sorry. Didn't mean to interrupt your movie."

"No worries. I've already seen it a million times." Even in this dim light, his Côte d'Azur eyes pierced the air like laser beams. "Did you need something?"

"Yes," she huffed dramatically. "For this flight to be over."

He chuckled. "I hear ya," then offered his hand. "I'm Billy."

"Yes, I know," she said as she shook it. He looked at her quizzically.

"My son is Nolan Abernathy. From Crestwood High?" She said the last part like a question, not because she was unsure, she knew where her son had gone to school. What she didn't know was whether Billy was willing to talk about it.

"Nolan! Of course I remember him." He flashed a smile bright enough to see from space. "It's nice to see you, Mrs. Abernathy."

She tried not to wince at being called "Mrs." They were both adults. "Please, call me Penelope."

"I'm pretty sure I've been to your house," he said, and she nodded. Everyone in Crestwood had been to her house. If her sons were going to hang out with friends, she wanted it to be under her watchful eye.

"We had a few shindigs back in the day."

"Nolan has a little brother, Ryan, right?"

"That's right," she said, pleased that he remembered. "And a little-er brother named Ace."

He knitted his eyebrows together. "I don't think I ever met Ace."

"He's here," she said. Then clarified, "In the main cabin, that is. He wanted to sit with his teammates."

"Yeah, I saw the Crestwood team was here. Tournament in Puerto Rico?"

"Yes."

"Lucky them."

"The team's not as good as when you were on it," she said to compliment him. And also because it was true.

"I can't take credit for that." It was an obvious nod to his and Nolan's former teammate, MLB superstar Trey Turnberry. But Penelope rejected the notion that the team's success belonged solely to Trey.

"One player cannot win tournaments all by himself. I think ASU would agree with me on that."

His smile wilted ever-so-slightly. Did he think she was stalking him? *As if!*

"I'm the president of the Booster Club," she explained, sensing his unease. "I track where all the good players go. Success stories are moneymakers for the program. I've been telling yours for years." It wasn't true, but whatever.

"That's kind of you," he said with a smile, and she couldn't tell if he was pleased or embarrassed.

"Did you see Coach Cal?" she asked so he wouldn't go back to his movie just yet.

"Only from a distance." She nodded, like it wasn't weird that he hadn't said hello to the man who'd coached him to a scholarship. "He looked like he had his hands full."

She knew the real reason he didn't say hello, but it would be distasteful to go there.

"He's so devoted to those boys," she said. "We're all in his debt for what he did for the program. And our town." Oops. She went there.

"For putting us on the map, you mean?"

She should have said yes and let the other part go. But she couldn't help herself.

"And that other thing."

"Not sure what you mean." He sounded genuinely confused. So, she clarified.

"Y'know . . ." She leaned closer and lowered her voice. "Not coming forward." His face was a blank. She dug in a little deeper. "After the accident."

"Come forward with what?" Billy asked.

Billy had to know what she was talking about, given that he was at the center of it. She interpreted the question as code for *"We're not going to talk about that."* And she graciously backed down.

"Don't worry. He would never do anything to harm you boys. You were his darlings. Still are."

Penelope saw the spooked look on his face. She tried not to get offended. Did he really think Nolan would have kept a secret like this from his own mother? And who did he think made it all go away? Yes, Nolan had been the intermediary, but she'd made the arrangements.

Penelope forgave the young man for his ignorance. Billy Wilcox didn't have a mother, poor thing, so it probably hadn't occurred to him that a mother knows when one of her babies needs to be rescued.

"One thing I know about Brendan Callahan is that he practices what he preaches," she said, to reassure him. "Team first, without exception."

And she leaned back into her seat like she had no idea Billy's whole world was closing in on him.

SPECIAL AGENT SAM COOPER: Good evening, Sheriff. Sorry to bother you again, but we've been going through some of your old police reports, and I found one I need to ask you about.

SHERIFF ALAN ECKLES: It's awfully late, Agent Cooper.

COOPER: Never too late for justice.

ECKLES: If this is about the sexual assault, I've only had the report for ten minutes. Rest assured I'll be following up in the morning.

COOPER: Yes, I have no doubt you will. We're actually interested in a different one . . . dated May 13, 2023. It seems a Mr. William Wilcox reported his car stolen.

ECKLES: You're asking me about a stolen vehicle report from three years ago?

COOPER: We trust you understand the significance of that particular date.

ECKLES: We get a lot of stolen car reports, Agent Cooper. People who took an Uber home from the bar and woke up to an empty garage. Parents whose kids went on a joy ride. You'd be surprised how many vehicles are reported stolen, many of which were never stolen at all.

COOPER: Right. Well I'm only interested in the one. The 2017 Ford Bronco that was reported missing by William Wilcox on May 13th, 2023—

ECKLES: Yeah, like I said, a whole lot of cars go missing—

COOPER: The day after Matthew Kessler was killed in a hit-and-run.
(Beat.)

ECKLES: Where are you going with this?

COOPER: I just arrived at the scene of the accident—

ECKLES: You're in Crestwood?

COOPER: That's right, lovely town. Anyway, I'm looking at the pictures from that night. I see there are some tire tracks visible. Did you ever have those analyzed? Because I'm not finding a forensics report.

ECKLES: Yes, our guy saw those. Unfortunately, he determined they could have belonged to any number of makes and models.

COOPER: We're having a closer look.

ECKLES: You're welcome to go fishing. But I think you'll find a lot of cars with that particular brand of tires.

COOPER: Yeah, it's probably a wild-goose chase. But I have to keep our forensic friends at the FBI busy with something.

ECKLES: Even if those treads are a match to the Bronco owned by Mr. Wilcox, it doesn't prove that's our perp car.

COOPER: Proving it's not would also be helpful. If that's what the analysis reveals, that is.

ECKLES: Just wouldn't want y'all to draw false conclusions.

COOPER: If we had a witness, it might button this thing right up.

ECKLES: Yes, it's a damn shame no one came forward.

COOPER: We're looking into that too.

CHAPTER 027

"22C wants coffee," Alphonso said, as he popped his head into the galley.

Cathy nodded. "On it." What was it with these passengers and coffee? Didn't anyone want to sleep?

She pressed the button to brew a fresh pot. As the amber liquid cascaded into the carafe, she found herself (once again!) obsessing about Francesca Kessler. *How could she just sit there and do nothing?* The second beverage service was complete, they'd traversed three states (Arizona, New Mexico, and Texas), day had given way to night, and the woman still hadn't confronted her lying ex-husband. Yes, they were going to be in Puerto Rico together for the tournament, there was plenty of time. But wasn't she dying to know what he'd seen that night?

The pot hissed as the last drops of liquid sputtered into the carafe. Cathy hated the smell of old coffee, so she always emptied the filter basket right away. If the little pre-measured pouches were loaded improperly . . . say, by a harried flight attendant whose mind was elsewhere . . . they would fill with water and explode. Which is exactly what happened when she opened the basket.

"Ow! Shit!"

Coffee-colored mud spurted out like water from a garden hose. As she raised her arms to shield her face, her elbow clipped the handle of the carafe. It hit the floor with a resounding clang.

As she jumped back—

A pair of hands swooped in toward the carafe—

"Gotcha!"

Just in time to stop the hot coffee from pouring out onto her feet.

"Oh my God, I'm so sorry," she said to Marco the tattooed rock-star–slash–air marshal who'd appeared out of nowhere just in time, as rockstars do.

"Right place, right time," he said with a smile. Rita was right. If something was amiss . . . like, say, a suitcase being loaded improperly . . . this Johnny-on-the-spot surely would have caught it.

He set the carafe on the counter. "You OK?"

"Not really," she admitted. "Sorry, that was unprofessional."

"If you want to serve that coffee, I won't tell anyone it was on the floor," he said with a conspiratorial wink.

"The coffee is the least of my worries."

"Oh?"

"My ex-husband is pissing me off," she blurted.

"Exes tend to do that, that's why they're exes."

She knew better than to air out her dirty laundry to an air marshal—or any passenger for that matter—but keeping things to herself wasn't her way. "He says I don't know the whole picture, but I know a coward when I see one."

"Maybe he needs a little push to be brave," Marco said. The comment flicked a switch in her brain. He was absolutely right.

"Thank you, Marco."

She delivered the coffee with the best smile she could muster, then marched toward the exit row where her chickenshit ex-husband was plugged into a movie.

"Hey, Cath," he said, pulling out his earphones. But she was not in the mood for pleasantries.

"Come to the back of the plane."

She nodded conspiratorially at Marco as she passed his row, grateful to her new friend for emboldening her to get tough. If he could hunt down hijackers, surely she could stand up to her ex.

She stepped into the galley. Brendan appeared a moment later.

"What's up?"

"I teed you up," she said, picking an empty Coke can off the counter and attempting to crush it in her bare hands.

"Teed me up to what, Cathy?" he asked dumbly.

"To tell Francesca what you saw, Brendan, and why you stayed quiet." She pushed her palms together and that soda can collapsed with a violent *pop!*

"I wish I could make you understand," he started, but she cut him off.

"This isn't about me," she hissed. She'd heard it all before. There was nothing to be gained from speaking out. Francesca's son wasn't coming back; more people would be hurt than helped if the truth came out; the situation was lose-lose, no matter what he did—or *didn't*—do; blah, blah, blah. Maybe all that was true. But a woman's life was unraveling right here, right now, and she wasn't going to let her husband sit on what he knew for a moment longer—not if it could ease Francesca's pain.

"I know you want to forget what you told me on that phone call," she continued, "but I can't."

"Where is this sudden outrage coming from?" he asked, as if she owed him an explanation for wanting to do the right thing.

"That woman's been in hell for three years. You can see it all over her face."

"Nothing I tell her will change the fact that her son is gone, Cath," Brendan said, intentionally missing the point. Cathy nearly threw that crumpled soda can at his head.

"I told her you saw the car," she said, to force his hand. "If you don't want her to call the police the second we land, you have approximately . . ." She looked down at her watch. "One hour and forty-two minutes to do the right thing." Cathy was bluffing. Francesca hadn't said anything about calling the police, but Brendan didn't know that.

Besides, if Francesca wasn't up to following this trail where it led, she'd do it. She wasn't a realtor for the stars anymore, but she still knew people in high places, including the assistant district attorney, who would surely make a call if she asked him to.

"The police already questioned me. I told them what I knew."

"Told who? Sherriff Eckles?"

"That's right."

"And he told you to forget what you saw."

Brendan looked down at his shoes. Cathy had no idea why Brendan thought he was doing their community a favor by burying the truth, only that in doing so he'd destroyed two families—Francesca's and his own. In his silence, he was denying the boy's parents the closure they deserved. If he had come forward, would Francesca and her husband still be together? And what about the two of them? Wouldn't they still be married too?

"I did what I thought was best for everyone, Cath," Brendan said, the *even if it was wrong* part understood but unspoken.

"What the hell kind of devil's bargain did you make with Sheriff Eckles?"

She was so focused on him that she didn't notice that a third person had entered the chat.

"Yes," Francesca Kessler said from the threshold of the galley. "I'd like to know too."

CAPTAIN BANCROFT: Good evening, folks, this is your captain speaking.

We've got a little weather brewing . . . a couple small storm systems, nothing to get too excited about. I'm hopeful I can fly around them, but if they develop into something more significant, I'm going to have to ask you to take your seats.

If you were putting off using the lavatory, I'm going to suggest you do that now, just in case. I'll update you all in just a little bit.

CHAPTER

028

Billy's movie was playing on his laptop, but he wasn't really watching. Jilly had snuck into the main cabin to hang with her "bitches" twenty minutes ago, and it was concerning that she hadn't come back. Maybe she was just having fun and lost track of time. Or maybe it was something else.

As he thought about that something else, rage wrapped around his ribs, making his chest feel like it was going to explode. *Fucking Angie.* Why couldn't she just let sleeping dogs lie? He couldn't blame his bad behavior on the booze because then he'd have to admit he had a problem. His dad would have a field day with that. Just imagining the *'I told you so'*s made him want to punch something. He poured another mini in his glass and downed it in one gulp.

There was no point asking why he'd done it, it was obvious. What is it they say about love and hate? They're not opposites, they're neighbors. Two sides of the same heart. He loved her so much he couldn't keep his hands off her. He hated her so much he had to hurt her for not loving him back. This wasn't about the booze. This was about what was really in his heart—*who* was really in his heart. And it wasn't the woman he was marrying.

So why had he asked her? It wasn't about the money—he could make his own fucking money. Maybe not his-and-hers Porsches kind of money, but enough to live well. He didn't need Versace sunglasses and shirts by Tom Ford. The only person he cared about impressing liked him best in a plain Jockey tee and joggers from Old Navy.

He'd deny it if you called him on it, but deep down, he knew his MO for marrying Jilly was not for pleasure, but to escape pain. After his mother died, he went from football to basketball to baseball in rapid succession. Crestwood needed his bat, his quickness, his ability to score. He needed *not* to be alone with his thoughts all day and night. Then school and sports were over, and there was nowhere to be and no one who needed him. Certainly not Angie. She was a modern, independent woman. She also worked nights. With no teammates or girlfriend to offer him something better, he reached for a bottle. And in a cruel twist of irony, the thing he used to comfort himself turned out to be the thing that drove the person he loved away.

Then along came Jilly. Unlike Angie, she didn't have a job and probably never would. Whereas Angie was determined to make him a better man, with Jilly he could do no wrong. Even the drinking didn't bother her—hell, sometimes he thought she needed it more than he did.

He didn't propose to Jilly to make Angie jealous, but he secretly hoped it had. Was he happy to be marrying Jillian? He wasn't sure. He just knew he was terrified of what might happen to him if he didn't.

He unclipped his seatbelt with sweaty palms. He'd been drinking since noon, and his insides burned like a campfire. The fact that Jilly still hadn't come back likely meant that she knew, she was pissed, and she expected Billy to come to her. If he wanted this wedding to go forward, he'd have to do some big-time groveling. God damn it, why hadn't he just told her himself? He knew from experience that the first rule of crisis management is to get ahead of your fuck-up, because the other person can't spin the situation to make you look bad if you spun it first. Angie had given him a whole week to craft a story of his sad sack ex-girlfriend begging for one last hurrah, but he'd put it off, and now it was too late.

Billy gripped the back of the seat in front of him as he stepped into the aisle. The ground swayed under his feet, and he wasn't sure if it was turbulence or the whiskey. The woman who'd identified herself as Nolan Abernathy's mother looked up at him.

"Are you all right?" she asked.

No, he was not fucking all right. He was fucked. He looked at her, with her big fucking hair to match her big fucking mouth. It had been three years since that boy had died. Why was she bringing it up now? Did she know he was marrying into money and thought she could blackmail him? It couldn't be a coincidence Nolan's mother wound up on the same flight as him, in the same row in first class . . . *could it?*

And why bring Coach Cal into it? He couldn't possibly know anything . . . could he? Unless someone told him. And who would tell him? Certainly not Nolan. Did that mean Coach saw something then? Heard something? And why was he just hearing about a possible witness now? The thought scared him, so he sucked it back into his reservoir of all the other scary thoughts. He had a more pressing problem to solve, and that was to talk to Jilly before Angie made him out to be a monster.

"I'm fine," he said flatly.

"I hope I didn't frighten you," Nolan's mother said. "I promise you, no one wants to upset the applecart. Certainly not me."

He looked down at her. Fury burned across his cheeks. She knew damn well that if he went down, Nolan was going down with him. So why was she tormenting him as if she had the upper hand?

"You have no idea what I want," he said, because fuck her and her applecart.

He felt like he was walking the rope ladder at the county fair as he teetered toward the bulkhead. He'd forgotten how altitude intensifies the effects of alcohol, just as he'd forgotten how to stop drinking once he started.

As he pulled back the curtain separating first class from coach, the first thing he saw was the sea of baseball caps—a dozen of them, maybe more. He wondered if these kids knew how lucky they were to play for Crestwood—bus rides with bottomless coolers of Gatorade, taking the field in front of cheering fans, a team hug after a hard-fought win, a "You'll get 'em next time" after a loss. Why is it that all good things come to an end and bad things stay with you forever? Would he once again weasel his way out of his fuck-up with a few bumps and bruises? Or would what he did to Angie be the thing to finally do him in?

He started down the aisle. It had been dark for hours now, and the light in the cabin was dim and uneven—a reading lamp here, a black hole of empty seats there. He didn't see Jilly until he was practically on top of her. She was hunched over and weeping into her palms. Angie was in the seat next to her, arm around her as she sobbed.

"Fuck," he muttered under his breath, but loud enough for Angie to hear. She looked up and shook her head.

"Go away," she mouthed.

But he didn't go away. He leaned over and put his face by Jilly's ear. "Jilly. Babe," he said softly, in that husky tone she liked. She tilted her head to look at him. Her mascara had smudged around her eyes. She looked like a sad raccoon.

"Let's go back to our seats, c'mon." He held out his arm. She didn't take it.

"She's staying here with me," Angie said. And Jilly cried harder.

Across the aisle, a boy was staring at him. This was so fucking humiliating.

"I don't know what she told you, but you owe me a chance to explain." He almost said something about being innocent until proven guilty, but that would imply he'd committed a crime. "Please."

She shook her head. "I have nothing to say to you, Billy."

They had fought before, of course they had—about dumb stuff like how come he was late to pick her up or couldn't be bothered to put the toilet seat down—but this was different. He couldn't smooth things over if he couldn't get her alone. And he couldn't get her alone while Angie was clinging to her like old chewing gum.

"You don't need to say anything. Just listen," he said.

She turned her face away from him.

"Go away, Billy," Angie hissed.

His hand twitched as he imagined balling it into a fist and smashing her perfect little face in. This was her fault. She ruined everything. She had already fucked up his life once, when she left him. He didn't know how he was going to fix this, just that he wasn't going to let her do it again.

CHAPTER

029

Federal Air Marshall Carlos Renaldo opened his phone and scrolled through his photos of the woman he loved. They didn't go out in public, so most of them—OK, *all* of them—were taken inside their hotel room. There were no selfies. He knew better than to upload a picture of the two of them together to the cloud. So they were all just her—in her uniform when he surprised her by booking the honeymoon suite and out of her uniform when she thanked him for it.

God damn she was hot. As he took in the curve of her waist, the gentle lilt of her breasts, that one dimple on her left cheek, his chest got tight like he was out of breath but worse. He never told her that he loved her. Is that why she broke it off? Because she wanted something she thought he couldn't give her?

He closed the phone. He needed to forget her, focus on his job. He knew without looking that eight rows behind him, the coach of the baseball team was chatting up the purple-haired flight attendant in the aft galley. Nothing concerning about that. Five rows in front of him, the bride from first class had displaced a male passenger and was sitting with one of her bridesmaids. Nothing concerning about that either. Also not concerning, but hella annoying, was the poor, lovestruck schmuck crouched beside her in the aisle. Carlos couldn't see either of their faces, but he imagined the lovebirds were giddy with happiness to be on their way to paradise to exchange vows of forever. If Katie were here, he might have thought it sweet how they couldn't bear to be apart. Today it pissed him off.

He forced himself to look away. He imagined the groom gazing up at the woman he loved, counting the minutes until the flight was over and he could ravage her—just like he should be doing. He closed his eyes and imagined Katie swishing up and down the aisle in her slim-fitting dress . . . if he timed his inhale just right, he could catch a whiff of her apple-pie perfume. God, he loved the way she smelled. He pictured himself breathing her in and checking his watch as sweet anticipation rolled over his skin, because *tick-tick-tick*—it wouldn't be long until he got her to himself.

Six years. That's how long he'd ping-ponged across the country at thirty thousand feet, watching and waiting for someone to commit an act of terror. It was a job—a damned important one—but not much of a life. Maybe that's why Katie called it quits. While she was traveling for Pioneer and he was traveling for the US of A, planning a life together made as much sense as shoveling the driveway in a blizzard. She was still young, just twenty-four, but he knew she wanted the American dream—two kids and a house in the suburbs, and a man to make them pancakes on Sunday mornings. He wanted those things too. With her. He didn't know how they would work it out, only that the first step was to tell her how he felt.

"Good evening, folks," the captain said over the PA. "We've got a little weather brewing. If you were putting off using the lavatory, I'm going to suggest you do that now, just in case. I'll update you all in just a little bit."

Renaldo opened his texting app. Yes, he should have been paying more attention to what was going on around him, but the captain was about to send everyone to their seats, and once they were buckled down, he'd be as useful as a screen door on a submarine. He had to write this message now, because to wait would convey lack of urgency, and getting Katie back was nothing if not urgent.

Dear Katie, he typed with his thumbs. I know you want more than a once-a-week romp. *Romp?* No, he couldn't call it that. What was he thinking? He hit the backspace key and tried again. Sitting on this plane without you here has been hell. *Too much?* Maybe, but it was true, and if there was ever a time to be honest, this was it. I want to give you all the things you want in life. I don't know what that will look like, but please, can we talk about it? I love you. He paused. He had never told her he loved her. Did he want the first time to be in a text?

His thumbs hovered over the keys. His heart was pounding. Someone's pantleg grazed his elbow as they walked by, but he didn't look up. Good God, would he give up his job for her? Or was he asking her to give up hers for him?

The hopeful feeling in his chest shape-shifted into despair. One of them would have to choose, and the person who gave up their career to play house would resent the other—maybe not right away, but in time. It happened so often it was a goddamned cliché. He didn't want to be at a stupid desk job any more than she did. So where did that leave them?

He thought about the consequences of professing his love. She'd already dumped him. Was he harassing her? Or just making a damn fool of himself? If this text made her feel uncomfortable, this could take a bad turn. A text like this would also prove beyond all doubt that he was compromised. Getting involved with a flight attendant was an absolute no-no. But texting her when he was on the job? Well, that was career suicide.

He sent it anyway.

CHAPTER

030

"She doesn't want to talk to you, Billy," Angie said, her fingers digging into Jilly's thigh. "Leave her alone."

Billy was too proud to grovel, so he straightened up like he was going back to his seat. And he would have, but he couldn't—a passenger had stepped into the aisle and was blocking his path. So he started walking the other way, toward the back of the plane, because he couldn't just stand there with his tail between his legs.

He was so mad he could barely see straight. What the fuck had Angie done? If she'd played that recording for Jilly, there was no way this wedding was happening. What was he supposed to tell all the people who were traveling across the country to watch them get married? He imagined the smug look on his father's face and how good it would feel to erase it with his fist. Where was his father anyway? Was he watching him? Laughing at him? He half-wanted him to pop out of his seat so he could unleash his rage because Lord knows that man deserved it.

He had to keep moving, so he continued toward the rear of the aircraft, between rows of bright-eyed boys in baseball hats. Under different circumstances, he might be happy for these kids, but today those emerald brims just pissed him off. Everything good had been taken from him—his sun-kissed wedding, his happy memories of baseball, the mother who'd never let anything bad happen to him.

His head felt like it was about to pop off. He needed to calm down. The bathroom off the aisle was occupied, but the one against the back wall was free. He was gunning for it when something hard and smooth rolled under his heel, causing him to stumble.

"Jesus, fuck!" He grabbed the seat tops on either side of him as he tipped backward like a cartoon character slipping on a banana peel. As he pulled himself back up, he looked down to see what he had stepped on.

He recognized the object immediately. Under different circumstances, the sight of it might have made him laugh. What a stupid thing to trip on, way up here, given how many just like it he'd handled in his life.

He tried to kick it under the seat, but it was bumping up against something and wouldn't go. He looked up at the kid dozing across all three seats, then shook his head and bent over. His hand curled around the shaft. The wood felt hard and smooth in his palm. It was strangely comforting, gripping the handle of a baseball bat after all these years. Made him feel powerful, like the homerun hitter he once was.

He was about to wake the kid to tell him to take care of his shit, but then he saw that sloppy chicken scratch of a signature on the shaft and changed his mind. This was no ordinary bat. Trey Turnberry, the MLB superstar he used to call friend, had anointed it. It was priceless now. No, he wasn't giving it back. After what he'd done to help that lucky shit live out his dream, he deserved that bat and a whole lot more.

It was just a few more steps to the bathroom. The purple-haired flight attendant was leaning against the counter, talking to two people with their backs to him. He didn't want her to see him filching that bat, so he tucked the handle up his sleeve and the barrel behind his leg to keep it out of her sight.

He kept his head down as he slipped into the galley. He had the lavatory door open and was halfway inside when someone called his name.

"Billy Wilcox? Is that you?"

He didn't have to look to see who it was, he would have known that voice anywhere. He'd heard it every day of baseball season for the best four years of his life. "Protect the bag! Your swing is late! Don't chase the high ones!" He'd thought by sitting in first class he would've made it to Puerto Rico without having to talk to his former coach—yet another foolish assumption on his part.

"Hey Coach," he said, peering over his shoulder. That's when he saw her. The birdlike woman in a crinkly blazer. He had no idea if she recognized him, but he sure as hell recognized her.

Blood waterfalled into his feet as his face caught fire. He always knew there was a chance he could bump into her—Crestwood was a small town, with only two supermarkets and a single movie theater. But to run into her up here, thirty thousand feet above the earth, on the eve of the most important day of his life, could only be the work of the devil himself.

"Just going to the head," he said, then tucked inside the bathroom and shut the door. This plane was like a funhouse of mirrors, reflecting every bad thing he'd ever done back at him. If there were a window in here, he probably would have jumped.

The plane shimmied, and the bat shook loose from his hand and tumbled to the floor. As he grabbed the sink for balance, the pilot's voice came over the PA.

"Good evening, this is your captain speaking," he said. "I'm afraid I have some bad news."

Bad news? He almost laughed. The news for him couldn't get any worse.

He sunk down on the closed toilet seat and put his head in his hands. The captain was still speaking. Something about putting away electronics, storm cells, and flying between them. He didn't want to face the dead kid's mom, so he stayed put until the captain stopped talking. And then for a full minute more.

The plane bounced as they hit a patch of rough air. He needed to go back to his seat. He was about to get up when the door floated open.

As he looked up into eyes that burned with fury, he remembered the bat on the floor by his feet, and how it wasn't just for baseball.

PART

Complications

003

CHAPTER

031

"Well, that was one for the memoir," Captain Bancroft said over the PA after the lights went back on. "Yes, that was lightning. It temporarily short circuited our avionics, but all systems are back online. Should be smooth sailing all the way to San Juan."

He hung up the handset and turned to his first officer. "Think they bought it?"

"We're not continuing on?" Drew Ridley, his FO, asked. Bancroft wanted to get to Puerto Rico as much as anyone, but it wasn't wholly up to him.

"Let's see what the company says. You have the controls."

"I have the controls."

Captain Bancroft lifted the sat phone from the cradle and dialed the pre-programmed number. A rep from Pioneer Airlines answered on the first ring.

"Pioneer dispatch, this is April."

"Hi April, this is Brett Bancroft, Pioneer 8-6-8 en route to San Juan. We experienced a lightning strike just south of Yankee Town. Our avionics went out for approximately two minutes, but we were able to reset the breaker, and the aircraft is flying normally. We need to know if Tech Ops wants us to continue on or divert."

"Stand by, Captain Bancroft."

Bancroft held the phone to his ear as he waited. There were no indications anything was wrong with the aircraft, but that lightning strike could have done unseen damage. If he were a betting man, he would put money on the company telling him to turn around and bring the plane back to the mainland to be inspected.

"Captain Bancroft, are you still there?" April asked.

"I'm here."

"Maintenance is advising you to declare an emergency and divert to Miami," she announced, as he'd anticipated she would.

"Roger that, diverting to Miami."

First Officer Ridley turned his head to look at him. "So we're going back through that weather system then?"

"They need to inspect the plane." He wasn't happy about it either. Diverting meant missed connections, upset passengers, and annoying layovers for the crew. But there was no way the company would take an unnecessary risk. They were ordering the aircraft to the mainland to cover their asses, and Bancroft would comply to cover his.

"This is Pioneer 8-6-8, declaring an emergency," the captain said into the comms. "We had a lightning strike and temporarily lost avionics. The company wants us to turn around. Requesting vectors to Miami."

"Pioneer 8-6-8 emergency, roger that," the air traffic controller responded. "Be advised, Miami is currently holding all planes due to crosswinds gusting up to four-zero knots. And thunderstorms in the vicinity. I've already got six aircraft ahead of you awaiting clearance."

Ridley raised an eyebrow but Bancroft ignored it.

"Then I guess we'll be number seven," he told ATC.

"Pioneer 8-6-8 emergency, how many souls on board and what's your available fuel in time?" Miami Central asked.

The captain looked at his manifest. "We have one hundred and thirty-two souls on board, and . . ." He glanced at the fuel gauge and did a quick calculation in his head. "Approximately two-and-a-half hours of fuel remaining."

"Roger that. I can get you moved up in the cue, you're my only emergency, but it's really storming down there."

"What about West Palm or Orlando?" the captain asked, because it was his job to explore all options.

"West Palm and Orlando aren't any better, weather-wise," the tower informed him. "We have clear air over Jacksonville, that's probably your best bet if you want to get to the mainland."

Ridley spoke into the boom, just to Bancroft. "San Juan's a lot closer than Jacksonville. We might as well continue on."

Ridley had a point. Jacksonville was three hundred nautical miles north of their current position, diverting there would add another hour of flying time. And turning around would send them back in the path of those thunderstorms.

"I have to admit, I don't love the idea of trying to beat out that weather system," he confessed. "It's going to be right on our tail the whole way."

"So what's our move?"

Bancroft considered his options. If they continued on to San Juan, there'd be no one to inspect the plane, but they'd for sure land in good weather and at their proper destination.

"I think holding the course is our best bet. We can let the company figure out about the plane."

"We're going onto San Juan, then?'" Ridley asked.

"As long as nothing else goes wrong, we'll be fine."

CHAPTER

032

Cathy Yap was seated in the middle of the main cabin when she heard the kid crying. Quick, uneven gasps, punctuated by the occasional whimper.

She unclipped her seatbelt. She was still woozy from being bounced around but managed to stand. Gripping the seatback in front of her, she slid into the aisle, then made her way toward the back of the plane, one wobbly step at a time.

The teen had his back to her, so she couldn't see his face. His legs were splayed out in front of him. His sloping shoulders heaved as he sobbed. The sound of him crying made her want to cry too. But she held it together because that was her job.

"Hey," she said, crouching down and putting a hand on his back. "It's OK." He was sitting on the galley floor, a pool of vomit between his legs. "It happens to everybody," she assured him. "That was some serious turbulence, I nearly lost it myself."

The boy cried harder. She made little circles on his back with the palm of her hand. She'd give him another minute, then help him back to his seat and—

"Oh my God," a voice said.

She looked over her shoulder at Fonzie, who was standing a few steps behind her with his mouth agape. She loved working with him, but he could be drama.

"He's fine," Cathy said, because she thought Fonzie's freak out was about seeing a boy sitting in a puddle of regurgitated french fries.

"Oh my God," Fonzie repeated. And that's when Cathy realized he wasn't looking at the boy or the puddle, but at something just beyond.

She swiveled her head. The lavatory door was partially open. The turbulence could explain that, they'd been bumped around pretty hard.

It was what was on the other side of that door that was incomprehensible. She flashed back to the exploding coffee filter, how it had sprayed the front of her uniform with mud-colored spume. Is that what she was seeing? How did coffee get on the lavatory walls?

"What do we do?" Fonzie asked, his voice quaking with fear. The boy was blocking her view, so she craned her neck to see around him. Panic zapped her chest when she realized that yes, that melon-sized orb on the floor was a human head and those spatters on the walls weren't coffee, they were blood.

Her heart shot into her throat. *Holy shit, holy shit, holy shit.* She closed her eyes and recalled the words of her instructor in Flight Attendant School. When in crisis, lean into your training. Follow the protocols. That's why they exist.

She went through the steps in her mind. *Step one: medical assessment. Check vitals and administer CPR if required.* By the looks of things, this person was beyond CPR, but she wouldn't know that until she got over there, and to do that she needed the kid out of the way.

"Who are you traveling with?" she asked the boy, trying to keep the panic out of her voice. "Are your parents on board?"

He shook his head. "No. I'm with my team." Of course. He was traveling with the baseball team. Brendan would take care of him. They just needed to get him back to his seat.

Step two: be decisive, authoritative, and project confidence. "Alphonso," she said as she stood. "Can you please take this young man back to his seat and grab Rita?" She wasn't his superior, but one of them had to do something, and he was frozen like a deer in headlights.

"Fonzie!" she said sharply. And his eyes met hers.

Step three: work as a team. "Help me get him up." She put a hand under the boy's armpit and indicated for her colleague to do the same. Together, they lifted the terrified teen onto his feet. "Fonzie's going to walk you back to your seat, OK?"

She looked sternly at Alphonso. He nodded.

"Sorry about the mess," the boy squeaked, and at first Cathy thought he was talking about the body.

"We deal with it all the time," Alphonso assured him, easing him away from the puddle he'd made. "We'll take care of it, not to worry. What's your name?"

"Kai."

"Hi Kai, I'm Alphonso, but you can call me Fonzie."

Cathy gave Fonzie a reassuring nod to let him know he was doing great. She was about to remind him to summon Rita, but the lead flight attendant was already in the aisle charging toward them.

"Everyone OK here?" she asked as she approached. Her eyes landed on the human head on the galley floor, and she let out a gasp.

"Alphonso's just taking Kai back to his seat," Cathy said in the calmest voice she could muster. "Kai is the one who opened the lavatory door," she explained. "We told him he could go back and join his friends."

"No!" Rita barked. "Sit him in an unoccupied row and stay with him," she told Fonzie.

Fonzie nodded and led the boy out into the cabin.

"If word gets out, there'll be hysteria on this plane," Rita hushed. "The passengers are already on edge." She spun around and reached for the interphone.

"Captain! It's Rita," she said into the handset. "We have a situation back here."

APRIL AT PIONEER AIR: April speaking.

CAPTAIN BRENT BANCROFT: Hi, April. This is Captain Brett Bancroft again. We've got a second emergency here, besides the lightning.

APRIL: Is the flight deck secure?

BANCROFT: Affirmative.

APRIL: What's your emergency?

BANCROFT: My purser is reporting an injury to a passenger in the main cabin. It might be serious.

APRIL: Is it turbulence related?

BANCROFT: Unclear.

APRIL: Does the passenger need medical assistance?

BANCROFT: Also unclear.

APRIL: I'll get the company physician to call you.

BANCROFT: I appreciate that.

APRIL: And I'll alert DHS.

BANCROFT: Is that necessary?

APRIL: Standard protocol, Captain. We'll be in touch. In the meantime, I suggest you keep those passengers in their seats.

BANCROFT: Roger that.

CAPTAIN BANCROFT: Good evening, folks. This is the captain speaking. Those storm cells are behind us to our west, but I'm going to keep that fasten seatbelt sign on a little while longer. Please stay in your seats while we clear any remaining bumpy air.

I will make one exception, if there is a doctor or other medical professional on board, the flight crew could use your help in the rear galley. Please make your way back there at this time and identify yourself to a flight attendant.

Barring any unforeseen holdups, we should be on the ground in San Juan in about ninety minutes. I'll update you with our exact arrival time as soon as I have it.

CHAPTER

033

The emergency medical kit was in the overhead bin closest to the galley. Cathy had never needed it, but she knew from her training that it contained, among other things, a stethoscope, a blood pressure cuff, an EpiPen, a defibrillator, an assortment of needles, syringes, and intravenous medications, several pairs of latex gloves, and enough bandages and gauze to wrap the entire plane. As Cathy reached up to retrieve it, a bespectacled woman with curly hair sidled up beside her.

Cathy turned her head to look at her. "I'm sorry, I'm afraid I need to ask you to return to your seat."

"I'm an emergency room doctor. I'm responding to the pilot's call."

"Over here, please," Rita called out, beckoning the woman toward the lav. Cathy grabbed the medical kit and followed the doctor toward the back of the plane. As she stepped into the galley, the interphone chimed.

"Can you answer that?" Rita said, taking the kit from her.

Cathy plucked the handset off the wall and pressed it to her ear. "This is Cathy."

"Hi, Cathy," the first officer said. "What's going on with that injured passenger?"

Rita had used the term "injured" because flight attendants didn't have the authority to pronounce a passenger dead, only a medical doctor could do that.

"A doctor just arrived back here. One sec."

As the ER doc pulled on a pair of gloves and leaned over the fallen passenger, the memory of the last time Cathy had stood this close to a dead body hit her like a tidal wave. By the time she'd arrived at the scene of the hit-and-run, the police had covered Matthew Kessler. She couldn't see his face, but his human-ness was unmistakable—long limbs, gently tapered chest, a tuft of dark brown hair peeking out from under the battered, yellow tarp.

"Cockpit is asking how the passenger is doing?" she said, forcing the image out of her mind.

Rita answered without looking up. "Tell them to stand by."

"Please stand by," Cathy parroted. She thought of Brendan, how she'd tried to comfort him. At first she thought he'd clammed up out of shock. Then he confided in her that yes, he'd seen the car, but he was choosing to keep it to himself. And that choice made it impossible for her to remain by his side. "Midlife crisis," she'd called it when her friends asked why she'd left him. Because she didn't just leave him. She left her town, her job, her hair, and everything she knew. Her friends understood that sometimes crises bring people together, and sometimes they drive them apart.

"Do you have a flashlight?" the doctor asked without looking up. Rita pulled her Maglite from her apron pocket and handed it to her. "And I'll take that stethoscope."

Cathy held her breath as the doctor put the stethoscope in her ears and extended the bell toward the body they all knew did not have a pulse.

"Cathy? Are you still there?" the first officer asked.

"The doctor is taking vitals," Cathy said into the phone. "Hold on."

"The physician on call just rang in over the sat phone. He said to relay those vitals when you have them."

"Copy that," Cathy told the FO. Then, to the doctor. "The cockpit is asking for vitals."

"No respiration. No heartbeat. Pupils are unresponsive and dilated," the doctor said, her voice devoid of emotion, as if she'd said these words a thousand times.

Cathy relayed the doctor's response word-for-word, doing her best to imitate her emotionless tone.

"Are you starting CPR?" Ridley asked.

"Cockpit wants to know if we're starting CPR."

The doctor shook her head. "It's too late for that."

"No," Cathy relayed. "She said it's too late." And now the tears came. Hot and silent, down both sides of her face. She cried not just for this person, but for Matthew Kessler, his mother and father, for everyone who'd lost someone too soon.

"Understood," Ridley said. "Stay on the line."

Cathy wiped her eyes with the back of her hand as she gripped the phone.

"Cathy, are you still there?" the FO asked.

"Yes."

"We need more information about what happened. Was it an illness? A cardiac event?"

"Stand by." Then, to the doctor, "They want to know what happened."

The doctor pulled the stethoscope from her ears and wiped the blood off the bell with a piece of gauze.

"It's got to be from the turbulence," Rita prompted.

"I don't think so," the doctor disagreed, leaning back on her heels.

"What else could it be?"

"I'm not a medical examiner, but the wounds to the face look . . . inflicted."

Rita scowled. "Inflicted?"

"By a blunt object. Maybe that?" She pointed to the baseball bat peeking out from under the wall-mounted toilet.

Rita's head snapped up. "Doctor, please find a seat nearby." The doctor nodded and backed away. Rita yanked the heavy blue curtain shut. Her eyes locked on Cathy's.

"Get the air marshal."

CHAPTER

034

Federal Air Marshal Carlos Renaldo dry-heaved into his airsick bag for the better part of five minutes. In six years in the air, he had never once gotten sick. To be losing it like this was fucking embarrassing. His only saving grace was that he was incognito and no one would know the candy-ass in 30C was the person responsible for keeping them safe.

He knew there were others in worse shape than he was. He'd heard some poor kid behind him crying, probably because he didn't make it to the bathroom in time. He felt bad for the flight attendants who had to clean up after him, but picking sick kids off the floor was not his job, and he wasn't going to blow his cover by doing it.

His nausea was finally subsiding, so he sealed the barf bag and stuck it in the seatback in front of him. His mouth tasted like the inside of a dumpster, so he pulled his water bottle out of the side pocket of his backpack and took a swig. He cursed this shitty flight as he swished the water between his teeth. He hoped bad things didn't come in threes, because getting dumped and struck by lightning was quite enough for one day.

He leaned back in his seat. As he settled in for what he assumed would be a boring next hour and a half, he heard movement behind him. He peered over his shoulder. The purple-haired flight attendant was talking to a passenger with dark hair and tattoos up his arms. He'd noticed them talking before—right before takeoff. But this was not flirty banter, so he listened this time.

"Sorry to disturb," he heard her say. "There's been an incident." *An incident?* "If you could please come with me?"

He watched as the tattooed passenger stood and followed her toward the back of the plane. There was nothing inherently alarming about a crew member talking to a passenger, so why were alarm bells ringing in his head like church bells on Christmas Eve? Maybe it was the urgency in her voice. Or the reluctance in his body language. Or that word—"incident." If there'd been an incident, shouldn't she be telling him?

He unbuckled his seatbelt and slid into the aisle.

"I'm sorry, sir," he heard the other female flight attendant say to the tattooed man—the one he met upon boarding. *What was her name again?* "We're having a medical emergency," she added, "you'll have to use the lavatory in the aisle."

Rita. That was it. And since when was a kid throwing up a medical emergency?

"I thought you said to summon him," Purple Hair told Rita.

"I told you to summon the—"

And then Rita was looking at him. And the purple-haired flight attendant let out a gasp, and good God, was that blood on the galley floor?

"Please return to your seat," Rita said to the tattooed man.

"No problem," the man said. Carlos stepped aside to let him pass, their eyes connecting ever-so-briefly.

"I'm so sorry," the purple-haired flight attendant said to Rita once Tattoos was out of earshot. Then to Carlos, "I got you guys mixed up."

"It happens," Carlos said, even though he'd never heard of it happening. "Carlos Renaldo, Federal Air Marshal." He offered his hand.

"Cathy Yap."

Renaldo looked down at the blood seeping out from beneath the heavy blue curtain. *Hello, medical emergency.* "You want to bring me up to speed, Cathy?"

"I heard a boy crying. So I got up to see why he was so upset. I didn't know what was wrong at first. It was Alphonso who spotted, y'know . . . the body."

Renaldo felt a tingle down his spine. "Body?"

She indicated the closed curtain with her head. "In the lav."

His pulse quickened. He reached for the curtain and cracked it open.

It was the smell that hit him first—sour and metallic, like a hospital emergency room, minus the antiseptic undertones. As he peered down at the lump of human flesh on the floor, he bit the insides of his cheeks to keep from crying out. There was blood everywhere—pooling on the floor, dotting the bathroom walls, soaking the victim's clothes and hair.

"Alphonso's our third flight attendant," Rita said. "There's just the three of us on this flight."

Renaldo let go of the curtain. "Where's Alphonso now?"

"I'm here," Alphonso said, emerging from the aisle. "The doctor took my place next to Kai."

"Kai's the young man who discovered the body," Rita said. "We're keeping him isolated. To keep him from talking with his friends."

"Yes, good," Carlos said, relieved she had thought of that. "Who else knows?" he asked, imagining the chaos that would ensue if people found out a fellow passenger had died while taking a piss.

"Just Kai, the three of us flight attendants, and the doctor who came back to help," Rita assured him. "And the cockpit, of course."

He flashed to the man the purple-haired flight attendant had mistaken for him. The curtain was closed. He would have reacted if he'd seen something. Plus, he was traveling alone, who would he even tell? This was contained. At least for now.

"Did the doctor give a cause of death?" he asked, knowing it was the first thing DHS would ask.

"I thought maybe the turbulence was responsible," Rita said, "because of all the blood. You can get pretty beaten up in bad air like that."

"But?" Renaldo asked, sensing she was holding something back.

Rita reached in front of him, pulled the curtain open, and pointed. "But then we saw that."

CHAPTER

035

Federal Agent Carlos Renaldo's stomach was in his throat as his brain struggled to process what his eyes were seeing. Blood-spattered walls. A crumpled corpse. An abandoned baseball bat lying there like it hadn't just obliterated someone's face.

A murder in flight was unprecedented. He hadn't been trained for this. But even worse, he hadn't been paying attention when it happened. Which meant he was about to be pummeled with a million questions he couldn't answer.

Rita let go of the curtain and it wafted closed. "Obviously our top concern is the passengers' safety," she said, as if she could tell he'd momentarily forgotten this wasn't about him.

"What's your best guess when this happened?" Carlos asked, even though he was the one who was supposed to know that. And would have, if he'd been doing his job.

Rita looked at the male flight attendant, who looked at the purple-haired one.

"I was here in the aft galley until the captain ordered us to buckle in," Cathy Yap said. "Turbulence is worse in the back, so I left to find a seat closer to the front." Her tone was apologetic, like she was the one who'd failed the dead passenger.

"What about you and . . ." He'd forgotten the male flight attendant's name. *Way to inspire confidence.*

"Alphonso," Alphonso said before Renaldo could read his nametag.

"We were both up in first," Rita said. *Translation: they couldn't help him either.*

"The, um . . . attack must have occurred sometime between when I left the galley and we hit that rough air." Cathy offered. "Because no one was walking around during the turbulence, it was too severe."

"Unless it happened right after the lightning strike," Rita interjected. "We were in the dark for two full minutes."

Renaldo thought back to those harrowing two minutes. It was dark as pitch. All around him, passengers were moaning and sobbing. Had someone snuck by him? He'd been too busy emptying his lunch into that airsick bag to clock anyone going anywhere.

"Did you notice any unusual passenger movement before the captain's fasten seatbelt order?" This was the question that embarrassed him the most. Because monitoring passenger movement was *his* job. And declaring his love to the woman who'd dumped him was a piss-poor excuse for not doing it.

"I mean, there were some hurried trips to the lav," Cathy said, "but nothing I would call unusual."

He knew from his training that a hijacker might pick off passengers one by one to force the pilot to divert the aircraft. But there were no indications of a change in course, and no one had come forward with demands. So maybe not a terrorist attack?

Whether or not this act of violence was part of a bigger plot, a passenger death was a big fucking deal, he had to call it in. He took out his phone to contact DHS. But before he had a chance to dial, it buzzed in his hand.

"Renaldo."

"Officer Renaldo, this is Deputy Administrator Vincent Garvey of TSA Los Angeles. We were just alerted by Pioneer Air of a medical emergency on board Pioneer Flight 8-6-8. Can you confirm?"

That was fast.

"Yes, sir, I can confirm." He didn't want the flight attendants to hear him floundering, so he opened the curtain and stepped behind it for privacy.

"Say more."

He was standing so close to the body he was practically on top it. "It appears a passenger was, uh . . ." *How to put this?* His eyes found the bat. "Bludgeoned to death in the aft lavatory. No one has come forward with any demands. I see no evidence that this was an act of terror."

"I'm sorry. Did you say bludgeoned to death?"

"That's right."

"Have you spoken to the captain?"

"Negative. I just got pulled into this one minute ago, sir." As soon as he said it, he knew it sounded like an excuse. The first person he should have spoken to was the captain.

"The cockpit reported a lightning strike at 22:24 Eastern Time. Can you confirm?"

"Yes, sir. The lights went out for approximately two minutes."

"And now?"

"Lights are back on, and the plane appears to be flying normally." With those words, his foot was so far down his throat he nearly choked on it. How could he know if the plane was flying normally unless he'd spoken to the captain?

"Hell of a coincidence," Garvey said, mercifully overlooking the blunder. "You get struck by lightning and someone winds up dead."

"We also went through some pretty rough air right before," Renaldo said. "Lose-your-lunch level turbulence. It was loud as hell."

"Could the attacker have used the turbulence for cover?"

Renaldo cringed as he conjured the memory of being neck-deep in his airsick bag. "Not my area of expertise," he said to sidestep the question. "But it's unlikely, given the severity of it. My best guess is that it happened right before it started, or right after, during the blackout."

"If it happened before, wouldn't you have seen something?"

And there it was. The tacit accusation. He swallowed his pride and spoke the truth. "It's possible I missed some passenger movement, sir." Shame percolated in his chest. He had one job—watch the fucking passengers. And he'd failed spectacularly.

"The good news is, there are a limited number of suspects," Garvey offered.

"Yes, sir." One hundred and twenty-five, if you didn't include him, the five-person flight crew, and the victim.

"We're bringing in the FBI. You'll be their boots on the ground. Or rather . . . in the air."

Carlos Renaldo was not a nervous fellow, but with those words, fear grabbed him by the throat. The FBI investigation would be all-encompassing. They would dissect the manifest, perform background checks on all the passengers, interview them one by one to ask them what they saw and heard. They would scrutinize the airport security footage. They'd track his movements to the crew lounge, see him grab Katie's arm as she stepped inside. They would ask him what the hell he was doing following that sexy flight attendant when he should have been at the gate with his fellow passengers.

And then they would seize his phone, and they would know.

"I'm here to serve," he said as was expected.

"Just do as they say and stay out of their way," Garvey said, and then he hung up.

Renaldo glanced at his watch. If the flight was on schedule, the FBI would be taking over the investigation in eighty-eight minutes. The only way to stop them from doing a deep dive into his negligence was to hand them the murderer on a silver platter. Eighty-eight measly minutes . . . and counting.

So where to start? He had no idea. There was no manual up here at thirty thousand feet, and no one to ask.

As he stood there infecting the crime scene, it occurred to him that he should take some pictures. He wasn't trained to look for clues, but that didn't mean he wouldn't know one if he saw one.

He opened his phone camera and started snapping. First, wide-angle shots documenting the scene—the blood spatters on the vanity, the mirror, the walls . . . was that blood on the ceiling? Yes, but not spatters . . . more like an imprint from a blood-soaked object. The body, perhaps?

He leaned over to take close-ups of the impact points. Bashed-in nose. Bloodied mouth. Then took a step back to get a full body shot. The victim's limbs were bent at odd angles. Carlos shuddered as he imagined the lifeless form being played like paddleball. Did that mean the attack happened before the turbulence, then? Because a baseball bat can't snap your neck, and there's no need to attack someone who's already dead.

He wasn't wearing gloves, so he photographed the bat without touching it. The make and model were down by the handle, he made sure to get a close-up of that. But there was something else, about halfway up the shaft. A signature. If not for the conversation he'd had with the big-haired lady in the lounge, he might not have recognized Trey Turnberry's loopy scrawl. This wasn't just any bat. It was one of a kind, hella valuable, and—*praise the Lord!*—traceable.

His phone buzzed in his hand.

"Renaldo."

"Officer Renaldo, this is Special Agent Sam Cooper of the FBI Violent Crimes Division. DHS briefed us on the situation up there, I'll be your POC going forward."

So this was it. His first legit emergency, and it was one he was not remotely trained how to handle. And also should have prevented. He briefed Cooper on what he knew, then stood by for his marching orders.

"You and those passengers are in a sardine can thirty thousand feet above the earth with a cold-blooded killer, Renaldo," Cooper reminded him.

"Yes, sir, I'm aware."

"Watch your back."

"I intend to, sir."

"Has the crew identified the victim?"

"Not yet.

"Have the flight attendants check the manifest against the passengers still in their seats." Embarrassment flooded his chest. He should have thought of that.

"Yes, sir."

"We're working with the captain to get the aircraft on the ground as soon as possible. San Juan is eighty-five minutes from your current position, but we're asking ATC to divert you to Florida. You'll be in the air a little longer, but I have twice as many assets on the ground there. The director wants a tier one response unit on this."

"Copy that." So more time to flail around up here, and an elite team of investigators to discover how he'd failed them. *Great.*

As he pocketed the phone, he told himself not to panic. They were in a confined space with no way in and no way out. He could keep these passengers safe. And wasn't that the most important thing? Stopping the killer from striking again?

Determination rose up from the pit of his stomach. And then he felt a wave of dread. How was he supposed to stop the killer from striking again if he couldn't figure out who it was?

And he almost laughed when he realized he had both too much time and not enough.

ATC: Pioneer 8-6-8 emergency, this is Miami Central, I just got word from DHS that we need to divert you to the mainland for security reasons.

CAPTAIN BANCROFT: What security reasons?

ATC: The FBI wants that aircraft where they can properly search it, and they don't have enough assets in San Juan.

BANCROFT: I see. OK.

ATC: Ground control will direct you where to park upon your arrival so investigators can board the aircraft away from the terminal.

CAPTAIN BANCROFT: Makes sense. We're grateful for their help.

ATC: Miami is the closest airport, but I can't land you there because of weather. I'm going to vector you to JAX.

BANCROFT: Jacksonville, roger that.

ATC: Please relay the number of souls on board and fuel in time.

BANCROFT: We've got one hundred and thirty-two soul—uh, correction—one hundred thirty-one souls on board and . . . just under two-and-a-half hours of fuel.

ATC: Diverting to JAX is going to add three hundred miles to your trip, but two-point-five hours of fuel is sufficient. And of course, you'll have priority,

BANCROFT: OK, thank you.

ATC: Turn left heading 3-3-5 for JAX.

BANCROFT: Left 3-3-5.

ATC: Be careful up there, Captain.

BANCROFT: Always am.

CAPTAIN BANCROFT: Good evening, folks. I'm afraid there's been a change in our flight plan. Out of an abundance of caution, the company has asked us to divert to Jacksonville to do a full inspection of the plane following that lightning strike. It's going to add a little flying time, but we should have clear air.

Apologies for the inconvenience, but we'll get you onto San Juan just as quickly as possible. In the meantime, please remain in your seats with your seat belts fastened.

CHAPTER

036

"Are you kidding me?" Penelope Abernathy huffed when she heard the announcement. The boys had a game in the morning, and if they missed it, it would be recorded as a forfeit, and they'd play all the losers going forward. *Not how she'd envisioned this trip.*

"I can't believe this is happening," she muttered to no one.

She took a deep breath and reminded herself what she always told her sons: *everything happens for a reason.* She thought about the possible reasons, and she felt a twinge of optimism. A layover would give her a chance to chat up the scout! Assuming he was one, she wasn't entirely convinced—but then again, she was predisposed to be suspicious. More likely he was just ignorant, as so many men are. In any case, best to act as if, because she was not about to miss an opportunity to turn lemons into lemonade.

Penelope looked over at Billy Wilcox's empty seat and her mood turned sour again. She hadn't intervened in the Matthew Kessler incident solely for his benefit, but she'd still gone to significant effort to make sure he couldn't be implicated. And he doesn't even invite Nolan to his wedding? Talk about ungrateful! Also, why did he and his bride book seats in first class if they were just going to skulk off to economy? This was a transcontinental flight, not musical chairs.

The fasten seatbelt sign was on. Countless trips to Catalina Island had given her hearty sea legs, but the events of the last ten minutes were next level. She needed a ginger chew to calm her churning stomach. They were in her purse in the overhead bin, so she unclipped and stood up. No one glared at her, probably because no one cared about her safety. Also, there were only a handful of people left in first class, all coupled up and comforting each other, while she was precariously alone.

As she fished the ginger chews out of her bag, she thought about her baby boy sitting alone without her in the main cabin. That blackout was nuts. She wasn't worried about Ace. As the youngest of three boys, he'd endured worse. His older brothers used to beat the living daylights out of him. One time he fell in a hole on a construction site, and instead of helping him out, they threw rocks at him, then left him for dead. It was only after their father threatened to ground them for life that they confessed to knowing where their little brother was. She wanted to castrate them, but her husband reminded her that "boys will be boys," so she let it go.

She sat back down, popped a ginger chew in her mouth, and closed her eyes. As the sharp tang rolled down her throat, her thoughts turned to the upcoming tournament—her last as the Crestwood Baseball Booster Club president. It was hard to believe her reign was coming to an end. When she took over the job Nolan's freshman year seven years ago, the program was limping along like a three-legged dog, barely able to scrape up enough funds to get a bus to Los Angeles. And now, thanks to her grit and determination, they were going to a tournament across the country to compete against teams from all over the world—Venezuela, Curaçao, Korea, Japan. The other baseball moms thought she was a saint for all the effort she put into it, but her dedication was largely self-serving. She wanted a son in Major League Baseball. And Ace was her last hope.

Her youngest son hadn't been courted by prestigious college programs like Nolan and Ryan, but he was the toughest of the three. If he played well in Puerto Rico, he could still get recruited, and he deserved to be! He had a better work ethic than his brothers, and a bigger ego, probably because of how they treated him. Letting them bully him wasn't strategic on her part—she was just exhausted—but wouldn't you know, the toughness he gained from being teased, smacked around, stuck in that hole, turned out to be his biggest asset. Unlike his brothers, he didn't quit when it got hard. More than that, he wanted to show them up, succeed where they had failed. Getting him recruited was not the only reason she was dragging the team to San Juan—they were all getting a grand adventure out of it—but it was the primary one, and she was determined that the opportunity not be wasted. Yes, the diversion meant they would be playing the losing teams, but playing losers gave him an even greater chance to shine. All she had to do was make sure the right people were watching.

In her career as a baseball mom, she'd never met a Major League scout—that hottie from the first-class lounge was the first, and she'd be a damn fool if she didn't take advantage. Maybe he wasn't the sharpest tool in the shed, but he was still connected, and everyone makes mistakes. Yes, she'd snubbed him, but not so egregiously that she couldn't win him back. Ace was only eighteen, getting him into the Major Leagues was a long game. And she would continue to play it because it was her passion. Also, she had nothing better to do in her looming empty-nester ennui.

She swallowed the rest of her ginger chew, then used her tongue to exhume the spicy bits that had gotten stuck in her teeth. She needed something to drink. Where were the flight attendants?

She reached up and pressed the call button, then got to work scheming how she would charm her way back into that scout's good graces.

CHAPTER

037

"Can I go sit with my friends now?" Ace Abernathy asked.

Federal Air Marshal Carlos Renaldo couldn't think of any more questions, so he stepped into the aisle so the boy could get out.

"Go ahead."

Carlos had no reason to think Abernathy was lying when he told him he'd moved to that empty row in the back to take a nap. Just because it put him closer to the crime scene didn't mean he was involved. *Did it?*

As Abernathy's seatmate stood up to let him in the row, he looked at Ace like, "what the hell was that?" Ace just shrugged. *Good.* That meant that so far, the only two people outside the flight crew who knew about the murder were the boy who found the body and the doctor who'd examined it. Keeping the murder under wraps and the passengers calm and out of the crime scene were his only orders. *Done and done.* He could have stayed parked in his seat with his mouth shut until they landed in Florida. Except he had another agenda: solve the murder, save his job. That meant getting proactive.

He dialed his phone before he lost his nerve.

"Cooper," Special Agent Sam Cooper said when he picked up on the first ring.

"Agent Cooper, it's Officer Renaldo."

"Go ahead, Renaldo."

"Sorry for the incoming call, but I was able to find out who that bat belongs to."

There was a beat of silence. *He'd overstepped.*

"Go on." *But the special agent would hear him out.*

"His name is Ace Abernathy," he said, then went on to tell him how his mother had snuck the bat through the security checkpoint, then handed it off to her son once they got to the terminal.

"Why would she do that?"

"Apparently she thinks it's lucky . . . you know how baseball players are."

Cooper dismissed the intel with a brusque, "I'll let you know if it proves helpful."

Carlos sensed the special agent was about to hang up, so he quickly added, "He asked if my questions about the bat on board had something to do with the death of Matthew Kessler."

And that got Cooper's attention. "Who's Matthew Kessler?"

"His teammate. Or rather, former teammate. He was killed in an unsolved hit-and-run. His mother, Francesca Kessler, is on this flight. Seat 11C."

There was a beat of silence, as if Cooper was deciding whether this was a lead worth following.

"I'll let you know if anything comes of it," Cooper said, but with a little more sincerity this time. Carlos felt a glimmer of hope. No, he wasn't an investigator, but if he acted like one, maybe the information would flow both ways.

"Thank you, sir."

And then came the reminder that he was just an airborne security guard.

"A team of twenty agents will be boarding the aircraft in Jacksonville to question the passengers and examine the crime scene. Please be ready to help maintain order."

"Yes, sir."

And then he hung up.

Carlos didn't know what to do next. He was nervous about

questioning the passengers, because what if he accidentally tipped off the killer and botched the investigation? Plus, there were rules about talking to suspects. If he solicited something improperly, it might be inadmissible. And he didn't want to do more harm than good.

He pressed his fingertips to his forehead. Defeatist thoughts were just excuses, he knew better than to give into them. He conjured the image of the framed poster hanging in his bathroom: *Certainty bends reality. Believe that you can do it, and you will not fail.* He may not have investigative skills, but he was *here*, at the scene of the crime, uniquely positioned to look for clues. And that's what he needed to be doing.

He opened his phone and started scrolling through the photos he'd taken. Was there something in them that might crack this case? He started with the wide shots. The lavatory was tiny. There was no room for a scuffle. Whatever happened in there happened fast and with great force. He imagined a wiry baseball player with quick hands, recalled the urban myth about the mother who lifted a car to save her child. Everyone was a suspect. He couldn't rule anyone out.

Murdering someone on a plane where there are dozens of captive, potential witnesses and nowhere to run or hide is incredibly risky. *So why here, why now?* Was the murderer afraid they wouldn't get another chance? Or was this a spontaneous act of violence prompted by something that happened in flight?

Then there was the matter of the murder weapon. Whoever did this had to have access. Ace Abernathy had brought the bat on board, but anybody could have found it and used it. Does that mean the murder was *not* premeditated? Because the only way it could have been premeditated was if the teen did it or was in on it. Could it be that simple?

He opened his manifest, scrolled through the names and photos of the one hundred and twenty-five possible suspects. How many of the passengers were mothers? Ball players? Athletes? How many had criminal records? How many had enough ice in their veins to kill in cold blood? As he stared down at the jumble of names that meant nothing to him, his phone buzzed in his hand.

"Renaldo."

"We're looking into the Kessler hit-and-run" Cooper said. "Nice work flagging that." He felt a twinge of pride.

"Thank you, sir."

"I just arrived in Crestwood," the special agent continued. "While I was driving, I got a call from Sheriff Alan Eckles's personal secretary about a police report that had come in earlier today. It was from someone on your flight.

Renaldo's heartbeat quickened. *Was Cooper about to share intel with him?*

"A passenger?" he asked.

"I just sent it to you. Have a look."

He opened the text and scanned the police report. Then toggled to the manifest to check out the photo of the woman who'd filed it. Angela Diaz was the woman he'd seen in a heated argument at the neighboring gate right before takeoff. He recalled her sparring partner's balled fist, her steely resolve . . . then felt a tremor of excitement that he might know something the FBI could use.

"We're doing a deep dive on everyone in the wedding party," Cooper said. "I'm pulling police reports from the last five years to see if anything else comes up."

"Thank you for keeping me in the loop."

"Keep the intel flowing. We're going to follow this investigation wherever it takes us."

Renaldo's heart trilled with anticipation. That was an invitation. And he was going to take it.

"About Ms. Diaz . . ." he started, because if he wanted to be treated like an investigator, he'd better start acting like one.

CHAPTER

038

"Has anything like this ever happened to you before?" First Officer Drew Ridley asked his captain as they headed northwest toward Jacksonville. They were entering the airspace above the notorious Bermuda triangle, but Bancroft didn't buy into the stories about ships and planes disappearing without a trace.

"If you mean the lightning strike—no," Captain Bancroft said. "If you mean the murder while in flight—also no. This is a day of many firsts."

Bancroft hoped the remark didn't sound glib. The situation in the main cabin was serious. And tragic. And dangerous. He had lost passengers in flight before—an elderly man on a nonstop to Tokyo, a coked-up businessman headed to Silicon Valley. It was not unheard of for a passenger to die midair. But a violent murder? No, he had never heard of that happening. Not unless terrorism was involved. But terrorists, by definition, don't kill for no reason. No one had threatened more violence if he didn't comply with a demand to change course. Yes, they were diverting. But the FBI had ordered that. Surely no terrorist could have anticipated they would be sent to Jacksonville.

"Sucks that we have to divert," Ridley said. Bancroft didn't like to inconvenience his passengers, but he wasn't broken up about it. Most people saw air travel as an undesirable means to a desirable end. What excited him was not *where* he was going, but *how* he was getting there. Flying was the love of Brett Bancroft's life, and he thanked his lucky stars every day that he got to do it for a living. He loved the dance with the controls, feeling the aircraft respond to his touch, chasing the sun, watching it fan out into rainbows of color. When he sat down in that captain's chair, he became a goddamned superhero, speeding through the air like a bullet, leapfrogging mountains in a single bound. Most people only felt safe when they were on the ground. For him, it was the opposite. There were so many things that could hurt you on terra firma. Up here, the dangers were relatively few, and the escape routes were infinite.

He thought about the danger that lurked outside the cockpit door. There was an armed air marshal on board, surely he could handle a lunatic with a baseball bat. He needed to focus on his job: flying the plane.

The airframe shuddered as they hit a pocket of unstable air. Nothing major, but enough to spook the passengers who had just been to hell and back.

"This is Pioneer 8-6-8 emergency," he said into the comms. "We seem to be entering a patch of rough air. Any chance you can get us out of these clouds?"

"Pioneer 8-6-8 emergency, radar indicates those thunderstorms top out at about three-one hundred feet. Climb and maintain flight level three-three-zero for a smoother ride."

"F-L-three-three-zero, roger that."

Bancroft gripped the side stick. As the plane started to climb, the master alarm went off like an exploding firecracker.

"Warning! Low fuel!" the onboard computer barked. "Warning!"

Bancroft looked at the fuel gauge and scowled.

"That's impossible," he said to his first officer. "We had nearly ten tons of fuel five minutes ago. The gauge must be malfunctioning."

"Warning! Low fuel! Warning!"

Bancroft silenced the alarm. "The avionics failure must have short circuited one of the sensors. This came on too fast to be a fuel leak."

"Unless that lightning strike split the tank open," Ridley countered.

The thought had occurred to Bancroft. But if that was the case, the fuel would have started leaking right away. He would have noticed it sooner.

"If our gauges are correct, what's our remaining fuel in time?" Bancroft asked, just in case it wasn't a gauge issue.

Ridley pulled out his iPad to do the calculation.

"Five minutes."

CHAPTER

039

"We should check on the passengers," Rita said, pointing to the call button panel where the light for seat 3B was flashing.

The passengers. Cathy had all but forgotten about them. She, Rita, and Fonzie had been huddled in the aft galley since the discovery of the body, waiting for the air marshal to tell them the murderer was in handcuffs and they could all breathe easily now. Just because that hadn't happened didn't mean they could shirk their duties. They had one hundred and twenty-five passengers who'd just gone through hair-raising turbulence, and one hundred and twenty-four of them deserved some hand-holding.

"Right. Of course," Cathy said, running her fingers through her close-cropped hair to fluff it. She couldn't wipe the worry off her face, but at least she could fix her hair.

"Fonzie, I need you to stay back here and make sure no one tries to peek behind that curtain," Rita ordered.

Fonzie winced, like he preferred to leave the dead-body-babysitting to someone else. "Copy that."

Then to Cathy, "After that turbulence, there are likely airsick bags that need collecting."

"On it," Cathy said, grabbing a trash bag. *Like her job was any better.*

"I'll do it," Rita said, taking the bag from Cathy's hand. "I want to take the temperature out in the main cabin, see how everyone's faring. Why don't you check on 3B?"

Cathy tried not to look pleased she got the easy task. "Will do."

"You're doing an admirable job staying cool under pressure—both of you," Rita said, looking at Fonzie, then at her. "Keep it up."

Rita motioned for her to go ahead. She stepped into the aisle. Three rows up, the air marshal was scrolling through photos of the murder weapon on his phone, presumably trying to find out how it got on board and into someone's skull.

"Any leads?" Cathy said, peering over his shoulder.

"We're working several angles," he said, closing the phone like she wasn't supposed to see. She knew she should keep walking, but she couldn't betray her yappy habits.

"I saw you talking to the boy who brought the bat on board," she whispered. "You don't think *he* did it?"

"I'm sorry," he said, not sounding the least bit sorry. "I can't reveal what we know at this point."

Cathy nodded slowly. Did that mean he knew something? Or was he sidestepping the question because he had no clue?

She hovered another few seconds to give him a chance to say more. "Right. Sorry to disturb," she said when he didn't.

She started back up the aisle. The discovery of the body had been so shocking, she'd almost forgotten about the drama that had preceded it. Telling Francesca her ex-husband had seen the car that struck and killed her son. Dragging Brendan to the back of the plane to inform him he could no longer stay silent. Then watching him squirm as Francesca demanded the whole truth right then and there.

Rita had said she was going to check on the passengers, but Cathy still took her time getting to first class. Among the one hundred and twenty-five remaining passengers was a murderer—*a murderer!* Yes, whoever plowed down Francesca's son was a murderer, too, but that was an accident. What happened in that lavatory was a vicious attack.

She walked slowly, checking out the passengers from behind as she made her way toward the front of the plane. *Is that coffee on 26C's pant leg? Or something else? Why does 24D look so relaxed? And 22A look so tense?* She felt a flash of anger. How could the murderer just sit there, playing Candy Crush like they didn't just smash someone's face in?

She crossed the threshold into first class. As expected, 3B's light was illuminated. She reached up and turned it off.

"Is everything OK, miss?"

The woman looked a little agitated, but then again, so did a lot of people.

"Did something happen back there?" the woman asked.

Cathy wasn't much of an actress, but she did her best to play dumb. "How do you mean?" The woman couldn't have seen them all huddled together in the aft galley from all the way up here . . . could she?

"We were just bounced around like popcorn popping, I would have thought someone would have come to check on us by now."

OK, so it was just about the turbulence—*good*. The criticism was fair. She opened her mouth to apologize, but before she could get a word out—

Rat-a-tat-a-tat!

Cathy stumbled backward toward the bulkhead. The sensation was like being inside a shaking maraca—loud and dizzyingly violent.

Cathy had never experienced total engine failure, but what happened next was just like she'd imagined. A jolt as their airspeed fell off a cliff. A sinking feeling as 150,000 pounds of aluminum and steel succumbed to the laws of physics. And then—

Silence.

Complete and total silence.

No hum of the engines, no whir of circulating air. Nothing but the sound of one hundred and twenty-five passengers sucking in their breath.

"What just happened?" 3B asked.

Cathy met the woman's wide-eyed stare. "Excuse me."

The interphone was six steps away, but getting to it felt like walking to the end of the earth. She tried to tell herself what was happening wasn't catastrophic. But her intuition knew otherwise.

She felt the passengers watching her, so she kept her face turned away while she reached for the handset. As she put it to her ear, her head felt as weightless as a hot-air balloon in flight. *Turbulence, lightning strike, power outage, murder* . . . she'd told herself nothing worse could happen now.

But of course there was one thing.

CHAPTER

040

"MAYDAY, MAYDAY, MAYDAY," Captain Bancroft boomed into his headset. "This is Pioneer 8-6-8. We're in total engine failure. I repeat, I've lost both engines. I'm not going to make it to Jacksonville, I need to land this bird now."

"Pioneer 8-6-8, roger that," the tower responded. "We'll find you an airstrip, stand by."

In his thirty-years of flying, Captain Bancroft had faced his fair share of emergencies—a loss of cabin pressure over the Grand Canyon, icing over Lake Ontario, stuck landing gear on an approach into JFK. The protocol for what to do during an in-flight emergency was unambiguous and known to every person who has ever flown a plane: One, aviate; two, navigate; three, communicate. In that order. No matter what obstacle a pilot is facing, his number one priority is to keep that airplane in the air. Ailerons, elevator, rudder, side stick—the captain toggled between them like a master chef cooking four courses at once. Each instrument had a role to play.

"Pioneer 8-6-8 emergency," Miami Center said, "your closest airport is JAGS McCartney in Cockburn Town."

Bancroft glanced at Ridley, who was going through the checklist for restarting the engines—standard protocol in this situation, but also futile.

"Stop what you're doing," he ordered. "We're not going to get our engines back online."

"How do you know?"

"We're out of fuel."

"I thought you said the low fuel warning was an avionics failure," his first officer said.

The low fuel warning was so incongruous when it went off eight minutes ago, he'd assumed it was an avionics failure caused by the lightning strike. Because eighteen thousand pounds of fuel doesn't just disappear.

"It was the most logical explanation under the circumstances," Bancroft replied. "But it was wrong." It was also unfortunate. Because while it's possible to restart a stalled engine, there are no gas stations at thirty thousand feet.

Bancroft turned his attention to the second order of business: navigate. Their two main generators quit when the fuel ran out, but the ram air turbine had kicked on and was keeping their essential instruments working. He had control of the airplane and, given their altitude of thirty thousand feet above the earth, a decent amount of glide range. They weren't in danger up in the clouds, but they couldn't stay aloft forever.

"Calculate our glide range so I can confirm our diversion into JAGS," the captain ordered.

"Roger that," Ridley said, taking out his iPad to do the math.

Third order of business: communicate. A crew member was calling, as expected. He pressed the Push-To-Talk button on his control stick. "This is the captain."

"Captain Bancroft, it's Cathy. What's going on?"

As he contemplated what to tell her—

"Estimated glide range is eighty-two miles," Ridley interrupted.

"Eighty-two miles, copy that," he parroted back. Then, into the comms, "Miami Center, how many miles to JAGS?"

"If we turn you now," the air traffic controller said, "it's one hundred and five, that's one-zero-five miles."

OK, so they weren't going to JAGS.

"That's the closest?"

"Affirmative."

The interphone chimed again. Cathy was waiting for an answer. "Captain? Are you there?"

He pressed the PTT button. "We lost both engines," he informed her, because there was no point sugarcoating this. "We're looking for an airstrip within range. Give me a few minutes."

He turned his attention back to his number one priority. "I'm reducing our speed to one-three-zero, knots," he told his FA as he increased the flaps and used the trim wheel to level the nose. In order to maximize his glide range, he needed to maintain optimal lift-to-drag ratio, and that meant slowing the aircraft down just the right amount.

"Pioneer 8-6-8 emergency, turn left heading two-three-zero for JAGS," ATC said over the comms, because the captain hadn't yet told them that's not where they were going.

"Negative. Too far," Bancroft responded, because JAGS was twenty-three miles beyond their range, and while he was a capable pilot, he could not bend the laws of physics.

"I have Puerto Plata in the Dominican. That's ninety-seven miles. But it's directly behind you."

The air traffic controller knew that turning the plane around would result in a loss of air speed and altitude. So while Puerto Plata was closer, it really wasn't.

"My maximum glide range is eighty-two miles. Need something closer," Bancroft told ATC. Then to Ridley, "Get out the charts. See what's down there."

"Pioneer 8-6-8 emergency," Miami Central squawked back, "I don't have an airstrip that can handle a jet your size within eighty-two miles."

It was eighty-*one* miles now. The longer they waited, the fewer options they would have. It was important to make a quick decision. But it was more important to make the right decision. It was storming out there. They couldn't do a water landing in choppy high seas—as soon as a wave hit the wing, the aircraft would tip and break apart. They needed a landing strip, a grassy field, any flat stretch of earth free from obstacles.

"Talk to me, Ridley," Bancroft said as he went to flaps five and trimmed the wheel.

"There's a bunch of private islands down there," the FO said, scrolling through his charts. "But they're not going to help us."

"Say more."

"The recommended airstrip length for the A320 is 6200 feet. None of them are even close to that."

"What's the minimum?"

"Checking," he said as he searched for it in the operating manual. "The absolute minimum is 3400. But that's with thrust reversers to slow the plane, which we don't currently have."

They'd lost the thrusters when they lost the engines. They had wheel brakes, but they'd be coming in so hot, if he hit them too hard they would catch fire. All Bancroft had were his ailerons, flaps, and the unflappable confidence of someone who'd landed F-14s on a one-hundred-meter flight deck.

"Take the controls."

"I have the controls."

Bancroft grabbed his iPad and looked at his options. Ridley was right. There were a lot of little islands down there, but their runways were tiny, some only twenty feet wide. These airports were built for Putt-Putt planes, not commercial jets.

He examined the charts one at a time. The longest airstrip within their eighty-one mile range—or rather, *seventy-nine* mile range now—was 2820 feet. Less than half of the recommended length, and six hundred feet short of the bare minimum for a fully operational A320.

He checked their position on the radar, then radioed Miami Center. "This is Pioneer 8-6-8 emergency. Requesting vectors to Martini Cay."

Miami Center was appropriately confused. "Pioneer 8-6-8, say again?"

"We want to go to Martini Cay, in Turks and Caicos."

"That airstrip can't accommodate a plane of your size," the tower replied. "It's only two thousand eight-two-zero feet."

"We're aware."

"There are no hospitals or support services. If you run into difficulty, you're completely on your own."

Bancroft knew all of this, but he had to play the cards he'd been dealt.

"It's either land there or not at all."

FIRST OFFICER DREW RIDLEY: Hi folks, this is your first officer. You probably felt that jolt and guessed that was our engines turning off.

We don't have enough glide range to make it to San Juan, but we've identified an airstrip in Turks and Caicos and are headed toward it. In the meantime, please remain in your seats with your seat belts fastened.

CHAPTER

041

Our engines turning off? Penelope blanched at the obnoxious turn of phrase. How stupid did the captain think they were? What happened was not like someone flipping off the light to take a nap, it was like smashing the lamp to smithereens.

The purple-haired flight attendant was white-knuckling the phone, and Penelope knew they were in deep shit. Like most people staring death in the face, she thought of her family. She loved her husband, of course, but the true loves of her life were her sons. Had she done right by Nolan, Ryan, and Ace in her twenty-six years of parenting? You're damn right she had! If they didn't survive the engines "turning off," she'd go to her grave knowing she'd done everything in her power to make her sons' dreams—fine, *her* dreams for her sons—come true.

Ace normally didn't need his mother to hold his hand, but there was nothing normal about what was happening, and—though she was loath to admit it—if she was going to die, she didn't want to do it alone. As she tucked her tray table so she could sneak back to the cheap seats, the curtain between main and first class whooshed open.

She turned her head to look. It was the scout from the first-class lounge. *What was he doing out of his seat?* As he whisked past her, she saw his right hand reaching for something shiny under the waistband of his coat. Good God, was that what she thought it was?

The synapses in her brain lit up like fireworks as the pieces came together. First was that gaffe in the first-class lounge. She'd wanted to believe he was a scout so badly she'd dismissed his comment about Trey Turnberry being a gift to the NCAA as a silly mistake. But everyone who followed baseball knew Turnberry was drafted straight out of high school. Then there was his odd behavior right after he'd boarded. Yes, she'd seen his camera app open as he moved his thumbs across his phone screen like he was texting, but she'd dismissed it as the guy just wanting to be left alone. Now he was charging the cockpit while reaching for what could only be a gun. Most people wouldn't believe a passenger could get a forbidden item through security, but she'd done it, hadn't she?

Click. She unclipped her seatbelt with the flick of her thumb. She wished she could huddle with her fellow passengers to make a plan to subdue the hijacker who was clearly trying to crash this plane, but there wasn't time to make friends. They'd catch on soon enough—once she revealed him for what he was.

She leaned over and plucked one of her stiletto-heeled boots off the floor. She knew if she met this man face-to-face in a dark alley, he would easily overpower her, but she had the element of surprise, and the rage of a grizzly bear when someone threatens her cub.

She wrapped her hand around the shaft of the boot with the heel poised to strike. As she crept toward the fake scout in her stocking feet, she summoned the memory of taking batting practice with her boys, and the cheers of "You go, girl!" when she hit it out of the park.

She snuck up behind him. Silently, she drew back her arm, the heel of her boot extended like the blade of a knife. Then, as stealthy as a lioness, she pounced.

"Ha!" she shouted as she brought the boot down toward the hijacker's head.

THWACK! The heel snapped, colliding with the cockpit door as the man ducked underneath it. As the impromptu weapon tumbled to the floor—

"Are you out of your mind?" the man shouted, wrestling her

outstretched arm behind her back and pressing her body against the bulkhead wall.

"I know you're not a scout!" she yelled. "And that you did something to this plane!"

Her gaze dropped down to his hip. She could see the gun clearly now, pinned to the waistband of his pants.

"Gun! He's got a gun!" She cranked her head around to look at the purple-haired flight attendant. *Why was she just standing there?* "Do something!"

"I'm a federal air marshal," the man said, pulling a zip-tie from somewhere unseen and wrapping it around her wrists. Then, before she could call bullshit, he unclipped that shiny thing on his hip and held it in the air for her and everyone to see.

At the sight of that badge, for the first time in her life she was too stunned to say a word.

His fingers dug into her arm as he pulled her back to her seat. She didn't resist. She was too busy putting her defense together. This man had lied to her face. He was charging the cockpit seconds after the engines "turned off." She had every reason to suspect someone was messing with this flight, and that it was him.

"Sit down," he commanded, and she obeyed, falling back onto her zip-tied hands.

She couldn't fasten her seatbelt with her hands behind her back, so he did it for her. She was humiliated. She was enraged. But more than that, she wanted—no, *needed*—to be with her son.

"You can't leave me like this!"

CHAPTER

042

Federal Agent Carlos Renaldo was too angry to respond. Not at the woman for attacking him—if he saw someone running toward the cockpit, he would have done the same thing. No, he was mad at himself. He'd botched this in-flight emergency at every turn. He'd failed to prevent the murder, failed to identify the murderer, and now failed to identify himself to the already on-edge passengers, one of whom had just tried to impale him with a boot. That was a helluva lot of failures, and they weren't even on the ground yet.

He looked down at the boot under the woman's chair—the mate to the one she'd used to try to impale him. He'd tried to tell the TSA that those security checks were theater—they should focus not on *what* could hurt you, but *who*. Half the passengers on this flight had something on their person that could kill a man. A hard-soled shoe was just as dangerous as that baseball bat, in the right hands.

"I'll deal with you later," he said to his attacker. She didn't meet his gaze, but he could see the fear in her eyes. Was she afraid he'd press charges? That they were all going to die? Or something else? He couldn't read her. But also, he had more pressing concerns.

He turned around, then strode up to the cockpit door and held his badge up to the camera. With this new development (double engine failure!), terrorism was back on the table, and if that's what this was, he'd better not make any more mistakes.

CLICK. The cockpit door unlocked. The pilot wouldn't let him in if he was hijacking the plane himself, but Renaldo kept his right hand on his gun, ready to draw if necessary.

"Is everything all right in here?" he asked as he stepped through the door. His eyes darted around the tiny space. The dash was lit up like a Christmas tree, every light flashing.

"We're in double engine failure," the captain said. "So things could be better."

Katie's perfectly imperfect face flashed in his mind. He felt a pinprick of shame as it hit him how different things would feel if she were here. Her safety would consume him. How could he tear himself away from her with a murderer at large and the engines on the fritz? In that moment, he understood—*really* understood—why relationships between air marshals and crew members were forbidden. Not that he had to worry about that anymore.

"We need to talk about the security threat on board," Renaldo said, telegraphing that if there was something the captain wanted to tell him, now was the time to speak up.

"Turning left zero-three-three," the captain said into his comms. Then, to him, "Happy to talk to you about that once we're on the ground, Officer . . . ?"

"Renaldo."

"Nice to meet you. I'm Brett Bancroft and that's first officer Drew Ridley." Then to Ridley, "Flaps two."

"Flaps two, copy."

"Where are we landing?" Renaldo asked, still on alert for indicators of sabotage. Was it possible the murder and the engine failure were unrelated? What were the odds?

"Martini Cay."

Renaldo had never heard of Martini Cay. "Why there?"

"We don't have enough glide range to go anywhere else."

"Is Martini Cay part of the Bahamas?"

"Turks and Caicos."

Turks and Caicos was a British Overseas Territory. The US didn't have any assets there. The FBI would need him to take charge. Given his incompetence to this point, he didn't know whether to be thrilled or scared shitless.

"Can you radio ahead to have law enforcement meet us on the tarmac?" Renaldo asked, because he couldn't guard the passengers and interview possible suspects at the same time.

"How about we figure it out once we're on the ground?" Bancroft replied. And Renaldo suddenly understood that making it to the ground was not a given.

"But there will be security there?" he pressed.

"Unlikely."

"Weather service reporting light winds blowing east-southeast to ten knots," the first officer interrupted.

"That's not going to do much to slow us down," the captain responded. "Visibility?"

"Three miles."

"We're not going to see that runway until we're practically on top of it," Bancroft said, and Renaldo felt a pinprick of unease.

"Correction: visibility is now down to two miles," the first officer said.

"Is two miles enough?" Renaldo asked.

"It is what it is," the captain said. Then, to his first officer, "If we want any hope of finding that runway, we need to get below these clouds."

"Agreed," the first officer replied.

"Stand by to increase our rate of descent to one thousand five hundred feet per minute. We can ease up if needed once we have a visual on the runway."

"That's going to make a lot of people very uncomfortable," the FO warned. Renaldo studied the first officer's face. Was that fear in his eyes?

"If the visibility gets any worse, we won't be able to see the runway at all," Bancroft said.

"Roger that." Yup, definitely fear. In his voice too.

Bancroft indicated the jumpseat with his head. "Mr. Renaldo, you'd better take a seat."

CHAPTER

043

“Pioneer 8-6-8, beginning final approach into Martini Cay,” Bancroft said into the comms, hoping that his decision to land on this tiny blip of an island was the right one. Were there any other choices? He’d find out at the inquiry. If he lived to be part of it.

“Copy that, 8-6-8.” If the air traffic controller was a God-fearing man, he was probably saying a prayer for them. They would be coming down hard and fast onto a runway a thousand feet too short. There was no way they wouldn’t go off the end of it. The only spot of good news was that it terminated at the beach, which meant they *might* get a few hundred feet of sand to slow them down. The bad news was, once they plowed through the sand, they’d torpedo into the ocean.

He pressed the PTT button on his boom. “Prepare the cabin for an emergency landing,” he told his purser. And then, because it would be irresponsible not to warn her, “We may end up in the water.”

He gripped the side stick. “Here we go.”

Bancroft pushed the stick forward. The nose levered down like the heavy end of a seesaw. Everything about this landing was risky. The steep approach angle. The poor visibility. The too-short runway with no speed brakes to slow them down. While in the navy, he’d landed F-14s on moving aircraft carriers, but this airplane was a totally different animal, even with the engines running.

"You all right, Officer Renaldo?" Bancroft asked the air marshal, who was clipped into the jumpseat behind him.

"I'm fine."

Bancroft checked his speed. As expected, they were accelerating with gravity.

"I'm going to full flaps," Bancroft announced. He had limited tools to slow the aircraft down. Without engines, if the nose dipped too low, they'd never get it back up.

"Full flaps," Ridley acknowledged.

They were teetering on the edge of a death spiral. If he lost control of the descent, they'd plunge headlong into the ocean.

"You see the island?" Bancroft asked, hoping his first officer's young eyes were sharper than his.

"Negative."

"What's our altitude?" he asked, not wanting to take his eyes off the horizon.

"Twelve thousand feet." If the visibility was two miles, Martini Cay should come into view any second.

"Count us down."

"Eleven-five . . . eleven thousand . . . ten thousand five . . ." They were at two miles above sea level now. Still no sign of Martini Cay. They knew its coordinates, but with only rudimentary navigational tools to guide them, the only way to pinpoint its location was with their eyes.

"Officer Renaldo, feel free to speak up if you see it."

"Looking," Renaldo said, leaning forward in his jumpseat. Then, a little more tentatively, "Is there really a chance we'll wind up in the ocean?" And the captain gave it to him straight.

"It's a mathematical certainty."

And then—inexplicably—the air marshal unbuckled his harness and stood.

"Officer Renaldo!" the captain snapped. "Get back in your seat!"

But the idiot air marshal ignored him.

CHAPTER

044

"Attention, all passengers," Rita said over the PA. "We are making an emergency landing. I need everyone in their seats with their seatbelts securely fastened." She looked over her shoulder at Cathy and Alphonso, and they understood that "everyone" included them.

"Are we going to die?" Alphonso asked Cathy as they slid into rear-facing jumpseats at the front of the aircraft.

"Not today," Cathy told him, because she hadn't busted her ass to live her dream to have it end like this. Yes, their engines had quit, but there were plenty of stories of planes surviving engine failure, it didn't have to be a death sentence.

As Cathy buckled in, she flashed back to the glee she felt when she got the call to work this flight. At the time, she thought what she felt was excitement to see someplace new, breathe sweet, tropical air, dip her toes in water that never grew cold. But as she looked out at couples young and old, all clinging to one another, she realized that under that excitement was something else: *relief.* Relief that she wouldn't have to spend another night trying to quiet her loneliness in a house that never felt like home. Because isn't that why she took this job? To stop missing Brendan?

"I need help!" the passenger in 3B cried out, snapping her back to the urgency of the moment. "Please, someone!"

"What's wrong with her?" Fonzie asked.

At first Cathy thought the woman was afraid for her life like everyone else. But then she remembered. "She's zip-tied."

"So?"

"She can't evacuate if she can't use her arms."

The nose of the plane levered toward the ground. The two flight attendants tipped backward in their seats.

"Please, help me!"

Cathy didn't have the authority to let her go. Still, she couldn't sit here and watch her die. She unclipped her harness.

"Cathy, don't," Fonzie pleaded.

"I'll be OK," Cathy said as she pulled herself up. She had a mini Swiss Army knife in her pocket that she could use to cut the restraints. She reached for it as she stood. But before she could take a step—

The cockpit door opened.

"I got it," the air marshal said, putting a hand on her shoulder as he passed. "Sit back down."

Cathy watched as the marshal cut his attacker free. As he slid into the empty seat across the aisle, his eyes ticked up to meet hers. A moment of silent respect passed between them. They had very different jobs, but their mission was the same: Keep these passengers safe.

"Please listen closely to my instructions," Rita announced over the PA. The air in the cabin grew eerily still, as if no one dared move or breathe. "The captain has informed me that we may wind up in the water."

And then came the collective gasp. Fonzie grabbed Cathy's arm. "We're not ditching, are we?" Ditching—also known as a "water landing"—was as dire as the name implied. Flight attendants spoke the word in hushed whispers.

"If we are, we're trained for it," Cathy said, in her best imitation of a pep talk. Two weeks of their seven-week training were spent learning what to do in a ditching. "We've got this."

"Your life vest is under the seat directly in front of you," Rita continued. "Please put it on, but *do not inflate*."

Passengers scrambled to find their vests. Cathy looked out as the young helped the old and the brave helped the scared. Experience had taught her that crises drive people apart. Today she was seeing how they could also bring them together.

"When it's time to deplane," Rita continued, "you will inflate your vest by pulling on the two tabs on either side or by blowing into the tube."

Most of these passengers had heard their spiel about what to do "in the event of a water landing" so many times they could recite it from memory. But they'd probably never listened, because what were the odds it would happen to them?

"When instructed, you will assume the brace position," Rita continued. "When told to brace, put your hands behind your neck, then lean over your lap and stay there until we tell you it's safe to move."

Emotion balled in Cathy's throat as she thought of all those teenage boys, how little of the world they'd seen in their young lives, how frightened they must be. And then she thought of Brendan, how he always knew how to keep them calm and steady. He did that for her too. She had just been too proud to admit it.

Her thoughts turned to Francesca. Was she afraid to die, or at peace because it meant, after three excruciating years, she'd finally be reunited with her son? The worst thing that could happen to a person had already happened to her. Would dying today just be the epilogue to a story that had already ended in tragedy? Or did she have a reason to live now that Brendan had told her what he knew and she might just get the justice she deserved?

"Cathy!" Fonzie said, grabbing her arm.

She looked to where he was pointing—at the woman in 3B, who had unclipped her seatbelt and was climbing into the aisle.

"Ma'am!" Cathy shouted. "Get back in your seat!"

The woman ignored her, began bear-crawling toward the main cabin. Cathy looked at the air marshal.

"Her son's back there," he said.

"She needs to be in a seat!" she shouted, putting a hand on her harness to release it.

"And I need *you* right where you are," Rita shouted back. And Cathy froze. With that command came a stunning revelation. She'd reviled her ex-husband for putting the so-called greater good above the well-being of any one person. But if she didn't survive the landing, Rita and Fonzie would have to do the work of all three of them. People might get hurt. People might die. She might be able to save one life, but in doing so, she'd be jeopardizing more. *A lot* more.

"I'm not ready to die," Fonzie whimpered.

"We're not going to die," she said, even though she had her doubts. Yes, an airplane could land on water, but it was near impossible in these conditions. All it took was one wave to catch the wing and the plane would rip apart, killing them all instantly. Still, she would do her job when the order came. And, two seconds later, the captain gave it.

"Flight attendants, prepare the passengers for impact."

Rita pushed the announce button on the interphone. Then gave the command that sent a shockwave of terror through the cabin.

"All passengers, assume the brace position."

And then she hung up the comms for the last time.

Cathy choked back her panic and focused on her job. Everything they would do from this point on had been drilled into them like a choreographed dance. And Rita had just given the downbeat.

"BRACE, BRACE, BRACE!" she called out. "Heads down, stay down!"

The three flight attendants chanted the command in unison, like cheerleaders at a football game. "BRACE, BRACE, BRACE!"

The airframe shook like a rocket ship piercing the atmosphere. The descent had become a nosedive. Gravity was Goliath and they were David, on the losing end of a fierce tug-o-war.

"Heads down, stay down! BRACE, BRACE, BRACE!"

Cathy chanted louder to drown out the wails of terrified passengers.

She peered out the window. The ocean was churning beneath them like a cauldron of boiling water. At this speed, hitting it would be like slamming into a wall of concrete.

All they could do was brace and pray.

CHAPTER

045

"Where's that runway?" Captain Bancroft asked his copilot, as he stared out the rain-blurred windshield into the dark night. He didn't mean to sound impatient, but if they didn't spot the airstrip on Martini Cay soon, they were going to wind up in the ocean. All approaches into these tiny islands were VFR—Visual Flight Rules—with no transponders or fancy navigational equipment to guide them. If they couldn't make visual contact—and soon—they might fly right over it.

"Looking," Ridley replied.

"I can't land on it if I can't see it," Bancroft warned.

"It's got to pop up any second now," Ridley said, straining to see through the soup. And then, like a Christmas miracle, the clouds parted and—

"There! I see lights!" Ridley shouted.

Bancroft's eyes were not as sharp as his young FO's, but he took him at his word. "How's our pitch? Do I need to pull up?" They were still in a steep descent. Possibly too steep.

"Negative, Captain. It's closer than we thought."

"Then let's get that gear down," he commanded.

"Gear down, copy."

Bancroft listened as the wheel box rumbled open and the gear snapped into place. A moment later, the parallel rows of landing lights came into view. It was a magnificent sight. Ridley was right. They were perfectly lined up. If they hadn't come down as steeply as they had, they would have overshot it.

"I think that's the most beautiful runway I've ever seen."

"Right there with you, Captain."

"Let's grab every inch of it," he said, communicating he wasn't going to decrease their rate of descent without saying the words.

"Roger that."

As the plane tore through the clouds, Bancroft grappled with the thought that this landing might be his last. No one could say he hadn't lived a full life. He'd traveled the world—seen historic cities, vibrant sunsets, storm clouds and treetops from above and below. He didn't have children, but he liked to think he'd cared just as deeply for the people he'd sworn to protect. As a former naval officer, he'd signed up to give his life in service to others. But his copilot had not.

"Put your life jacket on, Ridley," Bancroft said, eyes glued to the horizon.

"We're going to land this plane on solid ground, Cap."

"That's an order."

Ridley pulled his vest from under his seat and slipped it over his head. "I can take the controls—"

"Negative." Bancroft was not trying to be a hero. If there was time, he would have put his life jacket on too. But flying the engineless plane required every ounce of his attention. He couldn't risk even a few seconds of broken concentration—not even to hand off the controls.

"We're at three thousand feet," the copilot said so the captain could keep his eyes on the landing strip. "Two thousand five . . . two thousand . . ." Ridley's gaze flicked up from the instruments to the approaching ground. "Jesus, that runway is narrow."

Ridley was not overstating. The runway was thirty feet wide—a mere one-fifth of their wingspan.

"It only needs to hold the wheels," Bancroft reminded him.

The mention of wheels made Ridley gasp. "We're going too fast. We're going to blow out the gear."

Bancroft was aware of the risk. But they were already at full flaps, and without engines, there was nothing more he could do to slow them down.

"The gear will hold," he said, as if he could will it to be true. But it wouldn't be the worst thing. If both sides buckled, at least the plane would stay level. The bigger concern was that one would fail but not the other. A belly flop he could handle. A sideways skid on a thirty-foot wide runway, he could not. He had to bring this plane in straight.

"Count us down, Ridley."

Ridley's eyes were glued to the altimeter. "Altitude is five hundred feet . . . four hundred . . . three hundred . . ."

The crosswinds were picking up now. On an island as small as this one, an onshore breeze meant the wind was blowing from all directions. With a runway this narrow, there was zero room for error.

Bancroft made the micro-adjustments in rapid succession—left aileron, right rudder, soft turn to the left, hard turn to the right. He was flying by instinct now, there was no time to think.

"Two-fifty . . . two hundred . . ."

The earth rose up, up, up to meet the belly of the plane.

"Brace for impact," Bancroft ordered.

Ridley kept his eyes on the instruments. "One hundred."

"BRACE!"

Fifty feet, twenty-five, fifteen, ten . . .

The landing gear grazed strands of wild seagrass.

Ridley raised his knees to his chest and wrapped his arms around them. As he tucked his chin—

Bancroft yanked back the stick, and the nose of the plane jerked up like it was being pulled by a puppeteer.

And then, with the force of a wrecking ball—

FWAM! The rear wheels slammed into the asphalt, once—then again, *hard*.

A second later—

The front wheel slammed down, thrusting Ridley and Bancroft into their harnesses.

"We're down!" Bancroft shouted.

Under the belly of the plane, the wheels gobbled the asphalt, hurtling them forward at breakneck speed.

Bancroft looked out the windshield. The end of the runway was coming on fast. They had to slow down. But with no thrusters and their flaps and ground spoilers already fully engaged, they had no way to do that.

"We're going to run out of runway!" Ridley shouted.

Less than a thousand feet in front of them, the dark ocean loomed. As they careened toward it like a runaway train, Captain Bancroft remembered a trick he'd learned from a fellow pilot—a way to use the aileron and opposite rudder to make the whole aircraft work as a speed brake. He'd never tried it, and it was risky on a runway this narrow, but if they plunged into the ocean nose first, the aircraft would get torn to pieces.

He pushed down on the right rudder. As the plane began to turn, he engaged the left aileron. The plane went into a sideways skid.

"Captain! What are you doing?"

"Tell me when we're about to reach the end of the runway," Bancroft commanded, because even with the braking maneuver, it wasn't close to long enough.

Ridley looked out the window. "We're getting close. Two hundred feet maybe? Now a hundred. Fifty . . . thirty . . . we're just about there!"

Bancroft released the rudder and disengaged the aileron. The plane lurched forward, over the berm and onto the beach.

They felt a jolt as the front landing gear buckled. They were nose down, pushing through the sand like a snowplow in a blizzard. Granules rained down on the roof. For a second they were blinded. And then the deluge relented and he saw it.

The whitecapped abyss of the Atlantic Ocean.

Waiting to swallow them whole.

"We're going in the water!"

Bancroft took his hands off the controls. They were no good to him now. All he could hope was that he'd slowed the plane enough to keep it from torpedoing to the bottom.

The wheels cut through the foam as the nose sliced the ocean's surface like a shark fin. Water assaulted the windshield. It was like being in the rinse cycle at the carwash, all foam and spray and blinding chaos.

The captain and first officer slammed against their shoulder harnesses as the nose hit something hard. The plane thundered to a halt.

And then, silence.

PART

Stranded

004

CHAPTER

046

Rick Kessler was brushing his teeth under a skylight framing the full moon when his cellphone rang on the bathroom counter. He had a terrible habit of dicking around on his phone when he should've been getting ready for bed. It used to drive Francesca nuts. "Why do you need your phone to go to the bathroom?" she'd ask when she caught him doing Wordle on the throne. He'd stopped for a little while. But now that his phone was his only companion, he was back at it.

He spit out his toothpaste and looked down at the caller ID: "Unknown."

He felt a prickle of nervousness. It was after nine p.m. Who would be calling him at this hour?

"Hello?" he said, because the only thing more frightening than answering the call was not answering it.

"Mr. Kessler?" The voice was round and low, like a sports announcer or TV anchorman.

"Yes?" The towel around his waist was slipping. He pinched the phone between his ear and shoulder to re-tuck it.

"This is Special Agent Sam Cooper of the FBI. Sorry to call so late. I'm here in Crestwood. I was hoping to see you. Are you currently at home?"

"Yes."

"I should be there in about twenty minutes. I'd appreciate it if you could wait up for me." In sales, they called a person who could make a command sound like a request a "closer," and this guy did it as well as any salesman he'd ever met.

"I'm sorry," Rick asked, because he wasn't sure he'd heard correctly. "Did you say FBI?"

"That's right. I'm leading a task force in conjunction with DHS."

Rick didn't know what DHS was, but didn't want to admit that, so he asked, "What's this about?"

"I'd rather tell you in person."

"OK," Rick said, because what choice did he have?

"See you in twenty minutes," the FBI guy said. And then, without asking for Rick's address, he hung up.

Rick set the phone down and stared at it, as if it might come to life and explain what was happening. When after a few seconds it didn't, he hung his towel on the hook and went to get dressed.

The primary bedroom in his new condo was large—too large for one person—with vaulted ceilings and twin walk-in closets. Even with all that closet space, most of his clothes were piled on the overstuffed chair by the window. He extracted a pair of jeans that were mostly clean, and a T-shirt with minimal wrinkles. It was bedtime, he didn't need to look snappy.

He got dressed, then walked back into the bathroom to finger comb his towel-dried hair into a presentable shape. His unruly, salt-and-pepper mop was the envy of his friends, most of whom turned to exotic hair potions to make theirs look more voluminous. He had two days' worth of stubble. He felt self-conscious shaving for the man, so he left it alone.

His computer was in his home office, so he padded down the Berber-carpeted stairs. When the realtor showed him the place, his first thought was that it looked like a Holiday Inn. He wasn't looking for a home—he'd just left the nicest one he'd ever known—just an escape. So he cashed in his life insurance policy and bought it.

His friends tried to talk him out of it. "Give it time," they said.

"She's still grieving." But what they didn't understand was that he was still grieving too. Grieving *hard*. Matthew was his every breath. He was his sous chef, his fishing buddy, his backseat driver, the eyeroll to his dumb dad jokes. His death was incomprehensible. Losing him was like waking up on an unrecognizable planet, with gravity pulling you apart instead of holding you together.

For those first few months, he dragged his pain behind him like a gangrened limb. The stench of all that grief was choking him. He had to escape. Luckily, he had a special coping skill. He wasn't a professional actor anymore, but he still knew how to do it. He cast himself as the steely survivor, then adopted all the corresponding behaviors—assuring others he was all right, comforting them as they comforted him.

Like his idol, Robert De Niro, he went method with his acting, never breaking character, even when he was alone. Francesca accused him of being heartless, detached, unfeeling. He couldn't confess it was all just for show, because then he'd cease to believe the performance himself. Three years into the role, he still wore that stoic persona like a second skin, because shedding it meant unleashing grief that would swallow him whole. And so he left—his house, his wife, and the life they had together—before the performance wore off and he crumpled into dust.

"But what about Francesca?" his friends asked. "Don't you love her anymore?" Of course he did. That's why he had to become someone else. Someone who didn't fail his wife and kill his own child. No, the accident wasn't his fault, but he was the dad, the husband, the protector. He could have prevented it if he'd just done his fucking job. He knew it was cowardly to leave Francesca—cruel, even. But the only other thing he could have done to escape the suffocating guilt would have hurt her even more.

He sat down at the desk he'd bought at Wayfair and turned on his computer. He knew what the FBI did from watching *Criminal Minds*, but DHS? The special agent wouldn't have mentioned he was working with them unless it was important, and if it was important, Rick wanted to know who they were.

He opened his browser and typed: "What does DHS stand for?" 27,738,000 results popped up in .28 seconds, but by far the most popular one was THE DEPARTMENT OF HOMELAND SECURITY. He started reading. Their jurisdiction was enormous—border security, cyber threats, climate change, immigration enforcement, anti-terrorism. He clicked on the org chart. A bunch of acronyms he'd never heard of filled the screen: CISA, USCIS, USCG, FPS. But there was one he knew. Everybody who'd boarded a plane since 9/11 knew it too: TSA.

His breath caught in his throat. He tried to remember the last thing he'd said to Francesca when she called him from the airport. *Have a safe flight?* Doesn't everyone say that? He took his phone out of his pocket and dialed her number. It was still in his favorites—the only one. The call went to voicemail.

He didn't know what airline she was on—he hadn't asked, and she hadn't said—but he knew where she was going and approximately what time she'd left, and it only took a few clicks to find the flight. According to the Pioneer Air website, Flight 868 with nonstop service to San Juan had departed two hours late and hadn't arrived at its destination. Nothing unusual about a plane departing late. What *was* unusual was that there was no estimated arrival time. The column was blank.

He Googled "Flying time from San Diego to San Juan." By all accounts, it took about six hours.

He looked at his watch. If the plane left at 3:08 p.m., it should have landed twenty minutes ago. So where was it?

He opened another browser with trembling hands. That's when he found the YouTube link. A news report from San Juan.

The tears he'd refused to cry for three long years spilled from his eyes. He wiped them away with the palms of his hands. He wanted to end that painful chapter of his life—needed, begged, prayed for relief.

But not like this.

REPORTER MANDY CORREA: I'm here at Marin airport in San Juan, where Pioneer Air Flight 868 from Los Angeles, with a stopover in San Diego, was due to arrive at 12:02 a.m. local time, after a two-hour delay. The airline is being tight-lipped about the status of the airplane, saying only that there was some sort of in-flight emergency. We don't know if the plane has been diverted, and if so, where.

I'm being told by people on the ground here that among the passengers are eighteen members of the Crestwood High School baseball team. There have been hundreds of young players through this airport in the last twenty-four hours, here to participate in the Roberto Clemente High School World Series, which starts later today, and is scheduled to conclude at week's end.

More on this breaking story as updates come in. Reporting live from San Juan, I'm Mandy Correa.

CHAPTER

047

Cathy lifted her head slow as a sunrise. She flexed her fingers, wiggled her toes inside her shoes. It was eerily dark, with only the battery-powered floor lights to illuminate the cabin. As her eyes adjusted to the dim light, she could see the passengers hunched over like turtles with their foreheads on their knees.

She nudged Alphonso in the rear-facing jumpseat next to hers.

"Fonzie! Are you OK?"

Fonzie raised his head and blinked, three, four, five times. He flexed his knees, touched his face. "I think so."

She felt a cool sensation in her shoes. She looked down to see a puddle forming at her feet. The first-class cabin was taking on water like a leaky canoe.

"Oh my God. We're in the ocean!"

Rita was already out of her harness and on her feet. "We need to get out of here," she commanded. "Now!"

Cathy looked out the window, at the moonlit water lapping the glass. Her chest flooded with panic. "How? We can't open the doors, they're underwater!"

God bless Rita, she'd already thought of that. "Rear doors."

Cathy looked toward the back of the plane. It took her a second to realize the reason her head felt so heavy was that her rear-facing jumpseat was tilted backward. The aircraft was ass-up in the water, nose planted in the ocean floor. Which meant, while the forward doors were submerged, the rear doors were still operational—at least for the moment.

As Cathy unclipped her harness, Rita opened the closet and pulled out the bullhorn. But before she could raise it to her mouth, Fonzie grabbed her arm.

"If we take the passengers out the rear doors, they're going to see . . ." He didn't finish his sentence. Didn't have to.

"We'll cover it up," Cathy whispered.

"With what?" Fonzie asked.

The cockpit door opened. And Rita had the solution. "I need your jackets."

The pilot and copilot obediently slid out of their blazers and handed them to Rita.

"Go!" Rita barked, passing the jackets to Fonzie. "Cathy, go with him and prepare the doors."

Cathy nodded and took off down—or rather, *up*—the aisle, past shell-shocked passengers trembling in their seats. She wanted to stop and reassure them it was going to be OK, but if they didn't hurry up and get those rear doors open, they might miss their chance.

"Everybody, if I could please have your attention," Rita said through the bullhorn, her voice as steady as falling rain. "In a few minutes, we're going to begin deplaning through the rear doors. Please stay in your seat until it's your turn. Leave everything behind. I repeat. All personal belongings must remain on the plane."

As Rita spoke, heads rose up like flowers blooming. Cathy's heart was pounding with adrenaline. The landing was violent, she knew there would be injuries. She was concerned for all her passengers, but frantic to know if the one she still loved was OK.

She was three steps into the main cabin when a woman with a bloody nose grabbed her arm.

"What's happening? Where are we?"

"We've made an emergency landing and are about to deplane,"

Cathy said, pulling a napkin from her pocket and pressing it into the woman's hand. "Hold this to your nose and stand by for instructions." She didn't mean to be dismissive, but she had a job to do.

It was eight more steps to the exit row. Time moved in slow motion as she groped her way forward. *Five, four, three . . .* And then there he was. Relief flooded her chest as his eyes locked on hers.

"Are you OK?" she asked her ex-husband, giving him the once-over to make sure his arms and legs were all still attached.

He nodded. "You?"

"I have to get everyone out of here."

"Can we help?"

She glanced toward the rear of the aircraft. Alphonso had covered the body. You could still make out a human-sized mass peeking out from the half-open lavatory door, but the carnage was obscured.

"Come with me."

Brendan and Coach Brooks unclipped and followed her. The life rafts were in ceiling panels above their heads. In addition to the slide, which could be used as a raft once it fulfilled its primary purpose, the Airbus carried two octagonal, auto-inflating life rafts. Each could hold sixty people—almost enough. Fonzie had already grabbed one. She grabbed the other.

"Take the survival kits," she said, pointing to the golf bag–sized duffels in the open ceiling compartment. Cathy knew they couldn't be more than a few hundred yards from shore, but those kits contained first aid supplies, retractable oars, and emergency rations. It would be foolish to leave them behind.

"Brooks, help Fonzie on the aircraft-left side," Cathy said to Coach Brooks as they stepped into the galley. "Brendan, you're with me."

"Aircraft-left exit door armed and ready," Fonzie announced.

"Opening the right," Cathy echoed.

She pulled down on the lever. The door popped open and the evacuation slide inflated like a rectangular balloon.

"Deploying the raft!" she shouted, then tossed it out the door into the dark ocean.

Splash! The squirming ball of neoprene and rubber hissed as it sucked in air and the raft took shape.

"Aircraft-right exit armed and ready," she announced. Then, to Brendan, "You're going in first."

"No problem."

Maybe it was her newfound appreciation for the fragility of life, or maybe it was those world-weary blue eyes, but she suddenly missed him so much it hurt. This man was once everything to her—her dance partner, her confidant, the sun on her skin when the wind blew cold. She left him because she didn't understand—*couldn't* understand—how he could swallow evidence of a crime that left an innocent boy dead—even if, as he claimed, keeping it to himself would prevent further suffering. But now, with two lifeboats bobbing in the water below, she recalled the hypothetical she'd given him. *If you needed to push one person out of the boat to save the rest, would you do it?* She'd found his answer—*yes, I would*—reprehensible. But what if right now, to save all these passengers—mothers, fathers, grandparents, children—she had to sacrifice one? Would she do it? It was suddenly not so cut-and-dry.

"When you get to the bottom of the slide, I need you to direct everyone away from the aircraft into the lifeboat."

"Got it."

"If they can't get into the boat, have them hang onto the side. Just not on the airplane. Because if it gets sucked under . . ."

Fear flashed in his eyes. "I understand."

"You can inflate the vest now," she said, pantomiming the motion. He pulled down on the tabs and the vest puffed up like bread rising. "Go!"

He nodded. And before she could grab him and never let go, he leaped onto the slide.

Splash! He disappeared under the water. Cathy's heart stopped as one second became two became eternity.

Whoosh! His head and shoulders popped out of the froth and she found her breath again. He gave her the thumbs-up and she gave it back.

"You guys all set?" Rita asked, appearing at the threshold of the galley. Cathy nodded. They were ready: two doors open; two evacuation slides deployed; two sixty-person rafts bobbing in the chop; Brooks and Brendan treading water; Cathy and Alphonso standing by to direct traffic; and one hastily-covered dead body that, on any other day, would have been their biggest problem but now was an afterthought.

"All set," Cathy and Fonzie said in unison.

Rita raised the bullhorn. "Attention everyone! It's time to deplane. We'll start in the back and work our way forward. When it's your turn, please file in an orderly fashion toward the rear of the aircraft, life vests on but not inflated."

Marco, the tattooed rockstar Cathy had mistaken for the air marshal, was in the seat closest to the exit.

"You're first, Marco."

He unclipped his seatbelt and stepped up to the open door. "I just . . . jump?"

"Inflate the vest, sit down on the slide, climb into the raft."

One by one, Cathy and Fonzie directed the passengers down the slides. Besides a few minor scratches and the occasional bloody nose or lip, everyone seemed to be OK. Even the murderer, whoever that was.

Cathy felt a low hum of unease. She and the other passengers were about to crowd into lifeboats with a cold-blooded killer. Did he—or she—have something to do with the plane crashing? And what if they intended to strike again?

Cathy pushed the thought out of her mind. She had a job to do, and that was to get these people off this plane.

"Step forward. Inflate your vest. Jump!" The command became a chorus on repeat, and the passengers fell into an obedient rhythm. In the water below, Brendan and Brooks directed people into the boats, clearing the landing spot so the next person could jump.

"I can't swim," a sandy-haired teen in a Metallica T-shirt said when he stepped up to the open door.

"I got you," his dark-eyed teammate said, hooking his arm through his, and they went down the slide together.

Cathy peered down to make sure they made it to the boat. It was almost full. But that's not what alarmed her.

"Why does the slide angle suddenly seem less steep?" she asked Fonzie.

He'd already figured it out.

"Because we're sinking."

CHAPTER

048

Rick Kessler was in the kitchen waiting for the kettle to boil when the doorbell rang. Since moving out, he'd taken to drinking herbal tea to calm his nerves. Acting like he'd processed Matthew's death may have tricked his brain, but his body knew better.

"Good evening," he said to the absurdly tall, athletic-looking Black man standing on his front stoop.

"Rick Kessler?"

"Yes."

"I'm Special Agent Sam Cooper, FBI violent crimes division." He flashed his badge, but Rick was too alarmed by the word "violent" to register it. "May I come in?"

"Yes, of course," Rick said, opening the door all the way. In the kitchen, the teakettle started whistling. "I was just making some tea, may I offer you a cup?"

"No, thank you," Cooper said without a hint of a smile.

"Please, have a seat," Rick said, indicating the sofa. "I'll be with you in just one moment."

Cooper nodded and stepped over the threshold. Rick poured hot water into his cup, then joined the FBI agent in the living room.

"I have to say, I'm a little apprehensive to ask why you're here," Rick said as he sat down on the tattered recliner Francesca was all too happy to let him take. There was no side table within reach, so he was stuck holding the steaming mug that was burning the pads of his fingers.

"Sorry if I alarmed you," Agent Cooper said. He was sitting on the edge of the couch, leaning forward, elbows on knees, like he might spring to action any second.

"Oh it's fine, the FBI calls me all the time," Rick joked, then immediately regretted it. "When you said you were working with DHS, I presumed this had something to do with the flight my wife boarded earlier today. It should have landed almost an hour ago now, and I can't reach her?" It came out as a question, even though what he said was a fact.

"I don't have any information about that," Agent Cooper said, making it clear he was going to be the one asking the questions.

Rick felt his cheeks warm. He didn't like being talked to like a child. Or being lied to. "So why are you here?"

"It's late, so I'll get right to it," the FBI guy said, taking his phone out of his coat pocket and opening his camera roll. "Do you know this person?"

He stood up and walked over to Rick, held the phone so he could see the screen. The man in the photo was young and handsome, an actor maybe? He knew better than to guess.

"I don't think so. Should I?"

"His name is William Wilcox. Goes by Billy. Born and raised in Crestwood. Went to Crestwood High School."

Rick's pulse quickened at the mention of Crestwood High. "My wife teaches at Crestwood High," he said, because he was determined to find out what happened to her, and every bone in his body told him the stranger in his living room knew more than he was saying.

"Are you aware of any history between them?"

"History?"

"Yes. Did she ever mention his name?"

"No . . . I mean, I don't think so." The knot in his stomach tightened. "What's this about?"

Agent Cooper scrolled to another picture. "Do you recognize this vehicle?"

Rick didn't know much about PTSD, only that there was probably a reason the word "vehicle" made his stomach lurch. "Not offhand."

"It's a 2017 Ford Bronco. It belonged to Mr. Wilcox. He reported it stolen the day after your son was killed."

Rick raised the steaming cup to his lips, forced himself to take a sip. He felt like a wuss, drinking herbal tea in front of such a formidable person, but that's kind of why he needed it.

"We were looking through the police report filed by Sheriff Eckles—" the agent continued, but Rick interrupted.

"Why were you looking through Matthew's police report?" He thought the case was closed—*needed* it to be closed.

"I'll get to that. If you would just have a look." He zoomed in on the crime scene photo. "See these tire tracks?"

Rick peered at the photo. It looked like a crisscross of apple pie crust to him, but if Agent Cooper said they were tire tracks, who was he to disagree? "What about them?"

"At first we thought they were from two different cars, because these here are Firestone LE3s," he said, pointing to one set of squiggly lines, "and these are Goodyear."

His beating heart knew where this was going but he said nothing.

"We know from the title that Mr. Wilcox purchased the Bronco from a reseller in San Diego in 2019," Agent Cooper continued. "Luckily, the owner of the dealership was still up when we called him and had the original listing." Agent Cooper called up the listing on his phone. "See anything unusual about it?"

Rick saw it immediately. "It's a salvage title."

"That's right. It hit a light pole. Front right wheel had to be replaced."

Rick felt his skin tingle. "Let me guess. With a wheel with a different tire on it."

"Bingo. One car, two different types of tread marks. Doesn't definitively prove it was Mr. Wilcox's car, but it's awfully compelling."

"Are you saying whoever stole Mr. Wilcox's car killed my son?" Rick asked. Good God, did they actually have a lead?

"Well, that's where things get a little murky."

"Murky how?"

"Just because someone reported a car stolen doesn't mean someone stole it."

Rick stared blankly at the FBI agent. "I don't understand."

"It's possible Mr. Wilcox reported the car stolen to cover his tracks. Metaphorically speaking."

"You mean he lied about it being stolen?"

"We can't rule out the possibility."

"Why don't you ask him?" Rick asked, knowing he sounded insolent but suddenly not giving a damn.

"Under normal circumstances we would," Agent Cooper said. "But we can't."

"Why not?"

"Because he's dead."

CHAPTER

049

"How can I help?" Federal Air Marshal Carlos Renaldo asked Rita, who was standing at the bulkhead between first class and coach, bullhorn dangling at her side. The other two flight attendants were stationed by the open rear doors corralling passengers into lifeboats, while the first officer stood in the aisle making sure no one tried to exit out of turn. So far, no one was panicking—probably because they didn't know about the other looming threat.

"We'll get the passengers to the island," Rita said, meeting his gaze. "But we need you to keep them safe when we get there."

It was more of a plea than a command, and he heard her loud and clear.

"You can count on me."

He said it with confidence, even though his task was becoming increasingly difficult now that the potential suspects were scattering and the crime scene was sinking into the sea. There was no cell service here in the middle of the Atlantic, the comms were down, they were completely cut off. In a classic case of "be careful what you wish for," this murder was his to solve, on his own, with no help from anyone who knew what the hell they were doing.

He reflexively peeked down at his phone, as if it held the answers to how to proceed. To his astonishment, there was an unopened text message. *When did that come in?*

He clicked on it. It was from Special Agent Cooper.

> Murder victim Wilcox connected to Kessler hit-and-run

> Local reporter says Brendan Callahan in 21C witnessed, local police deny

> Crestwood Sherriff ignored evidence placing Wilcox's vehicle at scene

> Vehicle was reported stolen the next day

> FBI suspects a cover-up

> Call when able

Carlos reread the message twice, then a third time. It was the last communication he would get for a long time, and it was a lot to unpack. Did this mean his tip about Matthew Kessler proved helpful? Did the FBI think the murderer was connected to the unsolved hit-and-run? And if Cooper was telling him all of this, did that mean the FBI trusted him to take a more active role?

If he was grateful to be alive after that hair-raising descent, he was doubly grateful to have something to live for. The FBI had acted on his intel. That text indicated that they wanted—maybe even *needed*—his help.

And he would not let them down.

Buoyed by a renewed sense of purpose, he was eager to start questioning the passengers—the dead kid's mother, the possible eyewitness, the woman who'd smuggled that bat onto the plane—but they were busy jumping into life rafts. So he got up and walked over to the one person who, to his surprise, was available.

"Captain. A word?"

Captain Bancroft was standing by the open cockpit door, watching his flight crew evacuate the plane. The handful of first-class passengers were still in their seats waiting their turn to deplane, so Carlos beckoned him into the relative privacy of the cockpit.

"I haven't forgotten about the assailant," Bancroft told the marshal in a hushed tone once they were alone. "But my priority is getting the passengers off the plane. If it takes on too much water, it will sink like a stone."

"Understood." The captain was looking past him into the main cabin, as if the urgency in his eyes could make the evacuation happen faster.

"What's your theory why the engines failed, Captain?" Renaldo asked, because if there was a connection between the murder and the crash, that would be a significant development.

"Simple. We ran out of fuel."

"Sabotage?" Renaldo prompted. But Bancroft didn't take the bait.

"The plane was struck by lightning, Officer Renaldo. I think only God can do that."

Renaldo must have looked skeptical, because the captain added, "You're right to suspect a connection, but the fuel gauge told the story. We had eighteen thousand pounds of fuel before the lightning strike. Then, ten minutes later, we had none."

"When did you realize the fuel tanks were empty?"

Bancroft shook his head. "I should have realized it sooner. That's my mistake. I was hoodwinked by the avionics failure. I thought the gauges were malfunctioning."

"But they weren't?"

"They'll inspect this aircraft tail-to-nose, but the simplest explanation is usually the right one. The lightning strike punched a hole in the fuel tank. Gravity did the rest."

Renaldo didn't nod. Something still felt off. Double engine failure and murder were both extremely rare occurrences, could they really be unrelated?

"If this was an act of terror, there'd be signs," Bancroft continued. "No one made any demands of me. It was my choice how, when, and where to set the aircraft down. No one could have predicted I would do it here."

The airframe groaned and shifted beneath their feet. It was leveling off, the tail sinking to meet the nose.

"We should go," the captain said, indicating the cockpit door with a tic of his head, then extending an arm so Renaldo would walk through it.

The first-class cabin was empty now. The last few passengers were at the rear of the aircraft, queued up to jump. As Bancroft and Renaldo made their way down the aisle, Rita met them halfway with a life vest in each hand.

"The lifeboats are full," the breathless lead flight attendant said, handing them both a vest. "Some of the passengers are trying to swim to shore. It's only a couple hundred meters. Anyway, there's nothing I can do to stop them."

She looked at Renaldo, like that last bit was meant for him.

"There's nowhere for anyone to disappear to," Bancroft assured him. "It's an island. Barely five square miles and surrounded by water on all sides."

Rita grabbed a seatback for balance as sea water sloshed over their shoes.

"You'd better go, Rita," the captain said.

"Shall we hold the boats for you, Captain?"

"Negative," the former navy man replied. "Ridley knows his way around an airport and can help you when you get to shore."

"What about . . . ?" Her eyes darted toward the body.

"Officer Renaldo and I will take care of him."

Her face registered relief. "See you on the beach, Captain."

Renaldo watched as the first officer and three flight attendants hurried to deplane. And then he and the captain were the only two people left on board—well, *living* people.

A ghostly calm descended on the sinking capsule. The only sound was the patter of raindrops as the storm that kicked off this misadventure made an unwelcome reprise.

"We need to get out of here before that drizzle becomes a downpour," the captain said, beckoning Renaldo toward the rear of the plane. "Once the wings become submerged, they'll take the fuselage down with them."

Renaldo followed Bancroft into the aft galley and peered out the open door. The ocean swirled and spit. Yes, the worsening conditions were the most pressing concern. But not the only one.

"So?" Bancroft asked, reading his mind. "What are we doing with him?"

Renaldo was trained to handle just about any kind of in-flight emergency. He knew how to disarm an attacker, negotiate with a hostage-taker, and thanks to that walkie-talkie in the toilet incident, how to diffuse a bomb. But in his six years on the job, no one had taught him the *do*s and *don't*s of preserving a crime scene, and this one was next level.

"How long until someone rescues us?" Renaldo asked.

"Hard to say," Bancroft said as he gazed up at the gauzy, charcoal sky. "They're not going to send planes that can't land. And I have no idea where the nearest boats are. Could be hours."

Renaldo tried to imagine what the next few hours would bring. No one knew Billy Wilcox was missing yet, because while the plane was in the air they were all stuck in seats. But it wouldn't be long until someone noticed his absence and started asking where the hell he went.

"What does your agency want you to do?" Bancroft asked.

"I have no idea." *His agency.* He'd almost forgotten about them. What was the famous saying about crises? That they are an opportunity? Was this his opportunity to redeem himself? All he had to do was solve the murder and apprehend the murderer. By himself. With no experience or know-how. How hard could that be?

"We can detach the slide," Bancroft suggested. "Take him with us."

The tapping on the roof had become a steady drumroll. Renaldo didn't want to upset the crime scene. But he didn't want the poor guy to be fish food.

"How long do you think the plane will stay afloat?" Renaldo asked, practically shouting to be heard over the falling rain.

"We're lucky to still be standing here."

And Renaldo had his answer.

"Let's take him."

The captain removed the blazers. The victim was on his stomach, face pressed against the hard rubber floor. Bancroft rolled him over. His linen shirt was soaked with blood. His blue eyes were wide as soup spoons, and the whites rimmed with red. It was hard to tell in his current condition, but the man looked to be about Renaldo's age, maybe even younger. Renaldo felt a stab of guilt. If he hadn't been so consumed by his girl trouble, could he have prevented this?

Bancroft gripped the man's right arm. Renaldo swallowed his guilt and grabbed the left.

"One, two, THREE!"

Together, they pulled the dead man out of the lav.

"Take his feet," Bancroft ordered when they reached the door. Renaldo gripped the dead man's ankles.

"Easy now," Bancroft said, walking backward onto the slippery rubber while pulling the two hundred pounds of literal dead weight behind him. "We don't want to tip."

Rain was streaming from the sky. They were soaked within seconds. As Renaldo helped the captain maneuver the body into the center of the raft, he glanced at the man's face. Pink puddles of rainwater and blood were pooling in his bashed-in eye sockets.

"Let's cover him back up," Bancroft shouted over the rain.

Renaldo retrieved the blazers, then laid them over the victim.

"How are we going to get to shore?" he asked, shielding his eyes against the downpour to guesstimate how far it was to the beach. *Two . . . three hundred meters, maybe?* The other life rafts had survival kits with telescoping oars, but they only had themselves.

"We're going to swim," the captain said, then jumped into the whitecapped water.

Renaldo peered out at the one-hundred-some-odd silhouettes bouncing through the surf in their respective boats. In one of those packed life rafts, a cold-blooded killer sat shoulder-to-shoulder with innocent passengers who had no idea they were in danger. As rain battered the sinking capsule—a.k.a. his crime scene—he imagined the forensic evidence—blood spatters, skin cells, fingerprints—melting away like dirt at a car wash. Whoever bludgeoned that man to death was either an evil genius or the luckiest person on God's green earth.

"Jump in and push from behind," the captain said as he secured the tether to his waist then used his legs to push off from the sinking aircraft.

Despite a lighter load and no oars to steer it, the raft piloted by Captain Bancroft pulled ahead of the others. Its rectangular shape made it better suited for riding waves than the sixty-person octagons, and it was fast-approaching shore. Bancroft was pulling from the front, his arms windmilling through the water in a head-high lifeguard crawl. Renaldo was pushing from the back, flutter-kicking like a human outboard motor. Both were athletes and strong swimmers, but also let the motion of the ocean do the work, letting the waves pick them up and carry them toward the beach.

"I can touch here," Bancroft shouted.

Renaldo lowered his legs. "Me too!"

They were less than fifty meters out now—*almost there.* The full moon fought its way through the heather gray clouds, illuminating the sloping shoreline just beyond.

And something else.

At first Renaldo thought he was imagining it. His eyes were burning with seawater, and that gunmetal glint popping up out of the surf seemed incongruous. He wiped his eyes with the back of his hand, and the shape of the protrusion revealed itself—triangular, with the tip pointing straight up.

He blinked again. It was shiny . . . metallic? No not metal. Something much worse.

"Captain!"

He looked left: another one! Right: two more!

They were popping up all around him. He thought of his cargo, of the blood that was seeping off the raft into the water.

And he knew what they were.

CHAPTER

050

"Wave!" Coach Cal's failed pitcher-turned-outfielder, Ace Abernathy, called out as a wall of water rose up behind the life raft, lifting the back end then dropping it into the froth. With sixty bodies weighing it down, it was unlikely to flip, but Ace was his mother's son, so took it upon himself to tell everyone what they could see for themselves.

The ballplayers were split between the two rafts and brought the "team first" mentality Coach Cal had taught them to both. Ace was pinned to his mother's side—an indicator that he was a better son than he was a ball player. Cal was grateful to Penelope for growing his program, but he was not broken up that this was her last year. He wanted to put the devil's bargain they'd made behind him, which would be easier once she wasn't around.

Cathy, the unofficial captain of the lead boat, was perched on the bow, shouting occasional directions to "Paddle hard now!" and cheerleading, "You guys are doing great! Almost there!" Cal sat right behind her, arms poised to wrap around her waist if a big wave came, because he'd already lost her once, he wasn't going to let it happen again.

Also in his boat was the woman he'd betrayed—sitting at the back, where she didn't have to look at his lying face. Against his better instincts, when Francesca had confronted him in the galley an hour, but also a veritable *lifetime*, ago, he'd told her the truth. "I saw the car," he'd said. "And I knew who it belonged to. But I didn't come forward."

"Why?" Francesca had asked. "Why would you keep that to yourself?"

He'd wanted to explain that if it got out that one of his former players had killed a child right after they'd had a damn parade, his program—hell, the whole town—would forever live in infamy. The talented players would stop coming. The money would dry up. And that young man, who Coach Cal cared about despite the horrific thing he'd done, would get pulverized—by the press, his fellow citizens, a legal system that would show no mercy for this white boy who'd already had his fair share of lucky breaks. And, if the young man somehow survived all of that, he'd be left with no one but a father who'd never needed a reason to kick the shit out of him. It's not that he didn't care about justice, just that the price was too high.

But he hadn't told Francesca any of that. Instead, he'd simply said, "Because it would have led to more suffering."

"What about my suffering?" she'd asked. "Did you ever consider what it would do to me?"

He could have tried to blame Penelope, who'd masterminded the plan to make it all go away. Or Sheriff Eckles, who'd rubber-stamped it. But instead, all he said was "I'm sorry," because he couldn't tell her who he was protecting.

But also, maybe he didn't have to.

Because at that very moment, he appeared.

"Billy Wilcox?" he'd called out to him, disbelief spreading across his skin as if he'd conjured a ghost.

He'd watched Francesca's face as her former student scurried into the lavatory like a mouse who saw a cat. He didn't know how long it had been since Francesca had seen Billy, but there was no way she didn't remember the three-sport athlete whose face was perpetually dotted with bruises they both knew didn't come from errant foul balls. Was he right to talk her out of calling child services? Would her son still be alive if he had let her?

"Francesca? Are you OK?" Cathy had asked.

Francesca hadn't answered Cathy. Instead, she'd looked at him. He'd watched as suspicion engulfed her like a curtain falling. Before she could hold his feet to the fire, make him confirm what was painfully obvious, they hit a rough patch of air and were ordered to their seats.

"Here comes another wave," Ace shouted to his fellow raft passengers. "Hold on!"

Cal wrapped his arms around Cathy's waist as their boat buckled under the breaking wave. As sea water pummeled his skin, his body was a swirl of adrenaline and dread. He didn't know what Francesca would do now that she knew the truth, just that she was a woman with nothing more to lose.

CHAPTER

051

As the lifeboat carrying Francesca, Coach Cal, and the two Abernathys rode the swell like a wobbly dinnerplate, a few boat-lengths behind them, besties Angela Diaz and Jillian Azarian huddled shoulder-to-shoulder with their fingers threaded together like when they were five. Angie had thought her childhood girlfriend would disown her when she showed her that police report, but—to Angie's surprise—her best friend had seemed almost relieved.

"I knew he still loved you," Jillian had confessed as the airplane careened toward the sea.

"He was wasted," Angie had responded to ease the blow. She could have denied it, but if they were going to die in a plane crash, she didn't want the last words she spoke to be a lie.

"Don't make excuses for him!" Jillian had shot back. She was trying to get the life vest over her head, but it wouldn't go, so Angie reached up to help her.

"Hold on, it's stuck on your tiara."

Jilly's face reddened with embarrassment. "Can you take it off me?" she asked, because wearing a tiara while hurtling toward near-certain death was as absurd as marrying a man to make him love her. They both knew that was her plan. And that it would never work.

"I'm so sorry, Jills," Angie told her best friend as she untangled the tiara from Jillian's hair. She wasn't apologizing for her part in it, only the pain it had caused.

"I'm sorry too," Jillian had replied, taking that tiara from Angie's outstretched hand then squeezing it in her fist until it broke in half.

As the earth rose to meet the plummeting airplane, sorrow wrapped around them like a heavy cloak. The weight of their unspoken regrets was almost too much to bear. Angie wanted to apologize for so many things—for not telling Jillian about the lingering love in Billy's eyes; for filing that police report instead of coming to her; for letting the trust between them erode away; for letting Jillian construct a fantasy about Billy she knew was a lie. But above all of that, in what could have been her final moments on earth, Angie felt sorry for every woman who'd suffered at the hands of a man. Every woman who'd been degraded, assaulted, made to feel powerless. There were so many of them. All of them, perhaps. And her impulse to shove it under the rug filled her with shame, because if she didn't speak out, who would?

"What am I going to do now?" Jillian had asked her best friend as the sharp edge of the broken tiara cut into her skin. The wedding was off. There were a lot of unknowns, but that much was certain.

"We're in this together. Whatever you do, you'll do it with me by your side." And then it was time to brace. And neither of them worried about the future because the present was all they had.

But they'd survived. And now they were in a lifeboat with the other survivors—parents, cousins, bridesmaids, groomsmen—who would ask, "Where's Billy?" and they would have to get their story straight because there was no going back.

CHAPTER

052

Fifty meters from shore, Carlos Renaldo's fight-or-flight instinct kicked into overdrive.

"Shark!" he called out as shimmering gray triangles sliced through the ocean's surface. "Get out of the water!"

He slapped his palms down on the rain-soaked rubber. The top of the raft was slick. As soon as he pushed the ocean floor away with his legs, his hands slipped, and he was back in the water with a splash.

Adrenaline coursed through his veins as he tried again. Slipped again. He knew the more he flailed around, the more enticing he would be to his predator, but also that it was too late. Those sharks smelled blood. He was that doomed swimmer in *Jaws* right before the great white sunk his teeth into her ribs and tore her in half.

Rain was pelting his head, blurring his vision. He extended his arms and tried to grasp the raft with his fingertips one last time, but he couldn't get a grip.

All around him, shark fins were popping to the surface. "I can't get on the raft!" he shouted. Despite being from the island of Puerto Rico, he and the ocean were not friends. He'd never surfed or boogie boarded. If you asked him if he'd rather stare down an armed gunman or a shark, he'd pick the gunman every time.

"Whoa, whoa, take it easy," Bancroft called out from the front of the raft, where he was standing in chest-deep water. "Those aren't sharks, they're suitcases." He grabbed one and knocked on the hard casing. "They're not going to bite you."

Renaldo blinked and the metallic triangle poking out of the water came into focus. Embarrassment rolled over his skin. "I'm an idiot."

"There are definitely sharks here, you're smart to be on the lookout," Bancroft said so he wouldn't feel like a total dumbass. "Let's keep going."

Renaldo's legs churned beneath him as he guided the raft toward the beach. Chest-high water became waist-high became knee-high, and then they were standing on the shoreline, their shoes caked in clumpy sand.

"Over there!" Bancroft shouted, pointing to an overturned rowboat up the beach. "We can cover him with that."

It was much harder to push the squishy rubber through sand than it was through water. Renaldo's thighs and shoulders burned with the effort. At one point, the captain abandoned his tether and joined him in the back, and they pushed together until they reached the abandoned dinghy.

Wordlessly, they lifted the little wooden boat and placed it over the victim so that it covered him like a domed lid. It was inelegant, but an effective barrier against the rain and prying eyes.

"We'll leave him here for now," Bancroft said. "Let's go help the others."

Bancroft took off running down the beach. Several passengers had already jumped out into the froth and were steering the octagons through the shallow water. Renaldo shivered as he took in the D-Day-esque scene. One hundred and twenty-five passengers were marching, stumbling, crawling onto the beach. One passenger tripped in the surf, and another swooped in to help her up. A mother hugged her son, a husband held his wife as she wept into his chest. Failures, disappointments, mistrust had all been washed away by gratitude to be alive—at least for the moment.

And what about him? In times of crisis, it's natural—instinctual, even—to think of the person you love. What would Katie feel when she found out Flight 868 had crashed into the sea? Would the thought she'd nearly lost him make her realize that she loved him too? And what difference would it make? They couldn't be together, not if she wanted to stay in her career and he in his. And with passengers in danger and a murder to solve, he realized he was right where he belonged.

He swiped the rain-soaked hair out of his eyes and jogged down the beach. Everyone was out of the water now, but some were heading back in to grab the suitcases that were getting tossed around in the foam. A pile was forming at the water's edge. A few people were hunting through it, looking for theirs.

"Just grab one and we'll sort it out in the hangar," he heard Captain Bancroft tell the bewildered passengers, then looked to where he was pointing. Martini Cay "airport" was nothing more than a dimly lit landing strip that dead-ended at the beach. There was no terminal, no control tower, no signs of life. The only structure was a barn-shaped hangar beside the runway. It was the obvious place to seek shelter, given that it was the only place.

"Do we really need to take the suitcases?" Renaldo asked, as he joined Bancroft at the shoreline, because it was a recipe for chaos, and hadn't they had enough of that?

"We don't know how long we'll be here," Bancroft said. "They may contain useful items."

The baseball players were doubling up, taking a suitcase in each hand before heading up the beach. Renaldo realized the captain was right—those suitcases might contain medicine, food, clean clothes, and comfort items that would keep the passengers calm—so he followed suit, grabbing an oversized bag and joining the moving caravan. Of the one hundred and twenty-five remaining passengers, only the doctor and the kid who'd opened that lavatory door knew about the act of violence that had been committed—literally—behind their backs. Once they were crammed into that hangar, those boys were bound to start talking. Wilcox's loved ones would start looking. He imagined panic spreading like wildfire. He wouldn't have much time.

As he trudged through the sand, he went over what he knew. Angela

Diaz had filed a police report accusing Billy Wilcox of rape. She'd left out his name, but she had to know the police would figure out who it was from the other information she'd provided. She and Wilcox had argued in the terminal. She was clearly angry . . . *but angry enough to kill?* Or maybe someone who wanted Wilcox dead had witnessed them arguing, then filed that police report to cast suspicion on her. The fiancée, maybe? But why would she kill the man she was on her way to marry?

He considered the bride-to-be. She'd left her groom's side to visit her bridesmaids in the main cabin. Then, twenty minutes later, Wilcox came looking for her. At the time, Carlos thought it was because he missed her. Now he wasn't so sure. Wilcox knew what he'd done to Angela Diaz. But did his bride? What if she'd just found out? She never went back to her seat. Did she notice her man never did either? Or was she the person who'd made sure he wouldn't?

As wet sand crunched under his feet, he thought about the other potential suspects. According to Agent Cooper's text, Billy Wilcox was connected to that unsolved hit-and-run. The mother of the victim was on the flight. Was that a coincidence? Or had she boarded the plane with a mission?

And what about all those boys? Matthew Kessler had been their teammate. Had one of them decided to take revenge on the person they thought killed their friend? The murder weapon was a baseball bat, after all.

Finally, there was the mystery of Brendan Callahan. Per Cooper's text, a local reporter was claiming she saw Callahan at the scene. But the local police denied that. So was he there or not?

He cursed himself for his negligence. Who had slipped past him on the airplane? Francesca Kessler? One of the boys? Angela Diaz? The bride-to-be? Given how preoccupied he'd been, a mariachi band could have walked by without him noticing. God damn it, why had he chosen that moment to write that text?

The beach ended in a berm of loose rocks and seagrass. Just beyond that was the airport. If you could call that sorry strip of asphalt an airport.

Still, it was a place to gather. And once they were gathered, he'd go in search of answers.

As he reached the top of the berm, he spied a trim, sixtyish man struggling to get a suitcase up the incline. He put down the one he was carrying to give the man a hand.

"I got it," Carlos said, reaching down and taking the bag from him. As he set it down, his eyes caught the name and address on the luggage tag: *W. Wilcox, Crestwood, CA*. He knew from studying the manifest that there was another Wilcox on board, but not if they were related. The victim's father, perhaps?

"Thanks," the man said, clambering up beside him.

"You all right?" Carlos asked.

And for some reason, that made the man laugh. "Fucking helluva flight."

"I can carry that suitcase the rest of the way," Carlos said, to find out if this man was W. Wilcox from Crestwood or was schlepping someone else's bag.

"Nah, it's all right, I never pack more than I can carry," the man said, confirming that he was.

"I'm Carlos."

"Walter."

They shook hands. Walter Wilcox's grip was surprisingly strong.

"You part of the wedding party?" Carlos asked, curious why he wasn't with any of the other wedding-goers.

"There's not going to be a wedding," the old man quipped.

"No, I don't imagine," Carlos said, assuming he meant there was not going to be a wedding *this weekend*, because how could there be? Unless they had it here.

"He never deserved her," Walter Wilcox said as he picked up his suitcase. "No one's going to cry over him."

And Carlos wondered if he'd misunderstood.

CHAPTER

053

"I got you," Brendan said, reaching down from the top of the berm. Cathy had taken off her shoes before jumping in the life raft and was trying to climb up the jumble of rocks in bare feet.

"Thanks," she said, grabbing onto the hand she'd held during the best years of her life. Yes, she'd enjoyed her adventures as a flight attendant—this one aside—but she could never love anything as much as she loved her husband. Had she been too hard on him? Or was the trauma of the last hour messing with her head?

Brendan's palm was slick, but his grip was firm as he pulled her up the incline. The wind was sucking her rain-soaked pants against her thighs, making the skin on her legs raw with cold. She was soaked to the bone, but she was alive. *They* were alive. No, she and Brendan weren't a "they" anymore, but you'd never know it by the relief she felt that he was here with her.

"C'mon, let's go get dry," he said, putting a gentle hand on her back and steering her toward the shelter.

The airplane hangar was right off the airstrip—a no-nonsense rectangular building with rolling barn doors and a corrugated aluminum roof. Besides a few lonely-looking palm trees, there was nothing else in sight. The pint-sized parking lot had no cars. The grassy tie-down area had no planes. As far as airports went, this one was as rinky-dink as it got.

First Officer Ridley had gone ahead and was standing guard at the hangar door, checking out the passengers as they filed through it.

"What should we do with the suitcases?" Brendan asked the first officer.

"I'm asking passengers to line them up against the back wall," Ridley said, "so it's easier to spot whose is whose."

Brendan nodded, then started directing his suitcase-toting players toward the staging area. "If you find your own bag, you can take it," he told them. "Otherwise, leave them against the wall."

Cathy watched the man she'd vowed to love "for better or for worse" keep his boys calm by keeping them busy. He had such a great way with them—always patient and kind. She'd never looked to her husband to take care of her, but that didn't mean he hadn't. Today was a perfect example. Any number of passengers could have raised their hand to help her, but, like always, Brendan was the one who had.

"No bathrooms, no running water," Fonzie announced, joining her and Ridley by the hangar door. "The only thing in here besides us is that," he said, pointing to an aging Land Cruiser parked near the back. "And unless it can sprout wings or an outboard motor, it's not going to be much help."

"At least we have power," Cathy said, glancing up at the rusted pendant lights suspended from the ceiling like soda caps on strings. The light they emitted was dull and yellow, casting a spooky amber pall over the hangar's occupants.

"Well, hopefully we won't be here long," Fonzie said.

"From your lips," Cathy said, then walked over to where Brendan was overseeing the assembly line of players lining up the luggage.

"Hey," Brendan said, taking a step toward her. She breathed easier just being near him.

"Thanks for helping."

The corners of his eyes floated up in that smile she was certain he reserved just for her. "I like your purple hair," he said, reaching up to push a stray piece off her forehead.

"Some people think I lost my mind."

"You look good in purple."

"Not just because of the hair." Her cheeks warmed with the confession. Brendan Callahan was widely considered Crestwood's most eligible bachelor, and she a fool for leaving him.

"If anybody did something incomprehensible, it's me," he countered. As he lowered his arm, the backs of his fingers brushed her cheek. It was all she could do not to lean into his hand. *God, she missed his touch.*

She hadn't planned to tell him, but the words just spilled out.

"Brendan," she said, lowering her voice to just above a whisper, "something terrible happened while we were still in the air. Before the engine failure, I mean."

His face grew dark like the storm clouds overhead. "I know about the dead man in the lavatory. It's all the boys are talking about."

She pressed her lips together as the memory flashed in her mind—the lifeless body, the spattered walls, the rivulets of blood. A tremor of fear swirled with her grief.

"What happened to him?" Brendan asked. And Cathy spoke the scary word.

"He was murdered."

He nodded slowly, like she was confirming what he already knew.

"The air marshal is investigating," she continued, "but the circumstances aren't ideal, given that all the evidence is at the bottom of the ocean."

"Is that why the engines failed?" he asked. "Are the incidents related?"

She wondered about that too. "I don't think he knows."

"Poor Kai. What a thing to see," Brendan said, his voice cracking with emotion. As always, his heart was with his players. And that's why she had to tell him.

"You knew him," she said.

"Knew who?"

"The victim."

Brendan shook his head. "My boys are all here. I counted them."

"It wasn't one of the players," Cathy said, then corrected herself. "Not a current one, that is."

And this confused Brendan. "Then who?"

"Billy Wilcox."

Brendan's face turned to ash. Cathy knew how deeply he once cared for Billy—staying after practice to give him the love he wasn't getting at home.

But his confession still stunned her.

"It was Billy's car I saw, Cath. That night. I placed it right after I hung up with you. There was an ASU sticker on the back bumper. It was Billy's, I'm sure of it."

Cathy's mouth fell open. Not because she was surprised to learn whose car Brendan had seen, but because she hadn't figured it out herself. Who else would Brendan have protected no matter what the cost? Well, except for her.

"When I told Sheriff Eckles," he continued, "he convinced me not to say anything until he worked out how to protect him."

"Protect him from who?"

"I don't know. The media, his father . . . honestly, I can't remember. He asked for a few days to work some things out. Then a few days became a few weeks. The longer I waited to speak out, the harder it got. I know it was wrong not to come forward, but . . ."

He didn't finish the sentence—didn't have to. Everyone knew how Brendan had tried to protect the boy with the dead mother and abusive father. *Everyone.*

Cathy's hand flew over her mouth as the realization hit her.

"I know that's a piss-poor excuse," he started, misinterpreting her gasp.

"It's not that."

"Then what?"

"Francesca Kessler knows how you always had that boy's back."

"So?"

"You told her you saw the car and that you knew who it belonged to."

The air between them grew eerily still. "Wait a second. You don't think . . . ?"

"That a grieving woman with nothing else to live for would want revenge?" she asked like the answer wasn't obvious. "Wouldn't you? She was right there in the galley. And think about the timing. It happened right after you told her you'd seen the car."

He shook his head. But as he opened his mouth, no doubt to tell her there was no way—

"Brendan Callahan?" a man's voice interrupted, and Cathy turned to see the air marshal standing behind her, cupping his badge in his open palm. "I'm Officer Carlos Renaldo. Do you mind if I ask you a few questions?"

"What about?" Brendan asked.

"I'm working with the FBI on a case involving a former player of yours. Do you remember Matthew Kessler?"

Cathy's breath caught in her throat. Had the air marshal figured it out too?

"Of course," Brendan replied.

"We heard from a source that you were on scene the night he was killed." *Source? What source?* Cathy's heart thrummed in her chest. There was only one reason he'd be asking about that here, now, with Billy Wilcox lying dead on that plane.

"That's right."

"And that you may have seen the car that struck him."

Cathy stood soldier-still as they waited for him to confirm or deny. The notion that a person should always tell the truth seemed so juvenile to her now. Pilots lie to their passengers to avoid panic. Parents lie to their children to make them feel safe. There are many instances where a good-intentioned lie is preferable to the truth. But once Cathy climbed up on that high horse, she couldn't find her way back down. Should Brendan have told the truth about what he'd seen that night? Of course. But she understood why he couldn't bring himself to hurt the surrogate for the son he never had, especially if the sheriff himself told him they'd all be better off if he kept his mouth shut.

She tried to send him a message with her mind. *Don't tell him.*

"I was there, but I didn't see anything."

And she gave him an invisible nod of approval. Because while she didn't believe in an eye for an eye, she also had begun to see how putting an end to suffering might be a noble ideal, and that Francesca Kessler had suffered enough.

CHAPTER

054

"Thanks for speaking with me," Carlos Renaldo said to the baseball coach, even though their conversation had left him more confused. Brendan Callahan was either a witness who didn't see anything, or a witness who didn't want to say anything. If only he had the investigative skills to figure out which one it was.

Agent Cooper had texted that the FBI suspected a cover-up, and it certainly smelled like it. But he couldn't sniff out who the fine people of Crestwood were protecting and why. Billy Wilcox was not exactly a pillar of the community. So why would the local sheriff suppress testimony and evidence that implicated him in Matthew Kessler's death?

He took a minute to survey the passengers. The events of the last two hours had kicked the shit out of them. They were all exhausted and soaked to the bone. A few of them had their phones out, presumably using whatever apps didn't require an internet connection to pass the time. It was precarious being cut off from the world, but it was also an opportunity for him to solve this case and surprise everyone, including himself. It might be too late to save his career, but if Billy Wilcox's killer had another target in their sights, he might save a life.

He flashed back to what Billy's father had said about there not being a wedding. Did he mean postponed because of the plane crash? Or was he aware of trouble brewing? "No one would cry for him," he'd said.

Because he'd been dumped? Or killed? Were there others who knew the wedding might not happen? Or didn't *want* it to happen? And how far might they go to stop it?

His eyes landed on the baseball team, huddled together like they were meeting on the mound. Just beyond them, their coaches and chaperones kept watchful eyes. Whoever organized this trip had to arrange hotels, buses, and plane tickets. It had to have been planned months in advance. Just like that destination wedding. Was it possible someone in Crestwood knew Billy Wilcox would be traveling to Puerto Rico on the same day as the Crestwood baseball team and saw a once-in-a-lifetime opportunity? Could that someone be Francesca Kessler?

Matthew Kessler's death was an unsolved hit-and-run. But just because the police hadn't solved it didn't mean Francesca Kessler hadn't. She didn't look like the vigilante-justice type, but he knew better than to judge a book by its cover.

He knew what Francesca looked like from her driver's license photo in the manifest, so when he spotted her waiting in line to peruse the suitcases, he went over to talk to her.

"Hello," he said as he sidled up beside her. She smiled curtly at him, then turned her head away, balling her fists under her armpits as she crossed her arms across her chest. Was she hiding her hands? Or just cold?

"Rough flight," he said, taking in her profile. Her features were delicate—softly sloping chin, button nose. Her collarbone pressed into her still-damp silk blouse. He knew better than to think a slight woman couldn't be strong, but also, he was having a hard time imagining her driving a bat into someone's face.

"We're lucky to be alive, I suppose," she said without a hint of emotion.

"Is that how you feel? Lucky?"

She shrugged. "I'm working on it," she said, staring straight ahead.

"You're no stranger to trauma," he continued, following his instincts. Because in the absence of investigative experience, that's all he had.

"Everybody has trauma."

"Yes, but you lost a son."

Her head snapped around. "What do you know about that?"

"Carlos Renaldo, Federal Air Marshal," he said, flashing his badge. "I'm part of the team investigating what happened the night your son was killed."

Her expression grew hard, her body language guarded. "I was told the case was closed."

"We found cause to reopen it."

She blinked a few times. *Was she surprised? Or concerned?* "How can I help?"

"We've been tracking the movements of a fellow passenger named William Wilcox. Goes by Billy. Do you know him?" he asked, being deliberate about his use of the present tense.

"I'm a teacher at Crestwood High School," she said. "He was in one of my classes. Played sports, as I recall." It was risky, revealing evidence in an open investigation, but he did it anyway.

"Were you aware his vehicle was at the scene?"

"At the scene of what?" she asked dumbly, like the death of her son wasn't the defining moment of her life.

"The hit-and-run that killed your son."

"Who told you that?"

"The FBI placed his car there," he said, parroting Cooper's text message.

Her brow grew heavy with skepticism. "When? Why wasn't I told?" Was she trying to establish she didn't know Wilcox had been at the scene of the accident? Or was she genuinely confounded?

"The evidence was there all along. But nobody bothered to check it out." It was a wild theory, but he couldn't help but wonder if, in covering it up, the powers-that-be had given her a chance to exact her revenge.

"Are you saying someone covered it up?" she asked.

"Sure seems that way."

"Who would do that?"

MRS. BEATRICE "BEA" BOOKBINDER: Is this Special Agent Sam Cooper?

SPECIAL AGENT SAM COOPER: Yes. Hello, Bea.

BEA: I called Sergei, like you asked.

COOPER: Sergei?

BEA: Sorry. Sergei is our IT person. I thought I told you that.

COOPER: Go on.

BEA: I told him the FBI wanted to know what IP address that police report was filed from. You know, the stolen Ford Bronco?

COOPER: Yes, that's the one we're interested in.

BEA: Sergei said . . . hold on, let me check my notes. OK, here it is. He said the stolen vehicle report was filed at 8:06 a.m. on May 13th, 2023, and the IP address associated with the filing came from inside the building.

COOPER: Inside which building?

BEA: The police station.

COOPER: You mean . . . by someone in the police department?

BEA: Yes. And I can tell you, the only people at the station that morning were me and the sheriff. The deputies all had the morning off. Y'know, because of the parade the day before. And of course the accident that night. (Tsk, sigh.) That poor boy.

COOPER: So the only two people who could have reported that car stolen were you and Sheriff Eckles?

BEA: That's right. And it wasn't me.

CHAPTER

055

Francesca could feel anger erupting deep down in her belly. Cal had told her on the plane that he'd seen the car, but he couldn't go public with what he knew because it would "lead to more suffering." At the time it made no sense. But now it did. The word "cover-up" explained everything.

Her confusion turned to rage. She was so mad she wanted to punch that lying, two-faced piece of shit right in his big, fat—

"Miss?" the woman behind her said, tapping her lightly on the shoulder. "It's your turn," she said brightly.

"Oh, thanks." Francesca had been so distracted by her murderous thoughts, she hadn't noticed it was her turn to peruse the line of suitcases. She took a step forward, eyes cast down as her heart galloped in her chest. When the flight took off earlier that day, her mission was simple: Get one of Matthew's former teammates to tell her something—*anything*—that would help her figure out who killed her son. This trip was her last chance. The last few remaining kids who'd played with Matthew would be graduating in less than a month. After that, she'd never see any of them again.

There were eight boys on this trip who were at the game the night Matthew died. She had five days. She'd figured she could corner them one by one. Maybe even leverage something she got out of one to pressure another. But in the end, she didn't need five days. Or any trickery. It was that air marshal who furnished the clue that would crack the case.

She should have figured it out long ago. Sheriff Eckles was being way too nice to her, with those restaurant meals and that stupid tree planting ceremony. As if a tree could replace her flesh-and-blood son. She'd believed the sheriff when he told her the evidence was inconclusive. And that there were no witnesses. *What a fucking liar.*

Yes, she was furious at Coach Cal for suppressing evidence. But she knew he'd been bullied by the biggest bullies in town. Penelope wanted to protect her precious baseball program. Sheriff Eckles wanted to protect everything else. Plus, Cal said he'd seen the *car*, not the driver. They probably gaslit him into thinking he didn't see anything at all. She imagined them threatening him—"You'll lose everything you worked so hard to build," from Penelope; "Just keep your mouth shut and let us handle it," from the sheriff. Cal must have been terrified.

There was only one person important enough to make Alan Eckles and Penelope Abernathy do something so depraved. The sheriff and the Baseball Booster Club president would have gone to the ends of the earth to protect him—he'd turned Crestwood from a small-town laughingstock to the high school baseball capital of the world. His name was on the "Welcome to Crestwood" sign at the edge of town, his picture was in the barber shop, his uniform was behind glass in the school gym. If it got out that *the* Trey Turnberry had killed a boy—a baseball-playing boy, no less—the whole town would implode. Turnberry was the goose that laid the golden egg. Whenever the baseball team needed something—new sod, lights, a scoreboard in center field—all they had to do was ask him to sign something for them to auction off. Crestwood baseball even had its own store on eBay where fans could buy his signed rookie cards, baseballs, bats, jerseys, the mitt he wore in the All-Star game. Of course Billy Wilcox would loan his car to his old friend who'd arrived from Chicago by plane and didn't have one. But he wouldn't go to jail for him! So he, Penelope, and

Sheriff Eckles conspired to sweep it under the rug while Brendan Callahan looked the other way.

Rage coursed through her veins. Just because Sheriff Eckles wouldn't put Crestwood's golden boy behind bars didn't mean she wouldn't. Crestwood PD may have refused to properly investigate, but there were others who could—the District Attorney, the FBI, the DOJ, or—if none of them would listen—the local news. This story was too big for them to pass up. And she was too pissed off not to tell it. After three years of wandering aimlessly in and out of days, the justice she so desperately craved was so close she could taste it. She couldn't wait to see the look on Sheriff Eckles's ugly mug when she exposed him for what he'd done.

Her clothes were cold and heavy against her skin, and she couldn't do anything while she was stranded on a desert island, so she scanned the suitcases to try to find hers. As she walked between the dwindling piles, she thought about the troubled young man who'd gotten caught in the crosshairs of Sheriff and Penelope's evil machinations. They probably bullied him too. Poor Billy Wilcox had no family to speak of. He, Trey, and Penelope's oldest son, Nolan, had been like brothers—Crestwood's very own Three Musketeers—as admired as they were inseparable. So where was Nolan that night? How deep did this cover-up go?

Not all of the suitcases had made it, and many passengers were walking away disappointed. She thought she would be one of them, but then, right before she reached the end of the line, something on the floor caught her eye. A lavender ribbon. And just beyond it, a sand-encrusted black Samsonite.

She picked up her ribbon and reached for the suitcase, tying it back on the handle where it belonged. The tag identifying it as hers was missing, torn off in the crash, no doubt. The wheels were too caked with sand to roll, so she lifted it. Or tried to lift it. It was heavier than she expected. Did that mean it was filled with water? God, she hoped not.

She wanted to get out of the other passengers' way, so she flipped the suitcase on its side, then bent over and pushed it toward an unoccupied corner of the hangar. All around her, people were using their open suitcases as privacy shields to slip out of their soiled clothes. It was dark, and she was beyond caring if anyone saw her in her bra. Like everyone else, she just wanted to get warm and dry.

She crouched down and unzipped the bag. And what she saw confused her. Yes, she'd brought plain, white T-shirts, but she'd rolled hers and these were laid flat. She'd heard that TSA agents occasionally open bags to inspect the contents, had they done that to hers? She really wanted this to be her suitcase, so she moved the shirts aside to see what was underneath them.

That's when she saw the money. Rows upon rows of crisp hundred-dollar bills, jammed into Ziploc bags, piled one on top of the other in neat, little grids. Her hand flew over her mouth as she gasped. Her math-science brain couldn't resist doing the calculation. There are a hundred bills in a bundle. Each Ziploc bag held eight bundles, or eight hundred bills. There were two rows of three bags, and those two-by-three grids were stacked six rows deep. Thirty-six bundles would contain 28,800 one-hundred-dollar bills . . . or just under three million dollars.

She slammed the lid of the suitcase closed.

And prayed the owner hadn't seen her open it.

CHAPTER

056

"I found your suitcase," Angie said, pushing the brown-and-gold Louis Vuitton rolling trunk up to where Jillian was sitting. "I thought maybe you'd like to change into dry clothes."

The bride-to-be was tucked behind the Land Cruiser like she wasn't ready to face the wedding-goers. Or answer their questions about why she wasn't with Billy.

"You open it," Jillian said. "I can't look at that stuff."

Angie laid the trunk on its side and clicked open the latch. As she lifted the lid, her eyes landed on a sea of white: a floor-length Armani sheath for the reception; a silk negligée for bedtime; a Lilly Pulitzer shift dress for the next day's brunch.

"How about this beach cover-up with leggings?" Angie asked, fishing out the only clothes that didn't scream "bride!" They were even dry, thanks to the airtight seal on that fancy trunk.

Jillian took the outfit from Angie's outstretched hand. "Where am I supposed to change?"

Angie stood up and pulled on the passenger side door of the SUV. To her surprise, it opened. "How about in here?"

Jillian clutched her dry clothes to her chest and climbed up into the

Land Cruiser. As Angie closed the door behind her, she heard an unfamiliar voice speak her name.

"Miss Diaz?"

Angie spun around to see a man with tanned skin and light eyes staring at her. He wasn't with the wedding party and didn't look like he worked for the airline. *So how did he know her name?*

"Yes?"

"I'm Carlos Renaldo," he said, flashing the badge on his belt. "Federal Air Marshal. May I have a word?"

Her heartbeat picked up speed. "My friend's just changing inside the car," she stammered. "I have to stand guard."

"That's fine. We can talk here."

"What about?"

"A colleague on the ground relayed to me that you filed a police report earlier today. Right before takeoff."

Guilt washed over her like cold rain. Yes, what Billy did was wrong. And she had every right—a duty, even—to file that report. But she hadn't thought about how it would end. "What about it?"

"You declined to identify your attacker," he reminded her, in case she'd forgotten.

Angie didn't move or breathe. Did that mean she could pretend it wasn't Billy? The person who needed to know already did, the report had served its purpose.

"I'm not sure if you're aware, but the bar where you work . . . I believe it's called the Cliff Diver?" He paused to let her confirm.

"That's right."

"They still had the CCTV footage."

She didn't know what he wanted her to say, so she just shrugged.

"Does the name Billy Wilcox mean anything to you?" he asked.

There was no point trying to deny their relationship. Everyone in Crestwood knew they'd been a couple. "He's my ex-boyfriend."

"How long were you together?"

"Six years. The last two years of high school, and then the four years he was in college. But most of that was long distance." She told herself that it was law enforcement's job to follow up on a police report, this was all perfectly normal.

"Were you together the night Matthew Kessler was killed?"

Wait. What? Why was he asking about that?

"I can't access my notes because my tablet is still on the plane," he continued, "but I believe the date was May 12, 2023."

"Yes," she confirmed. "We were together then."

"What about that night?"

"What about it?"

"Did you go to the parade together?"

"No, I missed the parade. I was working."

"What time did you get off work?"

"I don't know exactly. Earlier than usual. Everyone was at the game, it was really quiet."

"So you met Billy at the ballgame, then?"

"No, after. I went home and showered first."

"He drove to your house to see you, then?" *Why did he want to know that?*

"No. I picked him up."

"From where?"

"The baseball field. He called me when the game ended. I met him at the Chevron station across the street because the school parking lot was a zoo."

"Did anyone see you guys there?"

"Where? At the gas station?" The air marshal nodded. "Billy tried to buy beer but the guy wouldn't sell it to him because of how drunk he was, so yeah, someone saw him."

"What about his car?"

"What about it?"

"How did he get to the game that night, did he drive there?"

"I mean, probably. Why?"

"Did you know that he reported his car stolen the next morning?"

And this surprised Angie. "I did not."

"Is that why he needed you to pick him up? Because someone stole his car?"

"Like I said, I don't know anything about his car being stolen. I picked him up because he'd been drinking and didn't want to drive. Couldn't drive." *None of them should have been driving*, she could have added.

"So you have no idea what happened to his car that night."

She shook her head. The truth was, she knew when he "couldn't find" that car for three days that something strange was going on. And, obviously, that a boy had been killed in a hit-and-run. She also knew who he'd been hanging out with that night. But she'd never connected the dots.

"Is it possible he loaned the car to someone? And then maybe forgot that he'd done that?" the air marshal pressed.

"It's possible, I guess," she said, because she only knew what Billy had told her, and he hadn't told her that.

Officer Renaldo nodded and asked her the question Sheriff Eckles should have asked her three years ago.

"Who do you think that could be?"

SPECIAL AGENT SAM COOPER: Is this Mohammed Ahmed?

MOHAMMED AHMED: Yes, please call me Mo.

COOPER: Mr. Ahmed, can you confirm that you own the Chevron station across from Crestwood High School?

MO: I do.

COOPER: My name is Special Agent Sam Cooper of the FBI Violent Crimes Division. I'm calling on the off-chance you remember the night of May 12, 2023. A boy was killed—

MO: Matthew Kessler. Of course I remember. All the Crestwood High boys used to come in for candy bars after school. A couple of them were troublemakers, but not Matthew. I was sorry to hear of his passing.

COOPER: Were you working at the gas station that night, per chance?

MO: Yes. Normally my son works the register. But he wanted to go to the baseball game at Crestwood, and I didn't have the heart to say no. Trey Turnberry threw out the first pitch.

COOPER: That's right. I'm trying to track the movements of a young man who was at the game. I'm going to text you his picture right now.
(Beat.)

COOPER: Please let me know when you get it.

MO: Oh, Billy Wilcox!

COOPER: You know him?

MO: Of course. He played baseball. I used to give him and the other boys Gatorade after the games.

COOPER: Did you give him any Gatorade the night Matthew Kessler was killed?

MO: No, but I probably should have. He came in here drunk as a skunk. I had to help his poor girlfriend get him in the car.

COOPER: Was that Angela Diaz?

MO: I don't know her name. She was a pretty little thing though.

COOPER: So the girlfriend, she drove him home, then?

MO: I don't know where they went, but they definitely left together.

COOPER: And there's no way he got behind the wheel.

MO: Absolutely not. I never would have allowed it.

COOPER: Do you remember what kind of car the girlfriend drove?

MO: Little sporty thing. A Miata maybe?

COOPER: Not a Bronco?

MO: I think I would know a Bronco from a Miata. I own a gas station.

CHAPTER

057

Captain Brett Bancroft didn't like being idle, but his aircraft was at the bottom of the Atlantic, so what else could he do but wait? It was still raining—hard. And with no way to communicate with the outside world, he had no idea how long until the cavalry came or who it would be. The Coastguard? Squids from Guantanamo Bay? The aircraft's transponder was relaying their location, they'd have no trouble finding the crash site. It was getting there that was the problem.

As he looked around at families huddled together, boys playing catch, passengers who'd found their belongings sharing their clothes and food with those who had not, he felt a mix of emotions—pride that he'd gotten these people to safety; sadness for the one who didn't make it; fear that the person who'd taken a life on his watch didn't plan to stop at just one. Now that he wasn't trying to land a plane with no engines, the reality that there was a murderer among them took center stage. He saw the air marshal talking to various passengers. Should he be helping him home in on a suspect? Probably. They may not have been in the air, but he was still responsible for these passengers' safety.

As he started across the hangar to collect his first officer who was similarly pacing with impatience, an incongruous noise broke through the steady thrum of rain.

"Do you hear that?" he asked Ridley.

"Hear what?"

"The airplane landing."

Ridley's face registered surprise. "Could the company get a jet here this fast?"

Bancroft shook his head. "Not a jet. No one would be foolish enough to land a jet aircraft on this runway," he quipped.

"So a prop plane then?"

Bancroft nodded. "It's taxiing now."

"Maybe they sent us supplies. Water, or blankets . . . ?"

"Who?"

"The Coast Guard?"

"Last time I checked, the Coast Guard travels by boat," Bancroft reminded him.

"So maybe it's unrelated. Someone visiting for the weekend."

"In this weather?" Turks and Caicos was a playground for the rich and famous, with luxury resorts on white sand beaches. People came to golf, scuba dive, and swim with the dolphins. They also came to disappear. If they had inadvertently invaded someone's hideaway, things could get prickly.

"I agree, it's an odd time for someone to visit their private island," Ridley conceded.

Bancroft was thinking the same thing. Not only was it storming out, it was also two in the morning.

"I'm going to go say hello," Bancroft said, downplaying his concern. They were trespassing. If someone had flown here in this weather, they probably weren't too happy about it.

"I'll go with you."

"It's awfully wet out there," the captain warned.

"Can't get any wetter than I already am."

The barn door squealed on rusty rollers as Ridley reached in front of the captain and pulled it open. Bancroft peered through the crack to see the tops of trees arching over in the wind. And once again he wondered, who the hell would venture out in this weather?

"You were right," Ridley called over his shoulder as he stepped out into the dark night. The rain was falling more *at* him than on him as the wind howled and swirled. "We have a visitor," he said, pointing at the sleek, single engine Mooney that was taxiing toward them down the runway.

"Well I'll be damned," Bancroft muttered as the plane came to a stop twenty meters from where they were standing.

"What do you think they want?" Ridley shouted over the idling engine.

"Your guess is as good as mine."

As they stood there staring, the Mooney's propeller stopped turning. A moment later, the door to the small plane opened and the pilot stepped out onto the wing.

"I'll go say hello," Ridley said, then took a step toward their visitors, using his open palm as a visor to shield his eyes from the rain.

Bancroft stared at the private pilot. The man's body language was odd. Why was he crouched behind the door like that?

Ridley raised a hand above his head and waved hello.

And that's when Bancroft saw it.

The barrel of a gun, pointed right at them.

"Ridley, get down!"

As Ridley froze in his tracks—

BLAM!

The gunman fired.

The first officer buckled at the knees. Bancroft ran out and caught him as he stumbled backwards.

"I'm hit!" Ridley said, grabbing his shoulder.

Bancroft snaked an arm around Ridley's ribs and pulled him toward the open hangar door. He didn't want to lead the shooter toward the passengers, but they were sitting ducks out there in the rain.

"What the fuck?" Ridley wailed as Bancroft ushered him inside. Blood was seeping through his shirt sleeve.

"You're all right," Bancroft said, depositing him on the hangar floor.

"It's just a flesh wound." He spun around to close the door, but a pair of steel-toed black boots were already stepping through it.

Bancroft put his hands up and backed away. Behind him, passengers gasped in horror. Some had heard the gunshot, but only one person knew beyond any doubt what it was.

CHAPTER

058

BLAM!

Renaldo's heart shot into his throat as the unmistakable sound of a gunshot echoed through the night air. With rain hammering the roof, he couldn't tell how close it was. Until he saw the captain dragging the bleeding first officer through the open hangar door.

"Shit!"

Renaldo ducked behind the Land Cruiser and reached for his Glock. He wanted to go to the captain's aid, but if they were under attack *(good God, were they under attack?)* his best course of action was to stay hidden until he'd assessed the situation. He'd been so preoccupied by the internal threat, the possibility of an external one never crossed his mind. Once again, he was playing catch-up.

His hand found his holster. But before he could draw, a man in all black stepped into the hangar and pointed his revolver into the crowd.

"Andrew!"

Passengers scurried for cover behind their suitcases and each other. Renaldo's right hand twitched at his side. He was in the gunman's line of sight, he couldn't pull his weapon.

As he waited for the gunman to look away—

A second gunman in a camo flak jacket stepped through the open barn door. *Shit. There were two of them.*

"Where is he?" Camo Flak Jacket asked.

"Annnn-drew!" The man in black called out again. "Come out, come out, wherever you are!" When no one answered, he pointed his gun in the air and—

BLAM! Fired off a round.

Passengers recoiled and gasped. Renaldo's heart hammered in his chest. It was killing him to just stand there like a bump on a log. But he couldn't risk the passengers' lives by starting a firefight.

"Don't make us do this the hard way, Andrew," the man in camo said, then unholstered his gun and pointed it into the crowd.

"I'm here," Drew Ridley, the first officer said, clutching his bleeding arm as he took a step toward them. *What did these thugs want with the first officer?* Renaldo glanced at the captain. His bewildered expression suggested he was equally baffled. The possibility of sabotage reared its ugly head. Did the first officer do something to the plane?

"I'll relax when I get my suitcase," Camo Flak Jacket said.

"I've got it right here," Ridley said, pushing a black Samsonite toward him with his foot. "Keeping it safe, just like I promised."

"Open it," the man in camo ordered.

Renaldo watched as Ridley unzipped the suitcase with his good arm, and turned it toward the armed invaders. As they eyed the suitcase, he eyed their guns. He wouldn't shoot unless they did first. Because maybe they just wanted what was in that suitcase and would leave the rest of the passengers alone?

The gunman in black squatted down and started pawing through the suitcase, then lifted it up and dumped the contents onto the floor—shorts, sundresses, sandals, a bathing suit.

"What the hell is this?"

Ridley's surprise seemed genuine. "I . . . don't know."

"Don't fuck with me," the man in black said, then raised his gun and—

BLAM! Shot him in the kneecap.

"Fuck! Jesus," Ridley said, collapsing to the ground as he grabbed his knee. Blood was seeping out between his fingers. "The bags must have gotten mixed up. It's not my fault. We were in a fucking plane crash."

"How convenient."

"You think I planned this?"

"Did you?" the gunman asked as Renaldo wondered the same thing.

Ridley cradled his knee with bloody fingers. "If it wasn't for me, your money would be stuck in Florida. You should be thanking me!"

Renaldo's ears pricked up. *Stuck in Florida?*

"So where is it?" the man in black asked.

"We'll find your fucking suitcase," Ridley said, pushing himself up on his one good leg. The first officer scanned the hangar, *looking, looking* . . .

"There!" Ridley said, pointing. "She took it!"

Renaldo looked to where Ridley was pointing. A tiny wisp of a woman was cowering behind an identical suitcase. Holy shit, it was Francesca Kessler. Her face was sheer terror. As the man in black started walking toward her—

Renaldo's fingers found the closure on his holster and unsnapped it. But he didn't draw, not yet. If he fired off a shot, he'd put everyone at risk . . . and be a sitting duck himself.

He watched with twitching fingers as the gunman in black stepped up to Francesca and pointed his revolver at her face.

"Open it," he ordered.

She obediently bent over the case and unzipped it.

He kicked the lid open. Pushed a T-shirt aside with the steel toe of his boot. Then reached down and pulled out a clear bag of money.

"How many did you take?" he asked Francesca, dangling it in front of her.

"What? No! I didn't . . . I wouldn't," she stammered.

He aimed the barrel of the gun between her eyes. "How many?"

"Please. No . . ."

Renaldo's hand closed around the handle of his gun. He couldn't just stand there and watch this asshole shoot someone, but what was he supposed to do? It was two armed men against one.

"No one steals from me," the man in black said.

As the thug cocked back the hammer—

Brendan Callahan, the baseball coach who seemed to have a knack for being in the thick of things, lunged for the gunman's legs—

"Brendan, no!" a woman's voice cried out.

—Then slammed into him, tackling him to the ground.

BLAM!

Across the hangar, the gunman in camo fired.

Brendan Callahan's chest erupted in a spray of blood.

"Brendan!" As flight attendant Cathy Yap fell to her knees—

BLAM!

Renaldo's bullet tore through the man in camo's neck. Blood sprayed out of his severed artery as he collapsed to the ground. Now there were just two of them. But the man in black had the edge. Because he didn't care who else died.

Renaldo pointed his Glock at the gunman, but he couldn't shoot, the gunman had pulled Callahan to his feet and was using him as a human shield.

Renaldo set down his weapon, raised his hands in the air. "No one else needs to die today."

"Except for you," the man in black spat, aiming the barrel of his revolver at Renaldo's chest. In that brief second between life and death, Renaldo thought of Katie, his beautiful Katie . . . what could have been if he'd had the courage to tell her how he felt.

The man in black cocked back the hammer of his revolver. But before he could get off the shot—

CRACK!

A bullet pierced his temple.

Blood ran down his cheek as he corkscrewed to the ground.

"Brendan!" Cathy rushed toward the wounded coach, catching him as he fell.

Renaldo looked toward where that fatal bullet had come from. And saw the tattooed passenger—the "rockstar" Cathy had mistaken for him—by the hangar door, his Beretta 9mm pointed at the fallen thug. *OK, so maybe not a rockstar . . .*

"Where's that doctor?" Bancroft called out.

"I'm here," the doctor replied, stepping out from the shadows.

"Please," Cathy called to her. "Help him."

As the doctor crouched down by Brendan Callahan's side, Renaldo's eyes found Francesca, hugging her knees and rocking back and forth. He holstered his gun and jogged over to her.

"Are you OK?" he asked. She was shaking all over. He kneeled down beside her and put a gentle hand on her shoulder. "It's OK, it's over now."

"I didn't try to steal that man's money. I grabbed the wrong suitcase. It looks just like mine." It was a Samsonite. He knew the model well. All the Pioneer Air flight attendants carried the same one.

"Yes, it does." Without touching it, he peered down into the main compartment. Nestled between neatly stacked, ziplocked bags of money was a slim, black box, with a pea-sized light bulb flashing green. A GPS tracking device. *So that's how they found them.*

He picked up one of the T-shirts the man in black had kicked aside.

On a hunch, he brought it to his nose and smelled it.

His heart exploded with grief. He would know that perfume anywhere.

Because it was Katie's.

FLIGHT ATTENDANT KATIE JEAN MACINTOSH: I have a problem.

FIRST OFFICER DREW RIDLEY: What kind of problem?

KATIE: I got bumped off the flight.

RIDLEY: Where's the suitcase?

KATIE: With me. I have it.

RIDLEY: Where are they sending you?

KATIE: I have no idea.

RIDLEY: You can't leave the airport with it.

KATIE: What do you want me to do? They might reassign me. I'm still on the clock.

RIDLEY: I have a guy who can get it on the plane, but you need to get it to him.

KATIE: Where is he?

RIDLEY: He drives the fuel truck. Hold on, I'm texting him.
(Brief wait.)

RIDLEY: He says to meet him on the lower level. Carousel five. Go now.

KATIE: You'll make the hand off in San Juan?

RIDLEY: Yes, just get it to my guy.

KATIE: Don't forget about the air marshal. I won't be there to distract him.

RIDLEY: It's fine. Those guys are useless.

CHAPTER

059

"Hey," Federal Air Marshal Carlos Renaldo said to the tattooed *not*-rockstar standing over the banged-up first officer, who was now bandaged and cuffed. "I'm Carlos."

"The air marshal, I figured that out up at thirty thousand feet." He held out his hand to shake. "Marco Reyes, DEA." *DEA? What was an agent from the Drug Enforcement Agency doing on his flight?*

"So . . . you're undercover too, then?" Normally he'd be pissed they placed another federal agent on his flight without telling him, but the man just saved his life, so he checked his anger.

"Technically I was just going to work," Reyes said. "But I travel with the guitar to fend off any questions."

"You're on a case, then?"

Reyes nodded. "The agency has known Pioneer Airlines was running drugs out of Puerto Rico for a while now. We just didn't know who all the players were. One might say we caught a lucky break. If you can call a crash landing lucky."

"I think I'm the one who got lucky," Renaldo said, eyeing the gun in Agent Reyes's waistband.

"Yeah, my piece was in my checked bag." He indicated the suitcase by his feet. "Glad it was one of the ones that washed up."

"You and me both." He wanted to ask about Katie, if they knew about her. But how to do that without revealing their relationship? "Do you know how the money got on board?" he said, hoping the question didn't arouse suspicion.

"We knew Pioneer had a network of employees smuggling contraband in their carry-ons. We had our eye on a few. But we chose to watch them, not arrest them. So they could lead us to the big fish."

Renaldo recalled seeing Katie rolling that suitcase into the crew lounge. But she never got on the plane. Plus, the bag was in the luggage hold, not an overhead bin. "I didn't think any of the carry-ons made it into the lifeboats."

"Yeah, they must have done it differently this time. Maybe because of the crew change. I'm guessing the mule was one of the flight attendants who got bumped in San Diego. We'll look at the crew that was supposed to work this flight, track their movements at the changeover."

Renaldo nodded slowly, tried to act like the thought of federal agents tracking his not-girlfriend's movements at the airport didn't terrify him. It made perfect sense that Katie had sent him away. She needed to get her carry-on onto the plane without him seeing. *Jesus, what a fucking idiot he was.* Katie didn't love him. He was a problem she had to solve. She set a trap, and he'd walked right into it.

He considered telling the DEA agent who just saved his life what he knew about the suitcase and the person it belonged to. But also, the cameras at the airport would tell the agency everything they needed to know. Unfortunately.

"You mind if I talk to him?" Renaldo asked, indicating Ridley. His superiors were going to have questions about the murder and the crash, and he wanted to get a jump on the answers.

"Be my guest," Reyes said, stepping aside.

Renaldo crouched down in front of Ridley. Anger percolated through his veins. He wanted to ask about Katie, how she'd gotten involved, if he was the one who dragged her into it. But he decided not to lead with that. "Tell me about the crash," he said to the first officer. "Was that planned?"

"Are you crazy? I wanted this plane to get to Puerto Rico more than anyone." Renaldo considered that. It made sense. If he was making a delivery, he'd want it to go through.

"What about the murder of William Wilcox?" he asked, because just because the DEA hadn't made a connection between Wilcox and the drug runners didn't mean there wasn't one.

"What about it?"

"Was that you?" Renaldo asked. There was no way Ridley could have murdered Wilcox himself, but there could have been other operatives on the plane.

Ridley shook his head. "I don't know who that guy is, just that him dying really fucked things up."

"Fucked things up how?"

"Him getting murdered is why we're here."

"I don't follow," Renaldo said. "How did Wilcox's murder force us to land here?"

"Because your friends at the fucking Fed wanted us to turn the plane around because of it."

Renaldo flashed to Ridley's flippant remark to the drug runners about how they should be thanking him, because "if not for him" their money would be stuck in Florida.

"What did you do?"

"We don't have any operatives in Florida. If that suitcase got unloaded by random baggage handlers in Jacksonville, we'd have lost control of it."

That still didn't explain the plane crash. "And so . . ."

"So I dumped the fuel."

Renaldo's blood turned to ice. "There were a hundred and thirty-one people on that plane—"

"I didn't mean to dump all of it," Ridley interrupted, "only enough to force us to continue on to San Juan. But then the captain had me take the controls. I couldn't shut the valve in time."

"So you *did* crash the plane."

"Not on purpose," he said, as if that made it any less repugnant.

"Why couldn't you just have let the plane land in Florida and pick up the suitcase from baggage claim?"

"Because we snuck it on. It's not tagged. It would have gotten seized and searched. Your girlfriend never checked it, there's nothing on it identifying who it belongs to or which airport it was bound for."

Renaldo bit the inside of his cheeks to redirect his anger—not at Katie for playing him, at himself for getting played. How could he have been so blind? Surely there'd been signs.

"She wasn't paid to fuck you, if that's what you're wondering," Ridley added. "That was her idea."

Renaldo's fingers curled into a fist. But he knew better than to waste a punch on this asshole.

"So what was her involvement?" he asked, corralling the fury that was pulsing through his veins.

"Just a lowly courier, like me. The cartel brought the drugs into Puerto Rico by boat, we put them on planes, then brought back the money. It's not fucking rocket science."

Renaldo grew suspicious. "Why are you telling me all of this?" He wasn't an investigator, but didn't it usually take more work to get a criminal to confess?

Ridley shrugged. "Because it's safer for me in prison. These guys don't tolerate mistakes. I figure tell you now, tell you later, it doesn't matter. My life is over either way."

The phrase "my life is over" boomed in his head like a bell ringing. As soon as the drug runners discovered their operation had been compromised, they'd go after Katie. There was no way she was coming out of this alive. He was sickened by what she had done, but he still loved her.

If he wasn't so busy feeling sorry for himself, would he have seen that suitcase being loaded onto the plane? Guilt wrapped around his ribs. The irony was so cruel he nearly cried. If Katie didn't make it out of this alive, it would be his obsession that killed her.

CHAPTER

060

Captain Brett Bancroft was not easily rattled. But seeing his first officer—the man who was supposed to be his trusted partner—on the ground in handcuffs made him quake with rage. They'd taken an oath to the airline to perform their duties faithfully and an unspoken one to each other to work as a team. To be betrayed like this rocked him to the core.

So he turned his gaze away, toward the brave coach who'd taken a bullet for his fellow passenger. Flight attendant Cathy Yap was beside him on the hangar floor, pressing a wadded up T-shirt into his gunshot wound. Bancroft bottled up his anger and walked over to where they were huddled.

"How's he doing?" he asked the doctor who stood up to greet him.

"He's lost a lot of blood," the doctor said in a hushed whisper. "If he doesn't get to a hospital soon . . ."

Bancroft's fury morphed into despair. Even if a rescue vessel arrived right away, the surrounding water was shallow—it would take hours to shuttle all the passengers out to it. Then several more to sail to a port big enough for a large ship to dock. And he'd already proved the runway was too short to land a jet. Any evacuation would take more time than this man had.

And then there was the matter of the weather. Yes, he'd landed in the storm, but only because he'd had no choice. Rescuers would come. But not until conditions improved.

"Captain!"

Bancroft turned to look at the air marshal who was running toward him. "What is it, Renaldo?" he asked, bracing himself for more bad news.

"I need to get a message to DHS," Renaldo said as if there were a way to do that. "It's urgent."

"I'm not in communication with the outside world any more than you are," Bancroft reminded him.

"A woman's life is at stake. We have to find a way."

The captain didn't like being a damsel in distress. But what could he do? He was not a quitter, but he was not a magician either.

He turned his gaze to peer out the open hangar door. And then he remembered. There *was* something he could do. It was insanely dangerous. But then again, so was doing nothing.

"Come with me."

The Mooney M20 was parked at the end of the runway. Rain was pounding the tarmac, blurring Bancroft's vision as he jogged toward it. That pilot had serious cajónes landing the small plane in the swirling wind. And taking off in it would be just as dangerous.

"Have you ever flown one of these?" Renaldo asked.

"Probably," Bancroft hedged, because now wasn't the time to inject doubt.

The single engine aircraft was a sleek four-seater, with a propellor mounted on the nose and retractable, tricycle landing gear. The captain walked around the tail to inspect it. The wings showed no damage or cracks. The tires were fully inflated. He checked the oil to see it was fresh and full. There were not many moving parts on this airplane. If it had gas, he could fly it.

The door was unlocked, so he opened it and climbed into the cockpit. A headset hung from the visor. And wouldn't you know, the keys were in the ignition.

"Stand back."

Bancroft flipped the twin master switches to power up the instruments. Opened the fuel valve. Moved the throttle one click to the right and the mixture to full. Then he turned on the lights and shouted through the open door.

"Clear!"

THRUMMMM. The propellor roared as the engine turned over. He listened to it for a long beat to see if his ears could detect a problem that his eyes had not. He checked the gauges, saw that he had nearly a full tank of fuel. Then he turned on the navigation system and finally, the radio.

"This is Mooney 2-5-2-Yankee Lima checking in from Martini Cay," he said into the headset. "Anyone read me?"

There was a beat of static. And then . . .

"Yankee Lima, this is Miami Central. What can we do for you?"

Success!

"I need to do an emergency medical evacuation from the island. I don't have my charts and didn't file a flight plan. Can you vector me to the nearest hospital?"

"Yankee Lima, you're eighty miles from Cockburn Town, they have a medical center with emergency services. Check back with us once you're in the air, we'll get you there."

Bancroft's chest flooded with relief. He could go eighty miles in less than twenty minutes. As long as the weather cooperated.

"Thanks much. Oh, one more thing." He turned off the mic and called to Renaldo. "Officer Renaldo!"

"Yankee Lima, go ahead," ATC squawked.

He flipped the mic back on. "I need to get a message to law enforcement regarding a developing situation on the ground in . . . ?" He looked at the air marshal.

"San Diego."

"San Diego. I'm putting Federal Air Marshal Carlos Renaldo on the comms. He may need you to make a phone call for him."

"Roger that, Yankee Lima. Happy to help."

Bancroft took off the headset and handed it to Renaldo. "Press here to talk. I'm going to go get my passenger."

Renaldo nodded his gratitude. "Thank you, Captain."

Bancroft hopped out of the plane and jogged across the tarmac.

"Boys!" he shouted as he crossed the threshold into the hangar. "I need your help getting your coach up and out of here."

The boys jumped to their feet, then hurried over to help their coach onto his.

"I can walk," the coach insisted.

"They're going to help you anyway," Cathy said.

Slowly, the players and Cathy eased Coach Callahan toward the open barn door. Rain pelted their baseball-capped heads as they stepped out onto the tarmac and moved en masse toward the idling plane.

"All good, Renaldo?" the captain asked as they reached the Mooney.

"I sent my message. Thank you," the air marshal replied, then moved out of the way.

"I'll go in first," Cathy said, pushing the pilot's chair forward and putting one foot on the step.

"Negative," Bancroft said. "Too dangerous." He was willing to risk his own life to save another's. But not Cathy's. "Please step aside." She held her ground.

"I know you want to protect me, but I have nothing to live for without him."

And, before Bancroft could stop her, she hoisted herself into the little plane. He could lose his job for letting her come. But only if they survived.

"All right, let's load him in."

Oh-so-gently, the ball players lifted their coach and eased him through the door and into Cathy's lap.

"Great job, boys," Bancroft said. "Now stand clear."

Bancroft climbed into his seat. He scanned the rudimentary instruments. *Was he really about to fly a plane he'd never been trained on into high winds and rain?*

"Captain, he's fading in and out," Cathy said from the backseat. "Please hurry."

Yes, he was.

"Strap in, it's going to be a bumpy ride."

The captain nudged the throttle. The craft inched forward toward the end of the runway. Using the foot pedals, he made a big arcing turn to point the nose in the right direction.

"Here we go."

Rain pelted the roof and wings like falling pennies. But rain wasn't his concern.

He looked up at the windsock. It was blowing due west. He smiled to himself. They had a headwind for takeoff. He said a silent thank you to the weather gods.

"Can we take off in this?" Cathy asked.

"You just worry about your man," the captain said. "I'll take care of the rest."

SPECIAL AGENT SAM COOPER: Good evening. This is Special Agent Sam Cooper of the FBI Violent Crimes Division.

LAPD DISPATCH: What can I do for you, Agent Cooper?

COOPER: There's a Miss Katie Jean MacIntosh arriving at LAX on Pioneer Airlines Flight 227 out of San Diego. Ms. MacIntosh works for the airline as a flight attendant. She's wanted in a federal drug running investigation.

LAPD: You want us to detain her?

COOPER:. Yes, please. We're faxing over her photo and a copy of the arrest warrant. You should have it any minute.

LAPD: I see it coming in now.

COOPER: The plane is due to touch down in fifteen minutes.

LAPD: We have airport police on site. Won't be a problem.

COOPER: I appreciate your help.

LAPD: Anytime.

CHAPTER

061

Federal Agent Carlos Renaldo watched through the open barn door as the single engine aircraft disappeared into the dark night. He knew he had gotten lucky. If there hadn't been an armed DEA agent on board, he'd have been the second casualty of Flight 868.

As he closed the door, his relief that he'd saved Katie's life was overtaken by frustration about the life that had been lost. If this was his last day as an air marshal—and it surely was—he didn't want his six-year career to end in failure. Solving the in-flight murder was his last chance to do something good.

If Ridley was telling the truth, Wilcox was not connected to that suitcase or the men who were after it. Yes, his death had played a role in the plane crashing, but only because Ridley dumped the fuel to try to force them to continue on to San Juan. Did that mean the murderer was someone from Crestwood, then?

He went back over what he knew. Angela Diaz had a clear motive, but the timing didn't make sense. Why file a police report a few hours before you intend to take your revenge? It was like putting on a T-shirt that said "It was me!" And he didn't believe she'd be stupid enough to do that.

So what about Jillian Azarian? She wasn't looking for her fiancé, which could have meant one of two things—she'd found out what he'd done and never wanted to talk to him again, or she knew he was dead because she was the one who killed him. But if she or Angela had done it, wouldn't they be putting on a show to make it seem like they were desperate to find him? If Miss Azarian was a calculating murderess, she sure didn't act like one.

Which led him back to the other debacle Billy Wilcox had been a part of: the unsolved hit-and-run. He knew from Agent Cooper that Wilcox's car had been linked to the scene. There were probably a lot of people from Crestwood who wanted justice for Matthew Kessler. But the one who wanted it most was here in this hangar. Perhaps it was time for one more chat.

The contents of Francesca Kessler's suitcase were strewn out on the floor, so he put them back inside, then zipped it up and carried it across the hangar where its owner was sitting on the floor with her knees pulled to her chest.

"I believe this belongs to you?" he said, setting the suitcase down beside her.

She looked up at him with weary eyes. "Thanks," she mustered.

"May I?" he said, then sat down beside her without waiting for an answer. "I know the last few minutes have been traumatic," he started. And to his surprise, she smiled.

"I'm no stranger to trauma," she said, parroting his words back to him. And he smiled too.

"I'm sorry to be a dog with a bone, but I was really hoping you could help me figure out what happened the night your son was killed."

She studied him a long beat. Like she was trying to decide whether she could trust him.

"You know something," he said, not as a question. "But you don't know if you can trust me."

"My experience with law enforcement has not exactly inspired trust."

He thought back to what Cooper had texted him about the Crestwood Sheriff pushing evidence under the rug.

"I get that."

"Do you?"

He decided to show his cards. "We think the local police may have tampered with the investigation into the death of your son. You and I want the same thing. To find out why."

"You were the one who helped me figure it out."

"Oh?"

"When you told me there'd been a cover-up."

"Any idea why the sheriff would want to protect Billy Wilcox?"

"Sheriff Eckles doesn't give a rat's ass about Billy Wilcox," she said.

"His car was on the scene."

"But he wasn't driving it."

Renaldo's pulse quickened. This jived with what Angela Diaz had told him about Billy Wilcox having been with her. "Then who was?"

She pointed at the woman from first class, the one who'd tried to impale him with her boot.

"Why don't you ask her?"

CHAPTER

062

Penelope Abernathy's silk shirt was clinging to her skin like Saran Wrap on raw meat. Her suitcase wasn't among the ones that had washed up on shore. Naturally. Her luck had gone the way of her looks and unfailing optimism—that is to say, it had run out. A few passengers had offered her dry items from their suitcases, but the indignity of wearing some random's beach *schmatta* was too much for her to bear.

"Ms. Abernathy?" a man's voice said. She turned to meet the gaze of the man who'd lied to her about being a scout, and who she'd tackled as a direct result, which really made the tackling his fault—at least that's what she'd tell the judge.

"Let me guess. You're here to arrest me." She said it in her most mocking voice, so he'd feel ridiculous for even thinking it.

"I'd rather talk, if that's OK with you."

"What about?"

"Billy Wilcox." Fear shot through her veins like electricity through a high-voltage wire. But she made sure not to show it.

"I feel bad for the boy. You know he lost his mother when he was just a child."

"So you knew him?"

"I've been the Crestwood High School Baseball Booster Club

president for ten years, I know everyone." Did she sound like a braggart? Maybe. But she refused to be humbled by some two-bit cop.

"Yeah, speaking of Crestwood," the air marshal said, "the FBI just reopened the investigation into the hit-and-run that killed Matthew Kessler."

Matthew Kessler. The sound of his name was as suffocating as the wind and rain battering their sorry excuse for a shelter.

"Shame that they never could solve it," she said like someone who wasn't the mastermind behind the cover-up.

"Some new evidence has emerged. Tire tracks matching the vehicle belonging to Mr. Wilcox were found at the scene." That so-called evidence wasn't new, but she tried to act surprised.

"How interesting."

"But the strange thing is, his girlfriend said Wilcox was with her."

She let out a snort. "And we all know the girlfriend would never lie to protect the man she loves."

"Where were you that night, Mrs. Abernathy?"

"Me?" She tried to look appropriately offended. "I was at the game, of course. My son Ace pitched the final out."

"And then where'd you go?"

Why was he looking at her like that? Surely he didn't know. How could he?

"Home."

"But not before stopping at the crime scene." She pressed her lips together as she considered whether or not to lie. "We have witnesses who put you there," he added. Yes, that was probably true, best not to deny it.

"Well, I saw all the sirens, of course I wanted to know what had happened in my town."

"So you followed the sirens?" he asked.

She hated repeating herself. But as she opened her mouth to say, *yes, she'd followed the sirens*, a woman's voice interrupted.

"Or maybe someone called you and told you to come?"

She snapped her head around. Francesca Kessler was standing

right behind her. Where the heck did she come from? That woman was like a cat.

Penelope felt a twinge of annoyance. She didn't want to lie in front of a cop, but she knew better than to admit to anything, not without a lawyer present.

"There were more sirens than an air raid," she said, evading the question. "No one had to tell me something had happened."

"It was Nolan, wasn't it?" Francesca said, hovering like a pesky fly. "He's the one who called you and told you what they'd done."

Penelope's jaw flexed in anger. "Don't you bring Nolan into this!" It wasn't like her to lose her cool. But her sons were off limits.

"You knew," she said flatly, and not as a question.

"Knew what?" she shot back.

"That Trey Turnberry was driving that car. You knew because Nolan was sitting right beside him when it struck and killed my son."

Fuck, fuck, fuck.

Penelope sucked in her cheeks and held her head high. Yes, what Francesca was saying was true, but she couldn't prove it. "I don't know what you're talking about," she said, reminding herself that she was a practiced liar. And the four other people—or rather, *three* other people now that Billy was dead—who knew the truth wouldn't talk because they were guilty of crimes too.

Francesca's lip was quivering. "Do you know what the not knowing has done to me? To my husband? To our marriage? Your lie ruined my life!"

"Oh for heaven's sake, I didn't lie." Penelope said, because keeping one's mouth shut is not the same as lying. And then, because she couldn't help herself: "It's not my fault you and your husband couldn't move on!"

Francesca's face turned tomato red. "How dare you?"

Penelope felt sorry for Francesca, but she was not about to sit back and let the woman slander her. "Just because my sons are still alive doesn't make me the villain here."

"What you did destroyed lives!" Francesca spat.

"And saved our goddamned town!" she shot back.

Yes, she'd concocted the plan to protect Trey Turnberry, because who else would have done it? Cal was too shell-shocked, and Sheriff Eckles was too stupid.

Behind Francesca, the ball players were all staring at her. "I didn't do it for me," she hissed. "I did it for them. So they would have a future. Just because your son died didn't mean he should take all of Crestwood down with him!"

THWACK! Francesca's punch landed with surprising force.

"Owww!" Penelope pressed the heel of her hand to her cheek. "What the hell, Francesca?" She looked at the air marshal, who was just standing there as useless as tits on a bull. "She just attacked me!"

He looked at her like, *and, so?*

"Aren't you going to arrest her?"

"No. But I'm considering arresting you."

"For what?"

"Obstruction of justice, for starters."

"Oh, please." With a good lawyer, she'd get away with a fine and a slap on the wrist. That other crime she'd committed, well, that was admittedly more serious. But luckily all the evidence was at the bottom of the ocean by now.

She hadn't planned to murder Billy Wilcox. She just wanted to talk. That's why she followed him into the main cabin. To apologize for throwing salt on old wounds, remind him to keep their secret a secret. OK, and also get her long overdue thank you for ponying up the five grand to fix the dent in his car and finding a body shop that would keep it on the downlow. But then she saw the fiancée crying. And she knew he just told her everything! He had to be silenced. Because if it got out what they did to protect Trey Turnberry, she, Sheriff Eckles, and her sweet, innocent Nolan would be up shit's creek.

Thank God her oldest son had possessed the good sense to call her and tell her what Trey had done. How neither of them saw the boy stepping out from that field. Because it was dark. And OK, yes, they'd been drinking—not as much as Billy, but too much to get behind the wheel of a car. She would have preferred her son hadn't been in the passenger seat, but she was grateful for his quick thinking.

She told Nolan to tell Trey to keep driving and not look back, then raced to the scene of the accident to make sure they hadn't left any evidence—a side mirror or piece of a headlight, anything that might have broken off on impact. She and Sheriff Eckles had arrived at the same time. At first she was confused why the sheriff was there. She'd told Nolan *not* to call the police. But then she saw Cal, holding his phone. And she knew she had to act fast.

Would Cal have kept his mouth shut if he'd known Trey was driving? *The* Trey Turnberry, who could have afforded fancy lawyers who could poke holes in the case? Hard to say. Not surprisingly, Cal had assumed the person driving Billy's car was Billy. Poor Billy with the dead mother and deadbeat father. She knew Cal wouldn't have the heart to send him to jail. Not after she and Sheriff Eckles convinced him he didn't have to.

She was quite proud of herself for painting such a grim picture of what would happen to Crestwood's beloved baseball program—and its coach—if it got out a former player had killed another. A program that did a lot of good for a lot of people—revitalized their town, kept kids off the streets, gave Cal the legendary status he hadn't achieved in the Major Leagues. You can't put the toothpaste back in the tube, she'd told him. Sheriff Eckles assured him he had no liability, he'd reported what he'd seen to the local police. He could walk away. And, thanks to her, that's what he did.

The bride-to-be was a potential loose end now, but even if Billy had told his fiancée everything, it was all hearsay without him to testify as to its validity. Besides, why would she want to defame her dead boyfriend by implicating him in a cover-up? Trey wouldn't tattle on himself, Eckles was as corrupt as Tony Soprano, and Nolan she could control. They could still keep this under wraps, as long as Francesca didn't start squawking.

"It's obvious what's going on here," she said, trying not to sound too condescending. "She's angry and she needs someone to blame. Understandable. Her boy was meant to be on this trip, did she tell you that?"

The air marshal was still standing there, sizing her up like melons at the grocery store.

"Grief can make a person crazy." She touched her swelling eye as proof. "I don't suppose you have an ice pack?"

"No, but I do have a theory," he said. "Would you like to hear it?"

"If it's that Francesca Kessler hates me because my three sons are all still alive, I couldn't agree more."

"No, that's not it."

She had zero interest in hearing his theory. What could he possibly know about the death of Billy Wilcox? Certainly not that he'd called her an old hag when she opened that lavatory door to apologize for dredging up bad memories; or that he'd tried to grab that bat but was too drunk and she got to it first; or that he'd laughed in her face when she'd threatened to hurt him—as if she were too weak or scared.

"That woman has more conspiracy theories than QAnon," she said, in an attempt to shut him up. But he just kept on yammering.

"If Francesca Kessler knew that Trey Turnberry was driving the car that killed her son . . ." he started . . .

"Francesca Kessler doesn't know her boney ass from her elbow."

"She would have no motive to kill Billy Wilcox."

"Kill Billy Wilcox?" She made sure to sound confused. "What are you talking about?"

"But you would."

CHAPTER

063

Renaldo watched Penelope Abernathy's face when he told her Billy Wilcox had been murdered. Her nostrils flared when she feigned surprise. Just as they had back in the first-class lounge, when she told him Trey Turnberry was a gift to the NCAA—something she knew to be untrue and he remembered a little too late. That nostril flare, that was her tell.

She knew Billy Wilcox was dead, because she was the one who murdered him..

All the pieces fit. Billy Wilcox didn't kill Matthew Kessler, but his car did, and Wilcox knew Trey Turnberry was driving it because he was the one who'd given him the keys. If he was ready to talk—maybe because he found himself face-to-face with the dead kid's grieving mother—the person desperate to keep it a secret would want to silence him—permanently.

If Francesca Kessler was right about Nolan Abernathy being in the passenger seat and calling his mother—something that was easy to confirm through phone records—Penelope, her son, and the sheriff were all obstructing justice when they declined to come forward with what they knew. And then there were all the perks of protecting a star like Trey Turnberry. If he were indebted to the good people of Crestwood for keeping his secret, the gifts to the town and its baseball program would keep coming. Penelope Abernathy, as the Baseball Booster Club president, had motive up the wazoo.

Carlos had no doubt this woman was capable of murdering a man in cold blood. She was aggressive—he'd learned that the hard way when she attacked him with a boot. She was also a former batting champion with the strength and skill to drive a softball to the moon. So yeah, totally capable.

She'd been seated in first class, but she could have snuck back to the aft galley right before the turbulence hit. A lot of passengers were making last minute trips to the lav. If she were among them, no one would've batted an eye. He hadn't seen her go back there, but he also hadn't seen Billy Wilcox, and clearly the man had walked past him, otherwise he'd still be alive. As for how she got back to first class after the bludgeoning, he had a theory inspired by seeing her crawling back to the main cabin as the plane was going down, which he would explore just as soon as he took care of the matter at hand.

"Penelope Abernathy, you're under arrest for the murder of Billy Wilcox," he said, pulling a set of flex-cuffs from his pocket.

"This will never stick," she said. "You have no evidence!"

As he cuffed her wrists for the second time that day, his eyes caught a dark red splotch on the sleeve of her blouse. That's the thing about blood stains—they're really hard to get out once they set.

She wasn't bleeding, so whose blood was it?

"We'll see about that."

FEDERAL AIR MARSHAL CARLOS RENALDO: I have a couple more questions for you, can we speak privately?

ACE ABERNATHY: Sure, I guess.

RENALDO: You holding up all right?

ACE: Kai told us about the dead guy. Is that what this is about?

RENALDO: I'll ask the questions, if that's all right with you.

ACE: OK.

RENALDO: You moved to an empty row near the back of the plane a couple of hours into the flight. Why?

ACE: I wanted to sleep.

RENALDO: Did you have the row to yourself?

ACE: Yeah, I mean, until my mom came.

RENALDO: Your mom came and sat with you?

ACE: I told her she didn't have to, I was fine.

RENALDO: So she came back to check on you, stayed for . . . how long?

ACE: She wasn't checking on me. She came back to use the bathroom.

RENALDO: That's what she said? That she came back to coach to use the bathroom?

ACE: She did use the bathroom. I saw her go back there.

RENALDO: Was that before or after the turbulence hit?

ACE: Right before. Then she got stuck, because by the time she finished in the bathroom, we were already bouncing around.

RENALDO: So she was sitting with you when it got really bad.

ACE: I didn't need her to. I wasn't scared.

RENALDO: When did she go back to her seat in first class?

ACE: After the lights went out.

RENALDO: She went back to her seat in the dark? What was the hurry?

ACE: She hates sitting in coach.

RENALDO: You think maybe she didn't want anybody to see her?

ACE: Why would she care about that?

MLB ALL-STAR TREY TURNBERRY IMPLICATED IN DEADLY HIT-AND-RUN

The Crestwood High alumnus is accused of fleeing the scene of the accident that killed rising baseball star
by Maryanne Kennedy, Staff Writer

Crestwood, CA, April 26, 2026—Chicago Cubs All-Star infielder Trey Turnberry was arrested this morning on charges of vehicular manslaughter and leaving the scene of an accident as new evidence emerged in the hit-and-run death of fifteen-year-old Matthew Kessler. The Crestwood High burgeoning baseball star was running to catch up with friends on the evening of May 12, 2023, when he was struck and killed. Despite a citywide search, the driver and vehicle remained unidentified for over three years.

In a related indictment, Crestwood Sheriff Alan Eckles pleaded guilty to two counts of evidence tampering and obstruction of justice when it was uncovered that he had known about Turnberry's involvement.

According to FBI Special Agent Sam Cooper, new forensic evidence coupled with previously suppressed witness testimony led investigators to a vehicle matching the one that fled the scene of Kessler's death. The vehicle, a black Ford Bronco with mismatched tires, was linked to a Crestwood resident who had loaned it to Turnberry the night of the incident, per a former teammate.

"This is a devastating turn of events for everyone involved,"

County Supervisor Rafael Nazario said in a press conference this morning. "We understand that Mr. Turnberry is a public figure, but that does not excuse him from his responsibility to remain at the scene of an accident, especially one with such tragic consequences."

Trey Turnberry, a two-time All-Star and Major League Baseball fan favorite, has not yet commented on the arrest. The Chicago Cubs released a statement this morning expressing their shock and disappointment.

"We are deeply saddened by the arrest of Trey Turnberry and are cooperating fully with the investigation," the statement reads. "The Cubs organization takes this situation very seriously. Our priority is justice, no matter what the consequences for our team."

Turnberry is scheduled to be arraigned on Thursday.

EPILOGUE

Justice

"Good morning, this is your captain speaking," the pilot of Pioneer Flight 305 announced over the PA, waking passengers from their naps. "We've begun our final descent into San Diego International Airport, so if you're not already buckled in, please do that now."

Three hundred and twenty-two heads tilted down toward their laps.

"Warmest wishes to the passengers of Pioneer Flight 868," the captain continued. "If this is your final destination, welcome home."

The airplane erupted in applause. The crash of the Puerto Rico–bound flight had dominated the headlines for the last forty-eight hours. As reported by the news media, after making an emergency landing in the Atlantic Ocean eighty miles south of Grand Turk, the passengers fought their way in lifeboats to Martini Cay, a remote, privately-owned island. After five hours without food or water, they were rescued by the HMS Wilmington, a naval cargo ship stationed off the coast of Venezuela. The evacuation had taken three hours, as rowboats shuttled passengers to deeper water where the navy ship was anchored.

The ocean voyage to Miami took almost eleven hours. The cargo vessel was equipped only with hard wooden benches, and many arrived in Miami without having slept for two days. But they were the lucky ones.

Not among the rescued passengers was Brendan "Cal" Callahan, head coach of the Crestwood High School baseball team, who'd been injured under undisclosed circumstances and flown by Captain Brett Bancroft to nearby Cockburn Town in a private plane parked on the island. Accompanying them was Callahan's ex-wife, Cathy Yap, one of three crew members who'd worked the flight. Per reports, the Mooney M20 landed without incident in Cockburn Town. Callahan was rushed to the medical center and is expected to make a full recovery.

As for Captain Bancroft, a joint task force of the FAA and NTSB determined that his decision to land in Martini Cay was sound and his execution beyond reproach, and Bancroft told the press that while he was devastated by the "betrayal" of his first officer, he was not going to let "one bad apple" keep him from returning to the job he loves.

First Officer Andrew "Drew" Ridley was detained in Miami after being treated for undisclosed injuries. Preliminary reports suggest his so-called betrayal involved dumping fuel in an attempt to keep the flight on course to San Juan, but investigators thus far declined to confirm the allegations.

Also not among the passengers on Flight 305 was William "Billy" Wilcox, who perished either as a result of the crash, or sometime before or after—the airline won't say, citing an ongoing investigation. Wilcox was scheduled to be married in San Juan. He is survived by his father, Walter Wilcox, and fiancée, Jillian Azarian.

The Airbus A330 with nonstop service from Miami touched down at San Diego International Airport at 12:02 p.m. It was a hazy afternoon, with low clouds and barely a hint of wind. The first passenger to deplane, Francesca Kessler, felt every emotion all at once as she walked down the jetway—gratitude to be alive; nervous anticipation for the media attention she was about to face; exhaustion from what she'd just endured; and yes, sadness for the solitary life that awaited her. But she was working on that.

As she stepped into the gate area, she forced herself not to cry when she saw all the balloons, flowers, and "welcome home" signs the passengers' loved ones had made. Her sister wasn't coming—she was a surgical nurse and had been called into an emergency appendectomy. But Francesca made a pointed effort *not* to feel sorry for herself. Rather than indulge those feelings of self-pity, she willed herself to dig deep, past the victim-speak, to find the seed of gratitude that was waiting to sprout. She was one of the lucky ones after all. All she had to do was choose to see herself that way.

Francesca was almost at the end of the line of well-wishers when the voice from every dream she'd had since she'd met him stopped her in her tracks.

"Francesca?"

She looked up. For a moment she thought her mind was playing tricks on her. But then her husband—yes, he was still her husband—stepped out of the crowd holding a bouquet of red roses.

"Rick? What are you doing here?"

"I want to come home, Francesca," he said, his voice quaking with emotion. "If you'll have me."

"But I thought . . ." she started but then chose not to remind him that the last time they'd spoken, it was about where he would send the divorce papers. "What changed your mind?"

"I never stopped loving you," he said. "I just couldn't handle all the feelings that came with it. But I'm ready to face them now."

Tears burst from her tired eyes as that seed of gratitude sprouted into full-blown joy. Was it nearly losing her that made him come around? Or the closure that came with finally having a suspect in their son's murder? She didn't need to know the reason.

"Will you take me back?" he asked.

"Yes," she said, falling into his open arms. "A thousand times yes."

As Francesca and Rick embraced, Angela Diaz and Jillian Azarian stepped off the jet bridge arm in arm. Jillian took little consolation that she wouldn't have to tell her friends and family why the wedding was off now, but at least no one would ask. As for how she felt about her dead fiancé, well, that was complicated. She was sickened by what he'd done to her best friend, but you don't just stop loving someone.

As for Angie, upon docking in Miami, her body let her know that she was not pregnant with Billy's baby. She would not forget the violence he'd inflicted upon her in his last week of life, but perhaps, in time, she would forgive him. Jillian had promised to stay by her side as she got the help she needed, just as Angie would be there to console Jillian in her grief.

DEA agent Marco Reyes was among the last to deplane. He'd lost his beloved guitar but earned a promotion for cracking his case and saving the air marshal's life.

On the DEA agent's heels was eighteen-year-old Ace Abernathy, who was greeted at the end of the jetway by his father, his lawyer, and an FBI agent. He had already told investigators in Miami how his mother had come into the main cabin to check on him right before the turbulence started, and then snuck back to her seat when the lights went out. He swore up and down he had no idea the real reason she'd come back there was to murder that man. When pressed, he admitted that he did think it strange that she'd used the lavatory in coach before sitting down next to him, but he wasn't in the habit of second-guessing his mother.

The last two people off the plane were Federal Air Marshal Carlos Renaldo and his prisoner, Crestwood Baseball Booster Club President Penelope Abernathy, who was facing charges of obstruction of justice and first-degree murder. Obstruction of justice charges had also been made against her oldest son, Nolan Abernathy, but eyewitness Brendan Callahan, who'd reported what he'd seen to local police, was off the hook.

If people assumed that shiner Mrs. Abernathy was sporting was from the plane crash, she wouldn't correct them. Her suitcase was never found, but new clothes had been provided—and not just for her comfort. Her bloodstained blouse had been confiscated by FBI agents in Miami, and, knowing what that DNA test would reveal, she was eyeing a plea deal to keep her oldest son, Nolan, out of prison. Two US marshals were standing by for the handoff, and Officer Renaldo felt a swell of satisfaction that he'd finally gotten a chance to fulfill the duties of the job he was trained to do.

"Officer Renaldo," Special Agent Sam Cooper said, reaching for his hand to shake it. As the US marshals hauled Mrs. Abernathy off for processing, the two men remained at the empty gate for an unofficial debrief.

"You performed admirably under difficult circumstances," Cooper said. "Agent Reyes told us about your bravery and good judgment in that hangar."

"Thank you, sir," he humbly replied. He'd made mistakes, he knew that. But also, he wasn't an investigator.

"Your instinct that the unsolved hit-and-run was connected to the murder was spot on," Cooper said, and Renaldo flashed back to the conversation when he'd passed on the tip.

"We raided Sheriff Alan Eckles's house this morning," Cooper continued. "Got his hard drives, his phone. But I don't think we'll need any of it."

"Sir?"

"He's already confessed. Plus we have a corroborating witness in Nolan Abernathy, who was in the passenger seat of the Bronco when Matthew Kessler was struck and killed. The case against Turnberry . . . well I don't want to say open-and-shut, but yeah, I think we got him."

Renaldo was pleased he'd helped to crack an unsolved case but also felt a twinge of trepidation. "So we're blowing up Major League Baseball, then?"

"So it seems."

The two men took a moment to process the gravity of that.

"There's something else, Renaldo."

"What's that, sir?"

His hesitation before answering telegraphed what was coming.

"We arrested Katie MacIntosh and went through her phone."

Renaldo felt embarrassment burn his cheeks. That phone had months' worth of text messages between him and Katie. Including that last one which was hella embarrassing.

"I think this is going to be it for you at the TSA," Cooper said.

Renaldo's heart dropped into his shoes. Yes, he'd felt underutilized at times, often longed to see more action. But he loved his job and believed in the mission of his agency.

"The TSA is expecting your immediate resignation," Cooper said.

Renaldo nodded. Because of course they were.

"But if you're interested in developing your investigative skills, there might be a place for you at the FBI."

Renaldo's head snapped up. "Sir?"

"Think about it," Cooper said.

Renaldo imagined his mother's reaction when he told her that her baby boy was working for the FBI. She hated how much time he spent on planes. And to be perfectly honest, so did he. But working for the FBI would be the best of both worlds. He could serve his country with his feet on the ground.

"I don't need to think about it, sir. If the FBI will have me, I'm in."

Cooper smiled. "You're going places, Renaldo," he said. "Places you don't need an airplane to get to."

And Federal Air Marshal Carlos Renaldo's heart soared.

ACKNOWLEDGMENTS

My father was a pilot. And boy, could he spin a yarn. Growing up, his dinner-table tales of sketchy takeoffs and hair-raising landings would hold me in thrall. I have been fascinated by these elegant, gravity-defying machines ever since. It was only a matter of time before I combined my long-gestating love affair with airplanes with my budding obsession with murder.

When I set out to write this book, despite all those stories, I knew very little about aviation. I enrolled in YouTube University, where I devoured countless ATC transcripts to bask in the mysterious and—let's be honest—kinda sexy banter between pilots and air traffic controllers. Of all the content I watched, none was more entertaining and informative than Petter Hörnfeldt's "Mentour Pilot." Thank you, Petter, for inspiring me with your superb storytelling.

Once the manuscript started taking shape, I had a ton of questions—some mundane (How do pilots talk to the crew during flight?), some technical (What is the optimal lift-to-drag ratio?). This book would not have been possible without the expert counsel (and superlative patience) of father and son pilots Rafael and Enrique Nazario, who helped steer me through dozens of possible scenarios toward the precarious nexus of unprecedented and plausible. Thank you to the Naz Five (and super-reader Angela Duddey) for all your support. I don't know how this book would have happened without you.

I rely on my early readers to tell me if I've gone off the rails. Thank you Debra Lewin (still first and fastest), Todd Schneider, Tyler Weltman, and Avital Ornovitz for always raising your hands to read those bumpy first drafts. And to my family, Uri Frodis, Sophie Frodis, and Taya Frodis, thank you for enduring my incessant "what ifs" as I grappled with the plot. I know it's annoying. And sorry, but I'm not going to stop.

Laura Dail, thank you for once again piloting my ship to its glorious final destination. To Addi Wright and my amazing team at Blackstone, thank you for the warm welcome and infusion of great ideas and energy. Celia Johnson, your insights during the developmental edit were nothing short of brilliant. I feel so lucky I get to work with such talented people who make my stories better at every turn.

I am immeasurably grateful to all the people who help spread the word about my books. Thank you Tonya @thrillerbooklovers, Julie @readingonthebrink, Carrie @carriereadsthem_all, Candice @candice_reads, Kristin @k2reader, Diana @dianas_books_cars_coffee, Krista and Brittany @thriller_book_sisters, Kim @itsallaboutthethrill, Linzie @suspenseisthrilling me, Katt @bibliopeeks, and everyone who posts and reviews. I see you. Thank you for including me in your Instaverse and for making the journey so fun.

In the past few years, I have had the incredible fortune of meeting and being mentored by some of the kindest, most talented authors on the planet. Thank you to all the amazing writers who have answered my emails, invited me to dinner, read, blurbed, and reviewed my work. Special thanks to the kindest of them all, mega-talent Hank Phillippi Ryan, who exemplifies everything wonderful about the writing community.

Finally, dear reader, a book is not finished until you crack it open. Thank you for spending time with my words, I'm honored to be invited into your imagination. Thank you for being the crucial, final piece of the puzzle.

Who are we doing it for if not for you?